John Smith was born in Shrewsbury, Shropshire, and has been a professional pilot for the last twenty years. He served in the RAF, in the Royal Saudi Air Force and, among many other flying jobs, was personal pilot to an Arab prince in the Gulf for one year. He features in the Guinness Book of Records as having achieved the fastest solo transatlantic flight. He now lives in Guernsey with his wife and two children.

SKYTRAP

John Smith

CORGI BOOKS

SKYTRAP

A CORGI BOOK 0 552 12491 5

Originally published in Great Britain by
Century Publishing Co. Ltd.

PRINTING HISTORY

Century edition published 1983
Corgi edition published 1985

This book is set in 10/11 Times

Corgi Books are published by
Transworld Publishers Ltd.,
Century House, 61-63 Uxbridge Road,
Ealing, London W5 5SA

Printed and bound in Great Britain by
Cox & Wyman Ltd, Reading

*This is the first
for James Gilbert*

'Sometimes gentle, sometimes capricious, sometimes awful, never the same for two moments together; almost human in its passions, almost spiritual in its tenderness, almost Divine in its infinity.'

Ruskin, *The Sky*

Prologue

A few inches away the world was not a friendly place. A typhoon roared out of the west Pacific bringing the usual spate of flash floods and lashing winds that twisted through the vast archipelago of the Philippines. Somewhere below, far down in an angry sky three miles deep, the town of Zamboanga was being pounded into insensibility. That life would be lost was inevitable in the worst storm of the century.

But for me and my crew the night was occasional stars and moon racing between wind-scattered anvils of cumulonimbus; the background roar of four Rolls-Royce Dart engines, and the comfort of worn leather seats as our Argosy freighter carried us back to our base at Manila. I cast an eye at the weather radar and watched the green sweeping paint on the screen, picking out the storm centres. A simple matter of zig-zagging our way northbound through the relatively clearer skies.

The flight engineer, Eddy Fuentes, pushed a paper cup of scalding coffee into my hand and promptly disappeared back to his station. A confusing array of dials and switches that monitored the well being of forty tons of aerial hardware. I half turned to Jake Ortega, who was riding as co-pilot, and offered him a cigarette. He gave me a twenty-four carat smile and shook his head. Ortega was ex-Philippine Air Force and well into his forties; although to look at, with his sleek blue-black hair and faultless olive complexion, you would have put him at no more than a handsome thirty years old. But that is usually the case with Filipinos, especially if they are airline captains and rich. The other face of third worlds is one you never get to know, unless you are unlucky enough to be born into it.

'Fifty pesos tonight?' Ortega's voice drifted into my headset.

'You're too rich already.'

He laughed. 'Perhaps you will win!'

'As I don't appear to have even a Chinaman's luck I very much doubt it . . . Ah, what the hell; as it's our last trip together, fifty it is.'

Ortega settled back in his seat and closed his eyes. I somehow knew they were still smiling.

The betting had started about a month previously, when Ortega switched from the twin-engined YS-11 fleet to the four-engined Argosy. That was also the time I had gained his lifelong friendship by becoming the first man, Filipino or otherwise, to eat more 'baloot' at one sitting then he did. 'Baloot' is basically a chicken egg which is incubated to near hatching. Whilst it is still warm you break away the shell at the top of the egg and drink the residue of warm liquid within. The next stage is a little harder; you eat the half-born chick – feathers, brains and all. That night I had eaten twelve. What the guys at that airline party didn't know was that I retched my guts out shortly after. It was the following day when Ortega started the wagering business. We agreed to split the number of landings on the day in question, and the one who did the best picked up the fifty pesos. Not that fifty pesos was much money, it worked out at around ten dollars. But after a month of steady losing I was beginning to have second thoughts. Today had been Ortega's final line check. He had flown the four-hour leg from Manila to Zamboanga earlier that day and as usual had pulled off a 'greaser'. Now on the return journey, it was my turn.

We had departed Zambo an hour earlier and spiralled our way up to 16,000 feet before the storm hit. Our cargo of farming implements, boxes of fruit, and one coffin – occupied by an army sergeant who had been murdered the previous evening in a bar-room brawl – lay in the cavernous hold beneath the flight deck. This then was one of those routine night flights which begin and end with monotonous regularity all over the world. One which had fifty pesos running on the final landing.

'I think we have a problem Steve!' Ortega said matter of factly.

'Problem?' He pointed at the radar screen. Sure enough we had a problem. Intense thunderstorm activity stretching from east to west and a long way up into the night sky. The options! There were none. We didn't have the performance to get over the top; we couldn't go back to Zambo as they were weathered in; and we couldn't fly hundreds of extra miles to get around it. Well we could – only problem was we would probably run out of fuel somewhere over the South China Sea. No, the only way was through it.

That aircraft bigger than Argosies have been known to break up in such violent weather is common knowledge in the flying game. That anyone should risk his neck to see that the freight gets through is an idea perpetrated by overweight airline flight managers from cosy little offices, their main concern being logistics and economics – that and the belief, 'if we did it once, why shouldn't you?'

I checked the range to the storm. Thirty miles. Thirty miles and we would be in the thick of it. Exactly how long we would be in there was anybody's guess, for at that precise moment the radar screen faded to a black nothingness. I muttered a few suitable obscenities and checked the fuse. It was serviceable! The damn thing was serviceable. I swore again and banged the set with the flat of my hand. Nothing, not even the faintest flicker, which meant we could fly into the biggest and fattest storm cell around and never even know it until it was too late. The adrenalin started with the realization we might never come out.

I turned to Fuentes. 'Eddy, get below and check the cargo lashings, then get yourself back up here . . . we're in for a rough ride.'

He disappeared down the hole into the cargo bay while Ortega and I started stowing loose articles. No point in being knocked out by a loose thermos flask, although if

11

we lost the wings in a structural break-up the point seemed somehow academic.

Without warning we flew into the gathering tempest. The rain was simply tropical, a wall of water which crashed against the screen adding to the eeriness of the dimly lit flight deck. No one spoke as I reduced power and fought to maintain a heading. But even if they had their voices would have been silenced by the deafening waterfall of rain which had now been joined by staccato drum rolls of hail. As the book says: reduce speed, maintain heading, and ride the storm.

Suddenly we hit a downdraught which slammed us earthwards at over four thousand feet a minute. The Argosy creaked and shuddered as I hit the levers to produce full climb power and hauled the nose violently skyward. Nothing changed. The rate of descent stayed firmly off the clock as the altimeter silently unwound towards the Sulu Sea. All I could do was sit and watch . . . and pray. Most pilots do at one time or another.

Thirteen thousand . . . twelve . . . eleven . . . ten. At five thousand things started easing up a little. But only a little. I wiped the blinding sweat out of my eyes and tried to firewall the power levers a shade further forward. They were already on the stops. The descent stopped as abruptly as it had started. The altimeter indicated 1,400 feet. I glanced across at the man with the gold fillings. He was smiling.

'Position?' I said shakily.

The airways chart was on his knee, attached to its clipboard. 'Fifty miles southsouthwest of Iloilo,' he said. He didn't even look at the chart; probably worked it out on the way down. Good airman Jake Ortega, always one step ahead of the aeroplane.

I went back to the instruments, my eyes tunnelling in on the altimeter and that miserly 1,400 feet. Fifty miles to landfall and high ground, which meant we had to go back into the storm. I reduced power and told Ortega to check the Manila weather with Iloilo. In the meanwhile I was

12

staying down here, in the relatively smoother air.

The weather report when it came was abysmal. Typhoon activity – airport flooded – surface winds over eighty knots. The stuff we were getting was the overspill.

'Diversion Jake . . . tell Iloilo we're coming in to them.'

Ten minutes later we had the city lights in sight. The weather was deteriorating fast. Surface wind gusting forty knots in heavy, squally showers. The other snag was with runway length; Iloilo was marginal on the best of days. Here and now on the blackest of nights it was going to be nothing short of entertaining. I called for the pre-landing checks and started walking the power levers back until I had pinned 140 knots on the airspeed indicator.

'Gear down,' I yelled as the Argosy pitched and rolled towards the rain-blurred lights of the city.

'Three greens,' Ortega confirmed.

I ran my hand through the sweat on my forehead. Every muscle in my body ached. I felt weak and tired and very, very old. Steady now . . . steady. Don't forget the runway length . . . it's short, remember . . . bloody short . . . just slam it on the numbers . . . it's easy . . . dead easy.

'Flaps approach,' I croaked. Outside the harsh sound of rain rose and fell as we passed through a heavy squall.

'Runway lights! Right! Turn right!'

'Where for Chrissakes? Where?' I screwed my head round searching for something Ortega could see and I could not. Then I had them. I kicked the rudder viciously and slewed forty tons of groaning metal to the right. Not the book way of doing things, but then I had my own idea about books.

'Jake . . . about a hundred yards this side of the threshold give me flaps land . . . got it?'

I caught his raised hand in my peripheral vision, his sign of acknowledgment.

Then he said: 'Don't forget the fifty pesos!'

'Get screwed.'

Ortega laughed, then reached across and snapped on the twin landing lights.

I thumbed the radio transmit button and called 'short

finals'. I didn't hear a reply, but then I wasn't really listening. I just wanted to put my two feet firmly on the safe earth and feel the cool, clear wind in my face.

The runway lead-in lights loomed dramatically beneath the aircraft as Ortega selected flaps land.

It was then that Iloilo disappeared. I tried to call out and ask what had happened to the runway lights, but the words remained paralysed in my throat. It was all too late. We were about fifty feet off the ground when the aircraft's landing lights picked out intermittent areas of shiny blackness. Tarmac? I pulled the power off and started to flare.

We fell out of the sky and hit hard. Too hard and too fast – then we were flying again. That was when I heard a voice screaming 'Trees!'

I saw them in the dying seconds. Tall, black, glistening wet . . . a rushing frenzy of death. The last thing I remember was the tortured, screaming sound of metal as the aircraft started coming apart in slow motion.

After that there was nothing. Nothing until I awoke and saw a white ceiling staring back at me and found I couldn't move. Six months of that as they put me back together; but at least it was only six months. Eddy Fuentes, the flight engineer, was killed on impact. Jake Ortega, the handsome man who had probably never done a bad landing in his life, died from his injuries three days after the crash.

An airport power failure at the critical point in our landing meant that Ortega had won his last bet. Ironically the exchange rate was just about right for a third world. Fifty pesos for a life.

Chapter One

The fourth anniversary had come and gone, spreading a few more centimetres of cancerous growth to the fast-weakening system. Some people recover from crashes, they just climb aboard a conveniently placed machine and within minutes everything is as it was. With me it had been different. Probably because of the six months on my back, and the left knee which had never quite healed up – a traumatic arthritic condition the specialist had said – to me it was a nagging pain, a cripple's limp, and an ever-constant reminder. Then there was the long ragged scar above my right eyebrow, and perhaps the strangest of all, how my hair had turned white practically overnight. I had become a young man in an old man's body; just about fit enough to hold my pilot's licence. Until today that was.

'I'm sorry Steve, looks like the old blood pressure's a bit high!' I heard what Jack Sullivan had said. Heard but didn't believe.

'What do you mean a bit high?'

'I mean it's one ninety over one ten, which means I'll have to refer you to a specialist at the Civil Aviation Authority.'

Now I had heard him. Steve Ritchie, forty-year-old freelance ferry pilot, a once upon a time ace, was finished, on the scrap heap. Not that it should have worried me because I had contracted that even rarer disease known to pilots. A fear of flying.

'Isn't there any way . . .'

'It could go back to normal Steve . . . but as I've told you before, give up the whisky. You could also try to lose a few pounds, all helps you know. Any family history of high blood pressure?'

'You know, Jack, if I didn't know you better I'd say

you were getting old . . . and as I'm not into spiritualism . . .'

'Ah Jesus, that's right, parents were killed in the war weren't they!'

I said, 'Something like that.'

He nodded sympathetically and began to fill in the medical report form on his desk.

'Is that it then?'

'Sorry pal, that's it. If you take this form up to the CAA guy . . . say next month. And in the meantime forget the booze.' The soft Irish brogue seemed to continue long after the voice had stopped.

I stumbled out of the surgery into a rainswept November day and started walking. I shouldn't have given a damn; I had grown to hate aircraft and everything they stood for. But somehow that pilot's licence was my last link with respectability. On paper I was a professional man . . . but not any more. Then I remembered the letter and the cheque for 4,000 US dollars. I'd promised Goldstein I would do the trip and what was more important I needed the money. People get understandably nasty about bouncing cheques.

What the hell, I'd go. There was always a way to get around an expired medical certificate. Of course if the Civil Aviation Authority found out I'd be in big trouble; but then at worst they could only revoke my licence. As I'd lost it anyway the point was purely academic. All I had to do was fight off the fear which gnawed at my intestines every time I approached an aeroplane. Fear? It was more like an incapacitating panic. An emotional state where rational thought and control disintegrated. All that remained was a very powerful urge to escape. It would be the reverse of a normal accident. The aircraft was fully serviceable, but the pilot was out of control.

I ended up in a pub not far from Sloane Square and ordered a large whisky from an overweight, peroxide blonde barmaid. Then I pulled the crumpled letter from my pocket and read it for the tenth time in two days.

Euroair International SA,
Rue de Francois Primiea, 177,
Paris,
France.

Attention: Steve Ritchie.

This will serve as a detailed instruction of how this trip should proceed.

We have given instructions to American Express, Haymarket 6, London SW1, Miss Doolittle, to issue a ticket London–Malawi, and to hold for your pick-up. Please identify yourself with your passport.

Enclosed please find cheque for 4,000 US dollars, being full and final payment for this ferry flight. I am also enclosing one Shell carnet for fuel purchases along the way.

Your final destination will be Ben Gurion airport, Tel Aviv. You will be received by Colonel Degani, who will sign a delivery receipt (see enclosed) and make arrangements for you to stay overnight and to return to Europe. It is important that all instructions be followed as precisely as possible, with safety, or good flight planning, being the only reason for deviation.

You will proceed to Malawi, where you will be met on your arrival by James Valentine, or his representative.

Address: Southland Aviation Limited,
    PO Box 272, Zomba Airport,
    Blantyre, Malawi,
    Tel: Zomba 9292 Telex: 324324 Wings Z

James will provide accommodation and see to it that you receive a Malawi validation for your British licence, as well as a check-out on the Dornier DO28. He will also help you with flight planning as he is very familiar with the route. It is important to make sure that all overflights and technical stops be requested in advance if required. James will assist on this. Generally speaking your route will be:

Blantyre
Nairobi

Juba
Khartoum
Wadi Halfa
Cairo
Cyprus

It is important that you avoid stops or overflights in Uganda and Ethiopia. Therefore careful flight planning and navigation is essential. The flight should be made in day VFR conditions.

You are not to go from your last stop to the final destination without telephone clearance from Colonel Degani. I.e. plan your last stop in Cyprus as an overnight stop and place a telephone call to Colonel Degani, before proceeding to final destination the next day. This is important.

It is of further importance that you do not discuss details of this trip. James is aware of your destination and there is no need for anyone else to know.

Upon your departure from Malawi and at each stop along the way, it is advisable that you try to send me a telex or a cable, or place a telephone call. Try to hold to this as much as possible. My business card (see enclosed) has all my contact numbers in Paris. This message should indicate next day's destination. Your flight plan should be worked out so that you do not arrive at destination between Friday noon and Saturday night. In other words plan to arrive before Friday noon or from Sunday on. In the event of difficult conditions, this can only be altered with my approval or that of the Colonel.

Enclosed please find delivery receipt. Do not leave without Colonel Degani's signature on this receipt.

There is a strong possibility that I will meet you en route and continue to the destination with you. If I am not present during the final part of the trip, you are to proceed to your home base with the delivery receipt in your possession, via Paris, where you and I will meet.

NOTE: Telephone numbers for Colonel Degani in Tel Aviv:

Office: 783 124   Res: 327 714

Good Luck

Very truly yours,
Max Goldstein

He seemed a careful man, Mr Goldstein. In the three-plus years I had been doing freelance ferry work this was the first time I had received such careful, well thought out instructions. Usually the only line I got was: 'Get the bloody thing there as quickly and as cheaply as possible.' The other thought that crossed my mind was, why me? There were a lot of well known ferry outfits in Europe. All he had said over the telephone was that my name had been given him by somebody or other. He didn't remember the somebody or other's name. Just that they had said I was good at my job.

What was also distinctly odd was that a man whom I had never met would send me full and final payment before I had carried out the flight. Even the regulars who hired me would only ever pay half in advance, with the remainder on completion. Max Goldstein, it seemed, was nothing like my regulars.

Chapter Two

The piped music started up with Lennon and McCartney's 'Yesterday' as the VC10 taxied off the runway. After about five bars it gave way to the muted metallic voice of a stewardess welcoming us to Blantyre Chileka airport and hoping we would fly with British Airways again in the near future. Some may be enticed, I thought, but if I had any say in the rest of my life I'd stick to ground pounding. Nothing against the flag carrier or the steely-eyed jet jockeys who sit at the sharp end, just an irrevocable decision that once I had ferried the Dornier to Tel Aviv and caught the first flight home the decree nisi would be absolute.

I looked out of the window as the '10' trundled slowly up towards the terminal. So this was Malawi. According to the well-thumbed information leaflet stuffed in the seat pocket in front of me, Malawi was formerly known as Nyasaland, being situated in the Great Rift Valley. It is bordered on the north by Tanzania, on the east and south by Mozambique, and by Zambia on the west. The capital is Lillongwe; official language English, and the domestic economy relies heavily on agriculture and forestry. The official religion is none – which I guessed was a polite way of saying that the poor bloody missionaries were eaten before they got this far.

'Yesterday' was back as I deplaned with the other passengers, patting my inside pocket as I went. I'd done a good job on the flying licence; might have missed my true vocation in life.

A lone figure was waiting on the airside of the terminal. Hands clasped behind his back, feet the regulation distance apart. He was stocky, sunburnt, leaning towards corpulence. The fawn trousers and matching bush shirt were crisp and immaculate, the brown brogues twinkling in the sunlight. As I got nearer I noticed the fleshy face and purple-tinged nose – drinker! The fine greying hair ruffled in the gentle breeze, then he snapped smartly to attention and took one precise military step forward.

'Mr Ritchie?' The inflexion in his voice was somewhere between Eton and one of those superior Guards regiments where family pedigree counts more than actual intelligence.

I stopped. 'Steve Ritchie,' I said. 'James Valentine?'

'Quite right old boy,' he replied, offering a strong, sunburnt hand. 'Thought it had to be you; only one carrying a flight bag.' The fleshy face creased into a grin. I nodded and followed him into the building. The white-washed customs hall was dusty and hot and full of flies; the black customs officers as inhospitable as their surroundings, checking and double checking every last item of luggage with a purposeful slowness. I refastened my flight bag and turned to Valentine. 'Keen lot!' I remarked.

'In the great British tradition, old boy. Damned shame we gave it all back . . . but there you are. Politicians and soldiers, don't you know; two different breeds what?'

I remembered Goldstein had mentioned over the telephone that Valentine was the former chief of police of Malawi. He now ran a small air charter service and had also branched out into aircraft sales. I started walking towards the door.

'This way old boy,' Valentine about-turned me and led me back to the tarmac and the world of flying machines. To a nearly new single-engine Cessna Skylane.

'Where to?'

'Home, Zomba . . . fifteen minutes that way.' He waved vaguely towards the distant purple mountains lying in the northeast. I threw my bags onto the back seats and fastened my lap strap. Five minutes later we clattered noisily into the tired noonday air and swung left on course. The thermal activity which affects a light single-engined aircraft is in marked contrast to anything you may feel in a jetliner. As I had thanked the Lord for my safe deliverance into Blantyre my system had wound down, thinking the flying for the day was over. I now felt the chain reaction of fear, sweating and the need for a drink, kick around in my guts. It was quite obvious that I was sobering up too fast.

Valentine said, 'See that place down there?' I followed his pointing finger. 'Tobacco plantation. The tall buildings at the back are the drying towers; where they hang the leaves.'

I made suitable noises to indicate that I was interested; at the same time fighting off the feeling of sickness that welled up in my throat.

The grass airfield which carried the misleading title Zomba airport lay at the foot of Zomba mountain, and was a few miles east of the neat little township. The airfield was deserted except for a pair of camouflaged Piper Apaches of uncertain vintage. It seemed natural to assume they would not win a lot of wars with that type of air force.

We rolled to an engine-off stop near an open-fronted shed which obviously served as a hangar. Lying inert in the shadows, the Dornier. All set it seemed for her long haul to Tel Aviv. I had the distinct feeling this was one flight I would live to regret. Even assuming I could get the heap of junk there in one piece, there was still the political instability between the Arabs and the Jews. Which could land me in the middle of a minor war. And minor wars have one thing in common with major wars – they shoot real bullets. I shuddered involuntarily and wondered what time the VC10 was heading back to London.

My left knee was hurting like hell after its prolonged period of inactivity, so my pronounced limp was reason enough for the grease-covered mechanic to question the sanity of the CAA in issuing cripples with flying licences. Well, he didn't actually say it, he didn't have to. I could read the message in his dark, angry eyes. That was my introduction to Rees-Williams, Valentine's chief engineer. And by the look of things the only engineer. I took an

22

instant dislike to the Welshman. It was nothing to do with his dark, angry features. More the feeling of trouble. The feeling that his threshold of patience was something like a lorry load of nitro travelling down a bumpy road.

'How is she?' I said, nodding towards the Dornier.

'Oh, a few problems,' he mumbled.

'For instance?'

'Left generator's on the blink and the auto pilot's bust.'

'Bust?'

'Spares man, can't get them.'

'Have you tried the Dornier factory?' His eyes flashed angrily at the question, but before he could speak a telephone extension bell started jangling erratically.

Valentine hurried off towards the door at the side of the hangar. 'Come through when you've finished old boy,' he called back.

As today was Friday I asked Rees-Williams if he would be working tomorrow. He muttered something about working every bloody day and stomped off towards a workbench in the corner of the hangar. 'I'd like to airtest it in the morning then,' I said.

He glowered at me. 'What about the generator?'

'Can you fix it?'

'Doubt it . . . anyway I've got other things to do.'

'But you will try?'

'We'll see,' he replied, and started throwing tools into a half-empty tool box. It was obvious I would get nothing else out of him so I went in search of Valentine.

His office was a small brick-built extension tacked onto the side of the hangar. At one end, a desk with an Adler electric typewriter, a telex machine which had seen better days, and one grey filing cabinet. In the centre of the room, a long high wooden structure which acted as a room divider cum bookshelf. Beyond that was Valentine's desk, a small safe, a coffee table, and three easy chairs. The chintzy curtains were hopelessly out of place. But then I hadn't expected the Ritz. I dropped into a chair and lit a cigarette. Valentine was doing little talking and a lot of listening; his face caught up in a worried frown.

'Right old boy . . . yes . . . I'll fly over straight away.'
He put the phone down, turning to me at the same time.
'Afraid I've got to go back to Blantyre.' He'd picked up
the phone again and was dialling. 'One of my Aztecs went
down last night and they've . . .' He stopped and turned
his attention to the phone. 'Hello. Hello Penny. Look, old
girl, have to go down to Blantyre and then on to
Tete . . . what? . . . No, they've found the Aztec . . . yes,
afraid so old girl. I was wondering if you could come
down and collect Steve Ritchie . . . yes, he's here at
Zomba . . . yes I will. Bye.' He dropped the receiver into
its cradle and started shuffling papers into a black
briefcase.

'My wife will be down to collect you in about an hour
or so. Terribly sorry about all this but as I was saying one
of our planes crashed last night and they've just located
the wreckage near to a place called Tete.' He hurried
towards the door. 'By the way,' he added, 'help yourself
to a cup of coffee . . . see you later.' With that he was
gone.

It took my brain about three minutes to engage, by
which time Valentine had made a noisy departure, taking
my flight bag and holdall with him. As my Scotch supply
resided in the map compartment of that flight bag it
looked as though I would have to settle for coffee after
all.

The sleepy silence of the African midday became too
much after about five minutes so I went back out to the
hangar. Might as well get the flight manual out of the
Dornier and check up on a few relevant speeds. My
research went unrewarded and as Rees-Williams had
obviously departed for lunch I went back to the office. It
had to be somewhere. The bookshelf drew a blank, which
left the filing cabinet. The top drawer of the cabinet was
marked A–F. I looked under D for Dornier and came up
with nothing. It was then that my inquisitive nature took
over. It was obvious that if Goldstein could afford to pay
me 4,000 dollars to do the trip there had to be a handsome

profit in the deal. All I had to do was find out how much it was purchased for and the selling price. It could even be a way out! The answer I'd been looking for. Get into aircraft sales. No need to fly them. If the profit is good you can pay someone else to do the delivery – just like Goldstein had done.

I found a part of the answer when I opened the second drawer of the filing cabinet. It was a part which made my blood boil. It was a file marked IAF – Israeli Air Force. Now I knew why Goldstein had paid over the odds, and cash up front. Undercover arms dealing! And I was the piggy in the middle. Now the detailed letter of instruction made sense. This was a purely military operation. I'd even asked Goldstein about Colonel Degani, but he'd fobbed him off as an Air Force type who wanted to buy his own private aircraft. The sales invoice in my hand stated the aircraft had been sold to the Israeli Air Force for 55,000 US dollars. The owner and selling agent was Southland Aviation Limited. There was no mention of Max Goldstein.

My anger slowly subsided when I realized I was in a strong bargaining position. All I had to do was confront Valentine with the facts and tell him that unless my fee was increased they could forget all about it. The other way, the easy way would be to catch the next flight back to London. That idea provided a problem. I would have to repay the 4,000 dollars, and as at least half of it had already been consumed by a bank overdraft . . .

I went across to Valentine's desk. I needed to find out more. Who had Valentine bought the aircraft from in the first place? What was Goldstein's connection? After twenty minutes of steady sweating I had established that Valentine owned two beaten-up old Aztecs, and a six-month-old Cessna Skylane, all of which he ran on ad hoc charter work. From the flying hours sheet I could see he was backing a loser, unless he was charging some exorbitant fee per hour. But then as there were sure to be other charter outfits over at Chileka airport he would be pricing himself out of the market. As for the engineering, it was obvious from his facilities that he couldn't offer much of a service. Which left aircraft sales, military or otherwise, a money-spinner if you do the right deals. There was nothing to indicate where the Dornier had come from in the first place; or for how much. I had to find out before I confronted Valentine. His profit margin was my bargaining lever.

I went back to the filing cabinet and returned the sales invoice to the IAF file. That was when the office door creaked open and a South-African-accented voice snarled, 'What the hell do you think you're doing, man?'

Chapter Three

I spun round and found myself looking at a giant of a young man. Six feet six I estimated, and solidly built at that. His hair was bleached blond by the sun. The eyes were ice blue.

'Looking for the pilot's notes for the Dornier,' I replied instinctively.

'You're Steve Ritchie,' he said.

'Right first time,' I said flatly.

The tension in his face subsided and he held out a huge bronzed hand and crushed mine in the process. 'Lucky Clay . . . fly part time for James.'

'Lucky?'

'Lucius really, but everyone calls me Lucky.'

'Bit tall for a driver,' I said conversationally.

He laughed. 'Not really man, I'm double jointed.'

'Yes, I suppose you'd need to be. You just flown in?'

He shook his head. 'No, been over at the military hangar. You must have noticed the two Air Force Apaches . . . I've got the Baron in their shed.'

'Didn't know Valentine had a Baron as well.'

Clay half smiled. 'He doesn't, it's mine.'

It was reasonable to assume that any part-time pilot who owned a Beechcraft Baron, which ran at about a couple of hundred thousand dollars new, had to be at least rich. 'What do you do apart from flying?' I said.

'Oh nothing much. Got a small farm over in Zambia.'

'Nice,' I said.

'Was that James leaving a short while ago?'

'Yes, something about an Aztec that crashed last night. He's gone down to Blantyre . . . I'm waiting for his wife to come and collect me.'

'No need, I'm heading up to the house, I'll give you a lift.' He went over to the phone and started dialling. 'Did

27

he say where the plane went down?'

I said, 'Sounded like Tete.'

'Christ, that far off track!' he exclaimed, then turned to the phone and spoke to the person on the other end.

The need for a drink was back with the thought of getting to the house. Anything to smooth down the jangled, fraying nerve ends.

Clay dropped the phone. 'All fixed then,' he said. 'By the way, did James say if there were any survivors?'

'No . . . how many were on board?'

'Six . . . full load.' He shrugged. 'Let's go then, got the Range Rover down at the other hangar.'

I limped after the long striding giant, silently cursing the pain in my knee. After four years I should have learned to live with it. But somehow I never had.

'Hurt your leg?' Clay stopped and waited for me to catch him up.

'Nothing,' I said. 'Ran out of runway one night.'

'Sorry to hear that, man. What were you flying?'

'Argosy, do you know them?'

'Twin-boomed jobs aren't they?'

'Right.'

'Military?'

'Ex-military, we were operating it out of Manila at the time. Philippine Airlines.'

'You ex-Air Force?'

'Ex most things,' I replied. 'And shortly ex-ferry pilot.'

'You're packing it up then?'

'It and flying,' I said. Clay looked suitably puzzled but didn't ask any more questions. As I had run out of legitimate answers I was grateful.

'How far to the house?' I said, as Clay gunned the white Range Rover down the dust bowl of a road.

He moved his head forward. 'See the top of that mountain . . . Zomba mountain . . . that's where the house is. About forty-five minutes' normal driving. I can do it in thirty.'

It took some time to sink in, and when it did it occurred to me that this trip was starting out like a commando survival course.

The route to the top of the mountain was via a red dirt, single-track road which switchbacked upwards to the 5,000-foot summit. At the halfway stage we passed through a pine forest. Neat piles of cut timber were stacked at intervals along the narrow road, and the heavy scent of pine forced into my nostrils with an unbelievable intensity.

We approached the top of the mountain around a sweeping right-hand curve, then turned into a long driveway which was lined on both sides by a low, white-painted wooden fence. Half a mile later we came to the house. A long, rambling, brick-built affair of the single-storey type. The setting was nothing short of most people's idea of paradise – perched on the cliff edge, it had endless panoramic views from west through south to east. The gardens were a profusion of bright flowering shrubs and rows of blue eucalyptus trees soaring majestically into the cloudless sky. From the verandah of the house I could see a swimming pool half concealed behind the flowering bushes. Valentine had to be selling a lot of aeroplanes, I thought, as I followed Lucky Clay into the house.

Penny Valentine was everything I had not expected. She was at least twenty years younger than her husband, which would put her in her thirties. But more surprising than that was the honey-coloured skin, the dark smouldering eyes, and the glossy black shoulder-length hair. Her slightly broad nose and widish mouth told me that this ravishing beauty was a delicate mixture of Caucasian and Negro genes. A mixture that was very pleasing to the eye.

Introductions over, I was ushered into the drawing room. Whoever was responsible for the decor had exquisite taste – from the polished parquet floor, the solitary Persian carpet, to the granite fireplace whose beaten copper hood disappeared into the beamed ceiling. The walls were white and carefully broken up by a number of expensively framed oil paintings. The settee

29

was a few thousands dollars of imported chesterfield and the sideboard, writing bureau and various chairs looked to be priceless antiques. All in all this one room could probably pay my salary for a lifetime and still come out ahead.

'Would you care for a drink?' she said in a cultured voice.

'Scotch if you have it . . . it's been a long journey.'

She smiled briefly and turned to Clay. 'Usual?' He nodded.

Apart from being very beautiful it seemed Penny Valentine was also long-suited in mental telepathy. She had only just finished speaking when the black, beaming face appeared in the doorway. He waited, respectfully silent.

Penny Valentine said, 'Sunday, this master is Mr Ritchie from England. He will be staying a few days. You can prepare the number one guest bungalow.'

'Yes Ma'am,' Sunday said.

'And would you pour two whiskies and a beer for Bwana Blue Gum.' Sunday giggled like a small child and hurried away.

'All the natives call Lucky Bwana Blue Gum,' Penny explained. 'After the eucalyptus trees.'

'Seems appropriate,' I replied.

'Keeps them amused,' Clay added.

Sunday returned about sixty seconds later and handed out the drinks. I suddenly felt a lot happier than I had for most of the day.

'You called your steward Sunday,' I said to Penny, as he went out of the door. 'Unusual sort of name!'

She crossed her legs with conscious elegance. 'James found him in the bush about twenty years ago. Apparently he had been abandoned, so James decided to take him in and as the day in question was a Sunday the name somehow stuck.'

I was only half listening, the other half was casually

inspecting the slender body residing in the pale green dress. I think she realized the effect she was having on me as she rose gracefully from her chair and allowed me the briefest glimpse of shapely thigh. 'If you'll excuse me, I must change and see to the horses.' With that she was gone. All that remained was the faintest trace of expensive perfume lingering tantalizingly in the cool mountain air.

I looked across at Clay. 'Horses as well!'

'She runs a small riding school, more out of boredom than anything else.'

I said, 'Not a bad looker is she?'

There was a moment of iciness in his eyes. The same iciness which had been there when we first met. Then he laughed. 'Not bad at all,' he conceded, unwrapping his long legs and climbing out of his chair. 'Well, I'm off for a few hours' shut eye, see you later . . . do you want me to get Sunday to show you to the bungalow?'

'No thanks, I'll just sit here for now.'

I listened to his footsteps receding along the verandah, then helped myself to another whisky from the decanter before moving over to the sideboard and the collection of silver-framed photographs. A younger James Valentine, very official in his police uniform, smiled back at me. Valentine again, still young, with a very English-looking lady. Another of Valentine in uniform, this time with a slimly-built fair-haired man – Germanic looks and rimless spectacles. Penny Valentine in the briefest of bikinis beckoning seductively from the side of a swimming pool. Valentine again, this time with his aeroplanes. I went back to the photo of him with the English-looking lady. His first wife perhaps? If so his taste had definitely improved with age. I went back to the studded leather chesterfield and finished my whisky. Then I lay my head back and within minutes I was asleep.

The room was tall, more like the inside of a church than an official government building. The bare whitewashed

31

walls were broken up only by the high open windows, through which the muted buzz of the Metro Manila traffic carried on the morning breeze. The court was in session. The charge being brought against me by the Civil Aviation Authority of the Philippines was one of gross negligence, causing the crash of Argosy aircraft RPC119, which had resulted in the deaths of two Filipino crew members. That was as much as my lawyer had told me a week before my hospital discharge. Now, nine days later, with the smell of hospital wards permeating my very skin, I heard the counsel for the prosecution say, 'Manslaughter under section 127a of the said act.' I nearly fainted as the implication of those words exploded inside my head. Manuel Luz caught me by the shoulder, then handed me a glass of water.

'Drink this, my friend. You will feel better.'

I took a sip and sat back in the hard wooden bench seat. 'What the hell does he mean, manslaughter?' I whispered.

Luz said, 'Do not worry, my friend, it is standard legal procedure.'

Standard legal procedure be damned. I looked around the courtroom at the unsmiling burnished faces; my snow-white complexion had me marked out in more ways than one. I could see it all now – found guilty on all charges. Then I would be taken to Fort Santiago; to the death cell. Jose Rizal had been taken there in 1896 by the Spaniards. The following day he had been marched through the streets to Bagumbayan Field. There had been a muffled sound of drums as Rizal said goodbye to the priests, then turning to the Spanish captain he requested to be shot facing the firing squad. His request was denied. They shot him in the back. His crimes had been rebellion, sedition and illegal association. Eighty or so years on life was still cheap and according to the prosecution I was solely responsible for the deaths of two Filipinos. And Luz was saying it's standard legal procedure! I only half listened to the remainder of the charges. It didn't make sense, not a single damned word of it. The trial lasted for a week. Through it all I had pleaded my innocence, or alternatively sat staring at the bare stone floor, then up at the high arch of ceiling; watching the rice birds trying to find their way back to the outside world. Back to freedom.

'Why hadn't you checked the weather reports before leaving Zamboanga?'

'I had checked them. The weather at the time was perfectly flyable.'

'What time did you check the weather?'

'About 15.30 local time.'

'What time did you depart Zamboanga?'

'18.30 hours.'

'You did not think fit to obtain more up-to-date weather before your departure?'

'I tried . . . it wasn't available.'

'I think you are lying, Captain . . . I think you never tried.'

'I am not lying, ask Don Luis Taviel de Andrade, the station manager at Zamboanga.'

Counsel for the prosecution smiled sardonically. 'I think you know that is impossible, Captain.'

'What the hell do you mean impossible? Ask him, he'll tell you the trouble I took to try to get an updated weather brief, he'll also tell you . . .'

'Captain, Captain,' the voice was condescending now. 'You know it is impossible. You know Luis Taviel de Andrade is dead!'

'Dead? What do you mean dead?'

'Dead! He ceases to live. He died on the night of the storm . . . many people were killed that night.'

'I didn't know,' I said quietly. 'I'm sorry. He was a good man.'

'You say he was a good man, Captain, and yet you are prepared to use him as a scapegoat for your own folly . . . isn't that correct?'

'To hell with you. You only have to check with the Royal Air Force and Philippine Airlines to see that I have never had a flying accident before this. And what is more if there hadn't been a total power failure at Iloilo the crash would never have occurred . . . you know that as well as I do.'

And so it went on; questioning, cross-questioning – back and forth. Then the final day; the day of judgment. By that time even Manuel Luz had lost some of his perkiness, now he wasn't so sure. He even went so far as to indicate I might possibly get a short jail sentence. But he would appeal against such a verdict . . . of course.

I just sat, weak and tired and old, feeling the sweat run in tiny rivulets down my face and neck. I had lost a lot of weight in that week, so that my grey lightweight suit hung like a rumpled shroud from my shoulders. High above, through the open windows the harsh glare of late afternoon was turning to red.

The verdict when it came was an unbelievable breath of fresh air, better than anything I had experienced in my life before. 'Not guilty of manslaughter, but guilty of infringement of articles . . .' the voice droned on in heavily accented English, but I didn't want to hear . . . I was free.

They loaded me on a DC10 flight later that evening. I had lost my Philippine flying licence and had been fined about 6,000 US dollars. The amount, oddly enough, corresponded exactly with the figure I had in the local bank. Then the airline vice-president arrived and said regretfully that under the circumstances the company could not pay me my three-month severance salary due to certain infringements in my contract. He also added they would be withholding my holiday pay and expense claims until the accountants had sorted them out – which was a roundabout way of saying they never would. Then he smiled, saying the first-class air fare to London was of course free. As was the champagne, but somehow it had lost its sparkle.

I awoke to the afternoon wearing slowly on, casting its long shadows across the drawing room. For a moment I sat quietly, wondering what would have happened if there had been no crash . . . no Iloilo!

I poured myself a whisky, pulled an old world atlas down from the bookcase and started planning my route to Tel Aviv. It was after dusk when Valentine returned with my bags, which contained the more up-to-date aerial charts I needed. They would show me exactly where my last flight with a heavier than air machine would take me. To hell and back I already knew, but that was only a part of it.

After dinner Valentine told of the scene he had witnessed at Tete, when one of his young pilots and five passengers had been tragically killed. I had listened without interrupting and went to bed seeing the pictures all over again. It was like an extract from a late-night movie, with the Aztec pilot finding himself lost after sunset somewhere over the vastness of Africa. Eventually the fuel ran out and the aircraft started its final engineless descent. Suddenly, unexpectedly, a moment of hope as a full moon broke through an opening in the sheet of cloud above. The pilot would have seen the bush road in the dying seconds and screamed to his passengers to 'brace – brace'. Then he would have hauled the nose up as the aircraft's landing light locked onto the makeshift runway. Holding the aircraft fairly flat now, waiting for the first impact. And then out of nowhere, the tall steel girders of a newly constructed bridge filling the screen. At nearly two miles a minute they wouldn't have known much. They would have known my worst enemy though – fear! Poor, sad, unlucky bastards. I hoped they had someone to

35

cherish their memories; the pilot did – a young wife and a six-month-old daughter. And that was the saddest part of all.

I fell into a troubled sleep, but instead of counting sheep, I found myself counting pilots. Ones I had known who were now no more. According to the law of averages I should have been dead a long time ago.

I was awake at five the next morning, courtesy of a car engine which shattered the dawn stillness. I lay listening as the gears grated and the noise slowly faded into the distance. Someone, it seemed, was up with the lark. I fumbled for the bedside light and my first cigarette of the day. Today was the day of the airtest. Oddly enough the thought didn't seem too bad; because I knew Valentine would be riding shotgun, ready to take over if anything went wrong. The jigsaw of flying fear stopped at that point. It seemed natural to assume that the crash had really finished me; I couldn't even fly into the smallest patch of cloud without fear shaking me apart. Then it had spread to night flying. I would never be able to do that again. Which left fine, clear sunny days – I could just about manage those – or could I?

I was still lying there trying to analyse the whole messy business when the bungalow door opened and Penny Valentine swept in. She was dressed in her horse-riding attire.

'Good morning Steve. I saw the light . . . thought you might like a cup of tea.'

'Thanks,' I said thickly. She placed the cup and saucer on the bedside table and withdrew far enough to be ladylike.

'Thought I heard a car leaving just now,' I said.

'James and Lucky. They've gone to the airport,

something about a charter. James said he would be back to collect you in about two hours . . . I believe you're airtesting the Dornier?'

'Something like that. What time's breakfast, by the way?'

'Whenever you're ready. Sunday will get you whatever you want.'

'I'll see you shortly then!'

'Afraid not,' she replied. 'I'm going riding.' She remained for a moment longer and then left me to my lukewarm tea and the seductive fragrance of her perfume.

The route down Zomba mountain was different, due to the red dirt road being a one-way system. As it was wide enough for only one vehicle this seemed a sensible sort of arrangement. The twists and curves and the sheer drops were quite awe inspiring, especially when being driven by Valentine. He had, like Clay, an affinity for speed, which on this particular highway I did not share.

'How do you get on for insurance out here?' I asked.

'Sorry, what was that old boy?'

'Insurance! On your crashed plane. Is it through Lloyds in London?'

'Insurance!' He looked genuinely surprised. 'No, afraid not. No insurance cover at all . . . never bothered.' With that he returned to his dreams of Silverstone, apparently unperturbed.

I couldn't believe it. Nobody in their right mind flies without insurance; especially if they're running a charter operation. Any normal operator would be wringing his hands at this stage of the proceedings, realizing he had just lost fifty per cent of his twin-engined fleet. In fact he would be looking for a quick way to end it all. Total financial loss on the aircraft, plus the third-party liabilities – one dead pilot and five dead passengers – not forgetting of course one partially damaged bridge at Tete. Valentine,

I concluded, was not a normal operator.

Hanging on to my seat as we developed a tail slide on a very bad hairpin I decided that he had to be into something a lot more lucrative than aircraft sales. Even if he was stealing the aircraft he was selling, he still couldn't make that sort of money.

Rees-Williams was wiping his hands with an oily rag as Valentine jerked to a stop inside the hangar. The heat and humidity away from the mountain were already having their effect. That clinging, damp, uncomfortable effect of having had a sauna with your clothes on. I climbed out of Valentine's Peugeot and limped over to the unsmiling Welshman.

'Just got to sign off the log books,' he said as I got nearer. 'I'm still not happy with the generator though, seems intermittent!'

'What do you mean intermittent?'

'Well, I changed the bloody brushes again . . . I reckon it's the field winding breaking down, though. In which case it's buggered.'

Valentine interrupted. 'Come through to the office when you've finished, old boy; one or two things to sort out before we go.' I nodded and turned back to Rees-Williams.

'What about spares?' I said.

'Christ man, this is Africa, not Fields' Aircraft Maintenance at bloody Heathrow. Half a century ago the bastards were still in the trees . . . and you're asking me about spares.'

'That's right. I'm the one who's ferrying this heap of junk back to . . . Europe. I want to at least start with a servicable aircraft.'

The Welshman's eyes flashed. 'I'll do what I can.'

I stood my ground. 'I want a serviceable aircraft or the flight's off . . . look, surely you can fill in a few requisition forms and send them off to the Dornier factory . . .'

Rees-Williams gave an ironical laugh. 'I bloody thought

38

so . . . ex-Air Force is it?'

'Once,' I said.

'Once is all it takes,' he said mockingly. 'This is the real world, boyo; it comes a bit harder here.' He turned and started to walk away; then paused and looked back. 'As I said before, Mr Ritchie, I'll do what I can.'

I found Valentine sitting at his desk. He'd obviously heard the raised voices. 'You'll have to take him with a pinch of salt,' he said as I sat down in the nearest chair. 'Good man really . . . just not what we're used to, eh? I mean if he was back in the ranks it would be a different story. As it is . . . well, you understand.'

'Maybe,' I said, 'but I'm not leaving here with an unserviceable aircraft.'

'Quite, quite. Just leave it to me, old boy, I'll handle it. In the meantime you'd better have a shufti at this.' He passed me the Dornier flight manual, the one I'd been looking for the previous day. Within these pages was everything I needed to know about a Dornier DO28. Just a matter of superimposing the written word over the feel and touch of the machine; then it all becomes familiar. The danger lies in the complacency which invariably follows. The old feeling that you know it all. And that's when you find aircraft are much like people; they have a killer instinct too. The day you forget it is the day they strike!

'All set then?' Valentine started towards the door.

'Right with you, just checking the fuel cross-feeding system.'

'I'll get her started up then!'

I lit a cigarette and stared blankly at the flight manual. Until I had found out how much Valentine had purchased the Dornier for I would have to play along. There was nothing else I could do. Nevertheless there was something about Valentine's entire operation that didn't quite add up. Something about Valentine living the life of a latter-day exiled king. And as everyone knows, latter-day exiled kings do not run shoestring aviation companies . . . unless! Unless it's a front for something else. Something more lucrative.

Chapter Four

The airtest was a minor disaster from beginning to end, and when we wrapped it up an hour later the Dornier had more electrical faults than Battersea power station during the blitz. Not that it worried me unduly, I was still dreaming of catching the VC10 flight back to London, and if the aircraft remained unserviceable for very much longer that was precisely what I would do.

Valentine asked me to find Rees-Williams and let him know the extent of the problems; then he left by road on some minor business errand. I remained in the oven of a cockpit, waiting for the post-flight shakes to subside to a more manageable level. I'd asked Valentine about the Dornier but he'd just replied he had bought it from a friend of his over at Chileka. Then I'd tried to get some information on Max Goldstein. Another blank. Apparently they had never met, having done all their business deals by telephone, telex and mail. Valentine had added, 'Excuse the French, old boy, but why the bloody hell would I want to go back to Europe?' Looking around I could understand his reasoning – even though I thought he was lying. Goldstein, in his letter of instruction, had said that Valentine would assist me with the flight planning as he was familiar with the route. It therefore followed that Valentine had at least been to Cyprus or Tel Aviv . . . why not Europe?

After half an hour of baking in the sun's heat I dragged my tired and sweating body out of the Dornier and limped over to the office. Perhaps I had missed something yesterday – something more in the filing cabinet! The clattering of the typewriter told me I had company long before I reached the door.

When I saw her I froze in disbelief. Froze, as twenty years of life telescoped into an instant. A billion photographic stills rushing back with the jerky-framed impressions of an old movie. It ended at Victoria station, London. The old Friday night meeting place. A long time and a lot of heartaches ago. What was even more amazing was she hadn't changed; well perhaps the waist had thickened a little, and perhaps there was the odd age line or two creeping into the still pretty face. But apart from that she was still the same girl. Girl! No, not girl, not any more. Woman – definitely woman.

She stopped typing, as if suddenly aware of being watched. Her eyes turned to mine. No warmth now; no searching, sensuous warmth. Nothing but that strangely distant way of strangers. I felt the lump in my throat harden as I went to speak. When the word came it was nothing more than a dry, questioning croak. 'Sally?'

The expression in her eyes changed immediately, sunlight catching the movement. She still didn't know. 'I'm Sally North,' she said. Still the stranger.

North! North! God, I couldn't be wrong, that wasn't her name. 'I'm . . . I'm sorry,' I said quietly. 'Just for a moment there I thought you were someone else, someone I used to know . . . but her name was Sally Cunningham.'

Surprise rippled through her eyes. 'That was my maiden name . . . Cunningham. Do I know you?'

The image of Victoria station faded suddenly to a sepia-printed yesterday, taking with it the young dark-haired boy in the blue Air Force uniform. The realization had struck home. The realization that although she had hardly changed, I had become a white-haired, scar-faced cripple. She wouldn't know me, not this way at least. I limped over to the desk, my hand reaching unconsciously to hide the hideous scar above my right eye. 'Steve,' I said, 'Stephen Ritchie.' The laugh was forced when I added. 'I suppose Victoria station's still the same!'

'Victoria . . . Stephen! God, it can't be. What . . .' she jumped to her feet, the question dying on her lips – but not in her eyes. I held out my hand with the awkwardness of a schoolboy.

'Don't look too closely,' I said jokingly. 'Comes of

42

burning the candle at both ends.'

She took my hand and held it for a long moment, 'Not you, Stephen. I don't believe that for one minute. And I don't believe any of this . . . I mean how long has it been? Fifteen years?'

'Twenty . . . this Christmas.'

The thought of all those years made her suddenly aware. Aware of herself. She smoothed down her skirt, then ran a hand nervously back through her hair. 'I'll make you a coffee . . . not much to say hello with . : .' I watched as she picked up the kettle from the top of the filing cabinet, made an excuse about getting some water, grabbed her handbag and rushed out of the door to the adjacent washroom.

Five minutes later she was back. Dark blonde hair perfectly in place, face carefully made up. Even the pale blue, short-sleeved blouse looked somehow fresher. She plugged the kettle in and switched it on. 'Where do we start?' she said.

'Start?'

'Yes,' she smiled. She always had a lovely smile and – what was it I used to say – 'come-to-bed eyes'. Brown, beautiful and very sexy.

'The memory lane bit, you mean?'

'God, don't say it like that, makes me feel positively ancient.'

'Not you Sally, you don't look a day older.'

'Compliments as well. Thank you kind sir.'

'Its lovely to see you anyway.'

'And you Stephen, and you. So what have you been doing with yourself all these years?'

I sat down on the typist's chair in an attempt to ease the painful throbbing which had started in my left knee. 'Not a lot,' I said.

She laughed. 'And I don't believe that for one minute either.'

'No, maybe not. If you've got twenty years to spare sometime let me know and I'll give you a blow by blow account.'

'Is that a promise?' she said lightly.

'That's a promise . . . anyway, what happened to you? Last I heard you were getting married.' The name suddenly clicked into place. 'North? Was that the guy?'

'Yes,' she said quietly.

'And you're still married I suppose!'

'Divorced.'

'Oh. I'm sorry.'

'No need to be, it was over a long time ago.'

'Yes,' I said absently, thinking of something else. 'Was that how you came to Africa?'

'In a roundabout way, yes. He was in the Australian Air Force, on an exchange posting to England. He was a pilot as well,' she smiled to herself. 'Must have had a thing about pilots. Anyway we married . . . whirlwind romance, everything. I went back to Australia with him . . . it's a long story but we eventually ended up in South Africa . . . Cape Town. That was after he had left the Air Force of course. Funnily enough I think that's when it started going wrong . . . when he stopped flying . . . he changed. Can you believe that?'

'Yes, I suppose so.'

'You know, I thought about it a lot at the time. It was as though aeroplanes gave him a more carefree attitude to life. He was like a boy who had never grown up; not in all ways but . . .' She looked at me, trying to force an understanding with her eyes.

'Most pilots are the same,' I said. 'A bunch of ageing Peter Pans. Flying keeps them young, mentally alert. In fact it's a great therapy for mortgages and bank overdrafts.'

'What, flying?'

'Well not so much the physical act of hauling the aircraft off the ground and then becoming engrossed in navigational problems – more the magic of soaring above towering white battlements of cumulus, watching the earth shrink into a distant nothingness. You get a feeling of power . . . as though you can reach out of the cockpit and touch the face of God; that's when your earthly problems simply melt away. They begin of course when you return.'

'And if you return for good?'

'Peter Pan grows old.'

She said, 'As simple as that!'

'As simple as that,' I replied.

She turned to the boiling kettle and started making the coffee. 'Good God,' she said, suddenly turning round to face me. 'You're taking the Dornier back!' I nodded. 'I must have seen your name a dozen times or more on telexes, and then it never clicked.'

'No reason why it should . . . all part of the other lifetime.'

Her hand was shaking as she handed me the cup of coffee. 'It was a nice time for all that,' she said softly. 'Are you married? You never said.'

'You never asked, but no . . . never found the time.'

'Don't tell me you're still breaking hearts!'

I looked down at my unsteady hands clinging to that white china cup and saucer. 'Young men break hearts, Sall, old men try to keep them together.'

There was something like sadness in her voice when she said, 'I haven't heard that in a long time!'

'What?'

'You called me Sall.'

'I always did, didn't I?'

'Yes . . . and while we're on the subject you're not an old man.'

'No, perhaps not.' I put my cup on the desk and fumbled through my pockets for a cigarette.

Sally looked at her watch. 'Look, I've got to get into town and post these letters; James said they were urgent. Why don't you come down to the house when you've finished . . . I've got some cold beer.' She gave a quick glance to check the reaction on my face, then added, 'If you feel up to calling on old flames, that is!'

'Love to,' I replied, watching her slip the dust cover over the Adler. She scribbled something on a sheet of paper.

45

'My address,' she said, 'and how to get there.'

I was standing at the window as her car disappeared down the dusty, tree-lined road. Beyond, the mountains swept gracefully up towards the sky. A sky that was darkening with storm clouds, as if heralding the start of the rainy season. For a moment Sally slipped out of my mind as the realization of leaving the safe earth struck a discordant note somewhere deep inside me. And that sky looked more of a killer than any black-hooded executioner. I made myself another coffee and went over to Valentine's desk and began a slow methodical search.

It must have been nearly an hour later when I heard the distant sound of aircraft engines. I limped out to the deserted hangar and looked up at the darkening sky. At first there was nothing, then the engines took on a more urgent note; almost a scream, as the pilot put the props into fine pitch. Pre-landing requirement . . . I lowered my eyes and picked up the low-wing twin almost immediately. It was a Beechcraft Baron, and it was travelling fast in a shallow dive. It crossed the runway threshold at no more than a few hundred feet, then pulled up in a dramatic wingover to the left. There was a touch of the military in that manoeuvre, the old buzz and break routine used by fighter pilots.

The Baron continued round, holding the tight angle of bank, losing speed as wheels and flaps were lowered. It held the turn until it was a few feet above the grass runway, then the wings smoothed out and the nose started easing up gently. It slid on to the ground with effortless precision, telling you that the pilot had done it all a thousand times before.

I was still standing on the same spot when the Baron thrum-thrummed up to the hangar. Mixtures to idle-cut-off and the engines sighed to a stop, sending a gentle harmonics vibration through the loosely fitted metal sheets of the hangar walls. I started walking towards the aircraft as the door swung open and the long athletic

46

frame of Lucky Clay emerged.

'Been far?' I said.

'Karonga, north end of the lake, that's all.'

'Weather looks a bit grim that way!'

He looked back at the sky. 'Yeah, some heavy rains moving in, should be here in an hour or so.' He jumped down off the wing.

'Tell me,' I said, 'how long have you been working for Valentine?'

He stretched his arms and scratched the back of his head before answering. Then he said, 'About a year or so . . . why do you ask?'

'As I mentioned yesterday, I'm packing up the ferry business; thought I'd have a go at aircraft sales. Valentine seems to be doing well from it . . . or was he a wealthy man originally?'

'James wealthy! Not as far as I know. Mind you he was the chief of police in these parts some years ago. I suppose that would carry a hefty pension.' He started walking towards the office.

'He must move quite a few planes through!' I ventured.

'Never really thought about it,' Clay replied.

'Any idea when he retired from the police force?'

Clay scratched his head again. 'Got me there man, you'd have to ask him yourself. Though from what he's said to me . . . I'd guess about six or seven years.' He opened the office door. 'What I need now is about a gallon of coffee.' He went over to the filing cabinet and switched the kettle on. 'So, how did the airtest go?'

'Don't ask,' I said, dropping into the typist's chair.

'Problems, you mean?'

'In spades . . . electrical mostly. And as Rees-Williams is noticeable by his absence I guess it will have to wait until Monday.'

Clay poured the water into the cups. 'James about?'

'Went to Blantyre.'

'Oh yeah, he mentioned that earlier.' He handed me a cup of coffee. 'Was Sally North here earlier . . . James's secretary?'

'Yes . . . she was here.'

'Didn't leave an envelope for me by any chance?'

'Not that I know of.'

'Damn,' Clay muttered. 'Still I guess she's got more important things on her mind than my pay cheque . . . poor old Sally.'

That made me look up. I said, 'Why's that?'

'Oh, the usual thing,' Clay replied casually. 'She was having a big affair with James . . . then he ditched her.'

'James?'

'James Valentine!'

'Doesn't seem the type,' I said.

Clay smiled. 'Don't let the old military bearing fool you; underneath all that he's an out and out romancer as we call them in these parts. Mind you, he soon tires of his women . . .'

'What about his wife?'

'Penny! Oh she knew all about it, and about every other affair he's had, but as they both go their separate ways . . .' Clay picked up his flight bag and moved down to Valentine's desk. I followed him.

'Going back to the house?' I said at length.

His pen was poised over the aircraft's technical log. 'Haven't got the wagon here. No, I'm flying over to Chileka.' There was a knowing twinkle in his blue eyes when he added, 'Got some business to attend to.'

'Who owns the pick-up outside?'

'Company hack, help yourself . . . but watch the brakes, they're bloody awful.'

'Thanks,' I said, moving towards the door. 'See you when I see you then.'

'Sure thing,' he replied absently.

I left a hurried note clamped in the vice on Rees-Williams's workbench, then cajoled the rattletrap of a pick-up into action. Sally's instructions were explicit and I found the house at the first attempt. Down the airport road towards town, first right after the National Bank and the last house down the road on the left. It was set back from the road, partially hidden behind a gathering of jacaranda trees and white-blossoming frangipani bushes. I parked the pick-up next to her dusty Ford and went up the steps to the verandah. The heavy scent of flowers, like the sultry sticky heat, was totally overpowering.

'Thought I heard a car,' Sally said, pushing the mesh screen outer door open.

'Nice little place,' I said.

'It's quiet . . . better than being in the middle of town.'

'And you never did like towns, did you?'

The brown eyes smiled warmly. 'I wouldn't have thought you'd have remembered.' She held the door open. 'Well, we're not going to stand here all day are we?'

Five minutes later I had an uncomfortable seat on the edge of the kitchen table, a tumbler full of whisky and the start of a potted history of her travels in Australia.

'Then we went to Alice Springs,' she was saying. 'Every year they have "Henley on the Todd".'

'What's that?'

'Well, every year during the dry they have a boat race on the dried-up river bed of the Todd. The boats are carried by the crews.'

'Sounds like Aussies,' I remarked.

'They blame it on their Pomm ancestry.' She smiled and went over to the sink and started peeling potatoes, the job she must have been doing when I arrived. I doubt if I will ever want anyone to ask me to stay to dinner as much as I did at that moment. But that afternoon, with the sky darkening with rain and the warm tingling glow of whisky running through my veins, I somehow felt at home. I suppose it was watching a woman peeling potatoes at a kitchen sink; something I hadn't seen for years. Then again it may have been the light untroubled conversation . . . or just a sudden bout of infinite nostalgia.

Sally finished the potatoes and returned to her seat at the table. 'Penny for them!' she said.

'Now if you'd said a whisky!'

She refilled my glass. 'Well?'

'Oh, nothing really . . . well, memories. Do you remember that holiday we had in Cornwall?'

'I remember.'

'And here we are twenty years later, and it all seems like yesterday.'

She smiled. 'When are you leaving?'

'With the Dornier you mean?'

'Yes.'

'Depends. It's got a lot of problems and I've got an aversion to old aeroplanes with problems.'

'Don't take it then.'

'Not as easy as that, I've been paid in advance . . . I've committed myself in a way.'

She studied my face for a long time. 'Do you mind if I ask you something; something personal?'

'Not at all.'

'What happened to your leg, I noticed the limp . . . and the scar.'

'One of those flying accidents you sometimes read about.'

'Were you still in the Air Force?'

'No . . . flying for an airline in the Philippines. Happened four years ago.'

She said, 'Oh.' Then changed the subject back to the Dornier ferry. 'So what happens if they can't fix the plane?'

I shrugged. 'I'll cross that bridge when I come to it. Spares seem to be the problem. Rees-Williams reckons it's impossible to get them.'

'He's right, you know. In the time I've been here I've noticed that. Apparently the blacks steal them off the airliners when they're unloading.'

'That figures. Not so much the blacks, but most international airports have the same problems. Mind you I would have thought the previous owners would have carried some spares.'

'Perhaps, why don't you ask them?'

'I don't know who they are.'

'The Malawi Air Force,' she replied. 'But I'm sure

David would have checked with them.'

'It's an ex-Air Force plane then?' I said, trying to hide the anger in my voice.

'Yes. Didn't they tell you that?'

'No, but it's not important.' Like hell it wasn't important. 'Who's David, by the way?'

'David Rees-Williams,' she said. 'Then of course there's Bill Kimberley. He might know something.'

'Who's he?'

'Oh, you'd like old Bill. He used to own Southland Aviation years ago. I met him at the expats' club in Blantyre a few months ago.' Her face became strained. 'James introduced me.'

'I see.'

'I don't suppose you do, but it doesn't really matter,' she said, twisting the diamond solitaire on her enagagement finger. It was by far the largest single diamond I had ever seen. I didn't know too much about diamonds, but enough to tell me that this stone was something like a three or four carat stone. And the open market price on that sort of diamond would be way out of reach of a secretary. Except she wouldn't have bought it for herself; women rarely do. No, it would have been from her former husband on their engagement. Either that or a gift from Valentine! I smiled to myself. He may be well off, I thought, but not that much.

By now Sally was on her fourth large whisky, which was about three too many for a non-drinker. The happiness which had been in her face earlier had long since disappeared; as with the sunny day outside. Now the eyes, the mouth, her whole face resembled the dark storm clouds – grey and full of tears. I thought about asking her for Bill Kimberley's address, but then realized I would probably find it in the telephone directory. I finished my drink and put the glass on the table. 'I'll be going then,' I said, moving over to her and putting my arm gently around her shoulders.

'You don't have to,' she said, looking up at me.

'I think it's better that I do.'

51

'Perhaps you're right.'

I leant down and kissed her lightly on the cheek. Her face was wet with tears.

I limped quietly out of the house to the first rains of the season and headed the pick-up towards Zomba mountain. I was passing through the pine forest trying to understand the changes years make in people when the rain started descending in a deafening wall. Up until now it had been heavy but manageable; now it could wash me over the side of the mountain with relative ease. I pressed on cautiously, the windscreen wipers clunk-clunking back and forth as they fought a losing battle with the tropical downpour. I stuck my head out of the window and squinted at the muddy track ahead; it was fast turning to a red river. Once through the forest, the total effect worsened considerably. Loose stones and rocks were being washed down from the rising ground on the left of the road, whilst on the right the sheer drop to a steaming bottomless pit became a frightening reality. A small boulder cannoned off the roof of the cab, stepping up the already fast-flowing adrenaline.

When I finally arrived at the house it was deserted. The blazing log fire and the topped-up whisky decanter were, however, better than people at that moment. I needed time to think, to collect my ragged thoughts together and put them into some semblance of order. Then I remembered Bill Kimberley and went through to the hallway to find a telephone directory. I made a note of his address and went back to the fire, settling my damp body onto the chesterfield. That was when I heard the feminine click of leather heels in the hallway.

Penny Valentine's sweeping entrance put an end to any idea I had about thinking. She was wearing the same clinging green dress as the previous day, and if anything was looking even more appealing.

She gave me a tight-faced smile. 'Hello, thought it was Lucky.'

52

'Afraid not, he's gone over to Chileka. Said he had some business to attend to.' Her face seemed to drop a little; or perhaps it was a trick of the late afternoon light. 'Looks as though the road will be out of commission if this keeps up,' I added.

'Usually the case,' she replied, and walked across to the french windows. As she stood there, legs slightly apart, I could see the shapely outline of her thighs through the thin material of the dress. As I'd said to Clay, not a bad looker. And she was getting better by the minute.

She remained there for a long time. Not speaking, not moving. A beautiful bird trapped in a gilded cage. Eventually she turned towards the door. 'Dinner will be at seven,' she said coldly.

She didn't wait for a reply, not that she had been expecting one anyway. It had been a statement of fact. Nothing more. With Sally it would have been different... once, anyway.

Chapter Five

Bill Kimberley lived in a broken-down old shack seven miles north of Blantyre on the Tudin Wada road. The shack was a white-painted wooden structure which had doubtless seen better days. The paint was peeling and odd planks were coming adrift from one of the walls, leaving it an uncared for and an unloved place. I parked the pick-up and followed an overgrown pathway leading to the house. Something rustled in the long grass at my feet, and just as suddenly was gone. They say a snake will never attack, they say it will always slither away; provided of course you give it adequate warning. If by chance you are unfortunate enough to step on it you could end up with problems. And those problems, like flying, I could do without.

The man who answered the door and the name of Bill Kimberley was nothing like I had expected Bill Kimberley to be. But then that is usually the case in life. He was short, wiry, and looked as though he had lived forever. His skin was weathered nut brown and resembled dried-up parchment. The hair, what little of it remained, was a salt and pepper mixture of white and reddish brown. The eyes, though, were the most remarkable feature in this little terrier of a man; they were small and brown and darted back and forth as if attached to invisible wires. I introduced myself and asked if I might ask him a few questions about Southland Aviation, the company he had once owned.

'Come right on in,' he said. 'Always nice to have a visitor. English aren't you?' Before I had the opportunity to answer he continued. 'Yes, thought so, tell by the accent you're not from these parts . . . anyway how did you find out about me and that "get poor quick" scheme down the road?'

I laughed at the reference. 'By accident really, I was talking to someone over at Chileka. They said you were quite a pilot in those days; so I thought I'd drop by and say hello.' Not quite true of course, but near enough.

'Quite a pilot eh! That's what they said did they . . . bloody liars the lot of them. Not quite a pilot at all; I was the best . . . but that was a long time ago. Anyway, have a seat. What part of England did you say you were from?'

'London, I . . .'

'London eh! I remember London, before your time of course. English m'self you know. Born and bred in Shropshire. Read poetry do you?'

'Can't say that I do,' I replied.

'Housman. A. E. Housman, wrote *Shropshire Lad*. That's me, all the way from Wenlock Edge. Nice place as I remember, but that's something else that's a long time ago. Anyway, what brings you to Malawi?' He sat back in his worn leather armchair and started filling an old briar pipe.

'Ferrying a Dornier out for James Valentine,' I said.

Kimberley's eyes darted up from the pipe. 'Thought he'd got rid of that lot years ago. Amazing, quite amazing.'

'That lot,' I repeated. 'I was under the impression there was just the one . . . the ex-Air Force machine!'

He sat for a moment eyeing the pipe and the pouch of tobacco. 'One you say. No, no, no. It was a batch of four, remember that quite clearly. Offered me the contract to buy them, the Air Force that is . . . told 'em to bugger off. Price y'see, much too high.'

I lit a cigarette. 'Perhaps Valentine just bought the one,' I ventured.

His eyes caught mine, then were off again like a pair of startled rabbits. 'No, bought the lot. There when it happened, y'see. While I'm thinking about it, would you like a drink? I can run to a warm Scotch if that's all right.'

'Warm Scotch sounds fine,' I said.

He chuckled quietly and shuffled over to an old varnished cupboard by the door. The heat of the morning was fast taking over the small untidy room, causing the sweat to run even more freely down my face, my neck and my back. The short rains of the previous evening had done nothing to relieve the heat in the lowlands, in fact quite the opposite. The humidity level must have been up by at least fifty per cent, and along with the hot, damp smell of decaying vegetation it was sickeningly oppressive. Kimberley returned from the cupboard with two decent measures of neat, warm whisky. He handed me one and settled back in his chair.

'Here's mud in your eye,' he said. 'Do they still say that?'

'Haven't heard it in a long time.'

'No, suppose not.'

'Why did you sell out to James Valentine?' I asked. 'If that's not a personal question.'

He chuckled again. 'That's easy,' he said. 'The silly bugger gave me too much money.' He put his whisky on the small side table by his chair and went back to filling his pipe. 'Been fighting a losing battle for years, trying to make ends meet, y'see. In fact if he'd waited another six months could have had it all for nothing . . . I'd have been bankrupt by then.'

'So he paid you a good price,' I said. Obviously I didn't sound too convinced; either that or he had noticed my eyes sweeping around the room, taking in the dusty, broken-down furniture.

'Don't take no notice of the place,' he said quietly. 'After Jean died, my wife that is, never got round to keeping it the way she did. Funny thing about women you know, you can say a lot of bad things about them but at the end of the day they're the ones who keep everything together . . . it's only when they've gone that you notice of course, and by then it's too late.'

'Yes, I suppose so. She's been dead a long time then . . . your wife.'

'Oh yes, quite a time now. Mind you, I think she was happy to go. Cancer y'see, nasty business that. It was a Christmas time as I recall. Pity. She'd struggled with me for years and years but somehow I never managed to turn the dreams into reality. You understand what I mean?'

'Not exactly.'

'Life,' he explained, 'it's the place to act out dreams. Of course you've got to have the courage; follow your instincts. I suppose I never had that brand of courage. Anyway Jean had a lot of faith, she kept on saying it would come right in the end. Wasn't far out either. It was the Christmas after she died that it did.'

He lit his pipe and puffed quietly away for a few moments before continuing. 'That was when I sold out to Valentine. He was adamant you know, not that I really wanted to change his mind; but I did warn him it was a risky business y'see. Told him the only way to make a small fortune in aviation is to start with a big one. All that did was to make him up his offer. Quite mad if you ask me. I remember thinking he wasn't much of a businessman, but then neither was I if the truth was known – just a pilot who thought it would be easier to work for himself. Not that easy, you know.'

I nodded. 'What about the Dorniers?'

'The Dorniers, ah yes. Told you the Air Force offered them to me, didn't I . . . yes, yes, course I did.' He puffed some more on his pipe. 'After Valentine bought the company he went along to the Air Force and in the very next breath took up the option. Made me think he was totally crazy. I stayed on with him for six months or so, showing him the ropes . . . even taught him to fly. Terrible as I recall, more of a driver, no feel for the aeroplane. It's in the hands, you know. They used to say I had the hands of an angel.' He held out his gnarled, sunburnt hands and surveyed them carefully. 'Perhaps not any more, but that once was enough. Made it all worthwhile.'

'I don't suppose you know if Valentine sold any of the Dorniers?' I said hopefully.

His eyes darted quickly around the room. 'Matter of fact he did sell at least one that I know of. Surprised me; no, that's the wrong word . . . confuse is better. But then I realized that was probably the reason I'd failed in business. Afraid to take a gamble, y'see. And that is the second secret. If life's the place to act out your dreams then business is the place to gamble. That's all it is, one great big game of cards. If they fall the right way you're home and dry. Anyway I was saying, he did sell the one . . . sad business that!'

My ears pricked up. 'Sad? Why sad?'

'Crashed, y'know. The plane crashed . . . somewhere north of Luxor in Egypt as I recall.'

I twisted uncomfortably in my chair. Tired old aeroplanes are prone to do that sort of thing. 'What happened to the pilot? Was he . . .'

Kimberley interrupted: 'Oh he was killed alright. It was a flamer, or so they said.'

I knew from that remark that Bill Kimberley was a wartime veteran; the word flamer being a wartime expression for aircraft going down in flames. I finished my whisky and stared blankly into the empty glass. The oppressive heat and the uncontrollable sweating were making me feel ever so slightly sick. I persevered. 'I don't suppose you would know the price the Air Force were asking for the Dorniers?'

'Now that's a question,' he muttered. He climbed unsteadily to his feet and shuffled towards the far side of the room. 'That is indeed a question!' After a number of minutes of searching through various drawers he found what he was looking for and returned to his chair. 'There you are, y'see,' he held up a pile of yellowed papers tied together with string. 'Might be in the final stages of anno domini but I still remember things.' He untied the string and flipped noisily through the pages, puffing gently on his pipe at the same time. 'There you are, there you are,' he waved a battered-looking document triumphantly in the air. 'Knew I still had it. Now let's see. Yes here we are, three hundred and sixty thousand kwacha for the job lot. As I said before too much . . . far too much.'

'Any idea what that is in dollars?'

'Don't know about then. Now it's one point two

kwacha to the dollar . . . or is it? Got the *Finanical Times* somewhere, last week's of course but it would be in there . . . do you want me to find it?'

'No thanks, not really important,' I said, doing a quick mental calculation on the figures he had given me. It worked out to exactly 300,000 US dollars for the four aircraft, which meant 75,000 dollars apiece. Then I remembered the sales invoice to the Israeli Air Force. The aircraft I was due to ferry had been sold for 55,000 US dollars. Something was wrong! Or was it? The exchange rate kwacha to dollar might have changed dramatically over the preceding years. Then again Valentine may have sold the other aircraft at a substantial profit and was accepting a twenty thousand dollar loss on the last one simply to balance the books . . . or help the cash flow situation. It still didn't explain his millionaire lifestyle though.

'You can't remember if he sold any more, then,' I said.

Kimberley climbed to his feet and took the two empty glasses back to the old varnished cupboard and refilled them. 'Oh I'm sure he did, but that would have been after I'd left the place.' He returned and handed me my refilled glass.

'Seems a wealthy sort of chap these days,' I said, lighting another cigarette. Kimberley took a long swallow of his whisky, replaced the pipe between his teeth and said, 'Funny thing that. Wasn't originally you know. Used to be the chief of police. Must have been after his first wife died . . . Jean; her name was Jean as well. Then he remarried that half-caste woman; nothing against her personally y'see, but it's frowned on in these parts. Course they all said he'd gone tropo . . .'

'Tropo, what's that?'

'Off his head, the tropics, y'see. Too much sun . . . you know the sort of thing.'

'Yes, I suppose I do.'

'Anyway he married the half-caste woman and then retired from the police. Next thing you know he buys this big spread up on the mountain, then the aviation

59

company from me ... then those Dorniers from the Air Force. Word was his wife had left him a lot of money.' A mischievous smile lit up his face. 'But then we know differently, don't we?'

'We do,' I said unconvincingly.

'Course we do ... y'see my wife Jean used to do a lot of social work with his wife. Apparently her father was a vicar in Guildford ... in England, but you'd know that, wouldn't you. Yes, yes, course you would. Anyway my wife used to say they were as poor as church mice, used to joke about it. He being a vicar and church mice, y'see.'

I gave a small laugh to show that I did.

'Mind you, she was a lady, say that much for her. Well-bred sort of woman ... not like the baggage he's got now, but there you are.'

I remained with Bill Kimberley for another half hour, listening mainly, as he rambled on about poetry and Wenlock Edge and boating on the River Severn. I didn't tell him it had all changed; no point really. He wasn't going back, not at his time of life, and at least this way he would die a happy man remembering an England uncluttered by progress.

I drove back towards Blantyre with a cool breeze circulating through the open window of the cab making the morning almost bearable. Amazing that Bill Kimberley hadn't asked me why I was so inquisitive; perhaps it was just that he needed a voice – other than his own. I hoped I would never grow that old and that alone; I could take it now, but I couldn't be sure about then.

As I had to drive through Blantyre on my way back to Zomba I decided to stop at Chileka airport and see if the bar was open. It was. It was also deserted except for a sleepy-eyed African who seemed to resent my order for a beer and an omelette.

'You want omelette?' he said, rubbing his eyes.

'One omelette and one beer,' I repeated with deliberate slowness.

'One omelette and one beer,' he said with equal

slowness, then padded off to the doorway at the corner of the bar. I found a seat directly under a squeaking paddle fan and lit a cigarette. Ten minutes later the sleepy-eyed African was back. 'One omelette and one beer,' he pronounced solemnly.

I said, 'Have you a knife and fork?'

His eyes rolled wide. 'Knife and fork?'

I mimed the actions of eating utensils over the greasy-looking omelette. 'Knife and fork,' I said tiredly.

The request sank in and he returned to the kitchen. Moments later he was back, polishing the knife and fork on his filthy, sweat-stained shirt sleeve. My appetite died on the first mouthful, so I lit another cigarette and took the Star beer out to the first-floor balcony. Clay arrived five minutes later.

'Thought it was you man, saw the pick-up outside.' He dropped into the next chair. 'What are you doing out this way?'

'Pilots and airports,' I said. 'Second home.'

'Yeah, guess so . . . when you leaving?'

'You tell me. How long's it going to take the Welshman to fix the kite? Once I can answer that part of the problem I might be able to come up with an answer.'

'Not the best engineer in the world is he?' Clay said.

'I'm amazed that Valentine puts up with him.'

Clay smiled knowingly. 'I think that's just a matter of engineers being thin on the ground in these parts . . . good engineers that is. And as Valentine doesn't pay too well . . .'

'We've all got our crosses to bear,' I said unsympathetically. 'As long as that Dornier is fixed that's all I care about.'

Clay said, 'Yeah, I'd make sure of that . . . not much in the way of servicing facilities between here and Tel Aviv.'

My jaw tightened. 'Who the bloody hell said anything about Tel Aviv?'

Clay was taken aback at my sudden anger, colour rising in his sunburnt face. 'It was James . . . he said something about it.'

After all the trouble Max Goldstein had taken in writing me a missal on the subject of secrecy, it seemed faintly ridiculous to think that Valentine was shouting his mouth off, even if it was to one of his pilots. If I had to do this trip it was going to be kept under wraps. As I would be staging through Egypt the last thing I wanted was for them to find out my true destination – it would be twenty years in a jail cell at least.

I turned to Clay. 'I'm heading back to Zomba now, are you flying up there?'

'Shortly,' he said. 'I'll be in around sunset.'

'One last word,' I said in a forced whisper. 'Don't mention Tel Aviv to anyone. For your information I'm going to Larnaca, Cyprus, end of story . . . got it?'

'Got it,' he replied.

The drive back to Zomba was very hot and very tiring. The wind had ceased and the sky was all over blue, framing a burning sun at its zenith. I didn't see another soul all the way, just a winding black ribbon of tarmac rippling with heat haze and edged by occasional gums and patches of dried-up grass thirsting for more rain. I had planned on going straight to the top of the mountain, but by the time I reached the township tiredness and the need for a drink had overtaken me. I drove to Sally North's house.

'I'm sorry about yesterday,' she said, handing me a long glass of whisky and water.

'No need to be, we all get our ups and downs. The answer is not to take it too seriously . . . life, I mean. One day at a time is quite enough.'

She smiled and dropped into the other verandah wicker chair. 'You didn't always use to talk that way,' she said.

'Victoria station you mean . . . but then I was twenty years of age and knew all the answers. Now I'm forty and haven't got a bloody clue. It's like the joke says, "Just when I thought I knew all life's answers they changed all the questions".'

'And that sounds like cynicism.'

'Not really Sall . . . I like to call it realism.' I took a

cigarette from a fresh pack and offered her one.

'Wrong lady friend,' she mocked.

I laughed. 'Chance would be a fine thing.'

She was silent for a few moments . . . pensive. As if trying to put together the right words. 'I'm leaving here shortly,' she said at length.

'Yes, I guessed you might be.'

There was no surprise in her voice when she said, 'So you know, then?'

I looked up from my glass and met her soft brown eyes. 'Yes, I know.'

'I won't bother to ask who told you, that doesn't worry me . . . he does though, he phoned me last night.'

'Valentine?'

'Yes . . . do you know what he said? He said he wanted this ring back,' she held out her left hand. 'It was the only present he ever gave me and now he wants it back.'

'He gave you that?' I said in astonishment.

She nodded. 'It was an unofficial engagement ring. Oh I had the lot, promises of divorce, marriage in the spring . . . when all he really wanted was to get into my bed.'

'So what did you tell him?'

'It wasn't very ladylike.'

'So you're not returning it?'

'No.'

'Is he likely to get nasty about it?'

'I don't think he's in much of a position to do that.'

'Why so?'

She looked at me steadily. 'Are you still the same Stephen I used to know?'

'Apart from the gammy leg and the bust-up face, you mean?'

Her face remained serious. 'No. Inside . . . what I mean is are you here to just ferry that aircraft or are there other reasons?'

'Other reasons? What other reasons? Take a look at me, will you? I'm a washed-up pilot who couldn't get a job with any decent company because I live in a bottle.

This is the only way I know to earn the rent money . . . and after this trip I won't even have that any more.'

'Why . . . what happens after this trip?'

I put my glass down and took her hand. 'I shouldn't even be here now . . . I've lost my licence.'

'Your flying licence?' she said in amazement.

'Yes.'

'How . . . why?'

'Medical grounds . . . high blood pressure.'

'But then why . . . ?'

'I'd already been paid for the trip, and half of the money had been swallowed up by a bank overdraft.'

'But won't someone find out?'

'Only if you tell them,' I said quietly.

She squeezed my hand. 'You know me better than that, don't you?'

'Come here,' I said. She leaned forward and I kissed her gently on the mouth.

'What was that for?'

'How about reliving old memories!'

'In that case welcome back, old memories.'

'You said Valentine wasn't in much of a position to get nasty about the ring. Why's that?'

She said simply, 'James Valentine is smuggling diamonds!' There was a moment's frozen and incredulous stillness. An African kind of stillness; the kind you find on windless days when the dank humidity and decaying vegetation only add to the uncomfortable feeling of excessive sweating. Beyond the verandah the incessant chorus of humming, zinging insects grew louder.

'Are you sure?' I said, feeling the blood drain from my face.

'I'm positive.'

'And Valentine knows you know?'

'I'm pretty sure he does . . . yes.'

My head was still reeling as my mind went through a rapid video rerun of previous events. The picture started taking shape. 'Where's he smuggling them to . . . do you know?'

'It's a long and complicated story, Stephen. It might be better if you forgot all about it and caught the first commercial flight back to England.'

'As I said before, not so easy; anyway I'd rather find out what the hell's going on.'

She didn't say anything at first and I had the feeling she wasn't going to. Then she took me by the hand and led me into the house and down the darkened hallway to the room at the end. It was a lounge, dining room, study all rolled into one. The dining table was littered with papers, books and various bits of office equipment. It was amongst the clutter that Sally picked up a photograph album and started flicking through the photo-filled pages. 'Read that,' she said, handing me a yellowed newspaper cutting. 'It's from a Jo'burg newspaper.'

I took it over to the window and started reading. The story had front-page coverage; but then a ten-million-dollar diamond theft would hardly be found amongst the ladies' underwear ads. I read it twice and went back towards the table. In a nutshell the story explained how ten million dollars' worth of cut and uncut diamonds – gem quality as opposed to industrial – had been cleverly lifted from the strongroom of the Williams Diamond Corporation. Chief Security Officer Felix Schmocker was assisting the police with their enquiries. A faded second-rate wire photo had accompanied the article. The face in that photo seemed vaguely familiar. 'You're saying that these are the diamonds; but according to the date on the paper here this all happened seven years ago . . . and anyway who the hell is Felix Schmocker?'

'He was James's deputy in the Malawi police force . . .'

'The photo, of course,' I looked at the newspaper cutting again. 'I've seen a photo of him at Valentine's house . . . both of them in uniform.'

Sally said, 'In a way that's how I found out. He used to bring office work here in the evenings, and then I started doing the books. I couldn't ever quite work out where everything came from . . . it seemed the company was losing far more than it was making. Then last Christmas he gave me this ring. It was some time after that when I was clearing some papers out of the office safe that I found the newspaper cutting. I was sure that he had forgotten about it so I kept it . . . more out of curiosity than anything, I suppose. A few weeks later I went up to the house to take some documents he had forgotten . . . that's when I saw the photograph of Felix Schmocker. Even then it didn't click, but when I started listening to phone conversations and reading through telex messages it all seemed to fit into place.'

'In what way exactly?'

'Well, I found out that after Felix Schmocker left the police force, which coincidentally was the same time that James did, he went to the Williams Diamond Corporation. About a year after that . . . the robbery.'

'What happened to Schmocker?'

'Got off apparently, insufficient evidence.'

'And you reckon he and James have the diamonds now?'

'Let's go to the kitchen, I'll make you a cup of tea.'

'Now if you'd said whisky!'

'Tea's better, cools you down.'

Ten minutes later we were sitting at the kitchen table. Me chain smoking and Sally pouring the tea. 'So,' I said. 'Going back to Valentine and Schmocker, you reckon they still have the diamonds!'

'Not Schmocker,' she replied, putting the cup before me, 'he's dead. No, I think James has got them all . . . or had them all.'

'What happened to Schmocker?'

'It was about six months after the trial. Apparently he was still in Jo'burg and being tailed every minute of the day and night. You see he was dismissed from his job, on full pension I was told, but the police didn't think the legal people had done their jobs properly so they decided to keep him under surveillance . . . hoping I suppose he would lead them to the cache of diamonds. They kept it up for six months and then one day – right in the middle of the city – his car was involved in a crash. He was burnt to death in the wreckage.'

'Amazing . . . how did you find all that out?'

Sally smiled briefly. 'The women's circles in Blantyre are notorious for gossip. Ask one question and you get a complete history.'

I inhaled deeply on my cigarette. 'But even assuming Valentine is mixed up in this, why would he wait all this time?'

'But don't you see . . . he's been moving them little by little.'

'Where to?'

'I'm not sure, but I did overhear a telephone conversation he was having with a man from Paris . . .'

'Not someone called Max Goldstein by any chance?'

'That's the name. Max Goldstein. I think he has something to do with this Dornier sale as well.'

'I know that, and there have been . . .' I stopped. And there have been three other such ferries. The perfect front! Buy aeroplanes from the military, stash a few diamonds in them and ferry them out to some other air force. Which makes the entire operation next door to a government transaction; and nobody, but nobody is going to question that.

'What did Valentine say to Goldstein exactly?'

'As far as I remember the last call was about two weeks ago, the time the sale of the Dornier was going through. James said something about the last "submarine goods" going through on the standard routing.'

'I don't follow, what are "submarine goods"?'

'It's diamond trade language for any goods that move along unorthodox routes. A polite way of saying smuggling, I suppose.'

'Don't tell me you got that from the women's circle in Blantyre!'

Sally smiled again. 'Matter of fact I did. Lucy Lockett's late husband used to be a *diamantaire* in Cape Town. She's a real old chatterbox but full of surprises.'

'Is that all?' I said.

'Isn't that enough?'

I drank my tea and thought. After a while I said, 'Might be. Do you know if Valentine still has the paperwork on the previous ferries?'

'At the office, it's all there.'

'Is it possible for me to have a look?'

There was deep concern in her eyes. 'Stephen, before we go any further do you think it's wise?'

'Probably not, but I'm not stopping now.'

'No, I didn't think you would. That's one thing that hasn't changed . . . once you've got your teeth into something you never let go.'

'I did once,' I said looking at her.

'Yes, you did, didn't you? I suppose you realize you broke my heart into tiny bits when you sent me that letter.'

'Another example of Ritchie screwing up his life.'

She reached out and took my hand. 'It doesn't have to be,' she said softly.

'Us, you mean?'

'Why not?'

'I couldn't offer you anything, Sall, I'm washed up. No money, no job . . . nothing!'

'We could change all that Stephen . . . at least we could try.'

I looked into the saddened, softened light of her beautiful eyes. 'Maybe!' I said. 'Tomorrow night! I'll take you out to dinner tomorrow night . . . we could go to Blantyre.'

'That would be nice . . . then we could come back here . . .'

I laughed. 'I remember that look.'

'What look?'

'The Friday night look you always gave me when you arrived at Victoria – the one that lasted until we arrived at that little hotel.'

'And seduced you I suppose . . .'

I said, 'That couldn't have been too difficult.'

'No, but I remember the first time . . . I don't suppose you do?'

'Your pink and black nightdress, you mean?'

She laughed. Deeply, warmly, lovingly; and I found myself wanting to go back. Life had been a lot easier then, less complicated. Perhaps it could be again. Or perhaps I was chasing moonbeams – looking for something which had died a long time ago. As if sensing my inner torment she came to me quietly, pressing my face into the softness of her breasts. I rose slowly and followed her to the bedroom.

It was late in the afternoon when Sally followed me out to the verandah and looked up at the reddening sky. 'No rain tomorrow,' she said.

'Perhaps not,' I said.

'Rather have the rains, at least it would be cooler.'

I was opening the door of the pick-up when she called my name. I waited as she came to me. 'Something you can do for me,' she said. 'Will you keep this?' She handed me the diamond ring.

'What am I supposed to do with it?'

'Just keep it safe; now if he asks for it back I can say I've lost it.'

'I doubt he'll believe that!'

'He can believe what he likes, but if I haven't got it there's nothing he can do, is there?'

'No, I suppose not.'

She reached up and kissed me lightly on the cheek. 'I'll see you at the office in the morning, I suppose.'

I climbed into the cab and closed the door. I wanted to say, how does every morning forever sound? Instead I said, 'Yes . . . in the morning.'

We were silent for a moment, then she said, 'Stephen!'

'Yes?'

'I love you.'

I reached out and touched her cheek. 'Tomorrow,' I said.

I drove slowly towards the mountain; caught up in a confusion of yesterdays. Remembering how things had once been. Remembering what seemed like a million weekends in London. Remembering how one weekend I had been unable to make it because of flying duties. The next weekend she had phoned and said she was busy. I went to town anyway, and for the first time found out how lonely London can be when you are by yourself. I even went down to Victoria station and stood by the flowerseller's stall, watching the unsmiling passengers bustling to and from the trains, and the inevitable pigeons dodging the footsteps as they searched for scraps of food.

And then I saw her. Radiantly beautiful, smiling, laughing. Sally! I started to move forward, then stopped. She was with another man. I couldn't even picture him any more, his image erased from my memory forever. But then! Then, I had shrunk back into the crowds, watching her walk out of the station, her laughter as she passed close to me somehow cruel and mocking.

I remained in London for the weekend and on the Sunday found myself back at Victoria station. Watching the passengers for the last train to Wendover. It was a bitterly cold winter's night, with a thin fog spreading up from the shiny black streets. A fog which stole the buildings and suspended the streetlamps in pools of yellow light. She arrived out of that same fog. Still smiling, still laughing, still radiantly beautiful – and still with the same man. I watched them board the last train and sit close together. Watched as the train pulled slowly down the dimly lit platform and clackety-clacked into the foggy night.

At twenty years of age and hopelessly in love, I found the pain had taken an eternity to die. I had never mentioned it, of course. What was the point? She was young and very beautiful and I somehow knew the idea of marriage would never appeal to her, not then at least. Three days later my application for a posting to Sharjah was rushed through. They needed pilots in the Middle East, and as nobody in their right mind volunteered for a posting to that particular hell hole . . .

That night I sat down and wrote to Sally. It was a long letter, full of memories and tender regrets. The sort of worthless drama only the young can dream up. It never occurred to me that my seeing her with another man could have been something totally innocent. I told her that as I would be away for at least nine months, if not longer, it somehow seemed pointless to continue with our relationship. Although I had never mentioned where I was going I still expected to find a letter, forwarded from my old station. But that letter never came, and nine months later Sally Cunningham, the face from Victoria station, had faded into a yesterday of painful memories. A yesterday that time had obscured, until now at least.

Now after all these years that yesterday was back; and with it the face. The still beautiful but older face. She would be at least forty. And at forty any normal unattached woman would be looking for a husband. In a limited field of middle-aged men I could be the answer. Not much of one admittedly, but one nevertheless. The distant nagging fear of flying and diamond smuggling were suddenly pushed aside as I tried to remember the pain from the first time around. The pain I had successfully avoided ever since.

Chapter Six

Valentine and Clay were deeply engrossed in conversation concerning a charter flight into southern Zimbabwe. Clay seemed less than happy about it.

'I don't think it's on, those rebels have got SAM missiles now,' Clay said.

'But it's right on the border,' Valentine replied with self-assurance, 'just a matter of in and out . . . you know the sort of thing.'

'Yeah, I know the sort of thing, but it was different then . . .'

Valentine cut him short, 'Yes, I realize that old boy, but this trip does need two crew . . . I wouldn't ask you, but after Anderson got the chop last week, you see the spot I'm in . . .' his voice trailed off.

They both looked up suddenly as I left the shadow of the verandah and entered the room.

'Steve, old boy, there you are . . . whisky?' Valentine was on his feet and halfway towards the whisky supply before I could answer.

I said, 'Thanks,' and went over to join Clay on the chesterfield.

'Just back then?' he asked.

'More or less.'

Valentine handed me a large Scotch and returned to his chair. 'Spoke to Rees-Williams today,' he said casually, 'looks as though you need a new generator for the port engine.'

'What are the hopes of getting one?' I replied.

'All sorted out,' Valentine said, 'managed to scrounge one from a chap in Lilongwe, said he'd drop it over tomorrow or Tuesday.' Then he turned to Clay, 'If you'd like to plan that flight, Lucky, we can talk about it after dinner.'

Clay got to his feet. 'Okay, I'll go and make a start on it now.' He left the room with concern written all over his face.

Once he had gone I turned to Valentine, 'What do you want to do about my licence validation with the Malawi authorities?'

'Have to leave it until Wednesday, old boy, I'll be away all day tomorrow, might not be back until Tuesday, actually. Still,' he smiled, 'if we can get the kite fixed on Wednesday, you can depart Thursday.'

'What about the diplomatic clearances?' I said.

'All in hand, I've put in overflight clearances for Tanzania and landing clearances for Kenya and the Sudan . . . the replies will be back before you leave.'

'What about Egypt?'

'That's in as well, but we never get replies normally, just dash the customs officers a bottle of Scotch or a few dollars and Bob's your uncle.'

I nodded, he wasn't far out on that observation. The common link of the third world, dash, bribery . . . call it what you like, it didn't really matter. All it took was the odd bottle, the handful of dollars and the right sympathetic ear. Worked like a dream every time.

Valentine moved over to the fireplace and started throwing logs into the dying embers. 'Gets cold up here in the evenings,' he said to no one in particular. He dusted off his hands and went back to his chair.

'About the routing,' I said, 'the one Max Goldstein gave me . . . I've checked them over, all the legs seem a bit short. Aren't you fitting ferry tanks?'

Valentine looked directly at me, and for the first time I noticed his eyes were a light green colour. 'Ferry tanks?' he said it as though the thought had never crossed his mind. 'No, we just thought the standard aircraft tanks would be enough. What did Max give you as the routing?'

'Blantyre, Nairobi, Juba, Khartoum, and then I think it was Wadi Halfa, Cairo, then on to Cyprus, which of course means Larnaca. Once there I have to phone the colonel in Tel Aviv before proceeding.'

Valentine thought for a moment, then said, 'Slight amendment to that, no need to go into Blantyre, just route Zomba direct to Karonga, up at the north end of the lake. I'll arrange a customs officer to clear you out of Malawi at that point. From there you go to Wilson airport, Nairobi, then as you said, Juba and Khartoum. After Khartoum direct to Luxor and then on to Larnaca. Cairo,' he added, 'is definitely out . . . spend all day trying to get the aircraft refuelled.'

'That was what I meant by ferry tanks,' I said, 'if I had an extra hundred or so gallons on board I could miss out half of those stops.'

'Most likely,' he said. 'Most likely, but we don't have the necessary bits and anyway the route I've given you is quite straightforward.'

'Yes, I suppose it is,' I agreed.

It was later, during dinner, that my chance came to work the conversation around to currency. By that time Penny was back from a hard day of horse riding, looking radiant and happy. Even Lucky Clay had lost the hangdog expression he had been wearing earlier in the evening. I started talking about the state of the British economy, which soon brought Valentine and Clay on line as pseudo political whizz kids. The conversation bounced around imports and exports, balance of trade figures, foreign trade, and soon ended up with Malawi. That's when I found out that Valentine had sold all the Dorniers at a loss.

The kwacha, Malawi's unit of currency, had apparently strengthened against major foreign currencies in the preceding half dozen years and as I doubted Valentine had sold the aircraft at much more than the asking price he must have been losing all the way. Either way, it was still the perfect front for smuggling.

I returned to my bungalow late, having joined Valentine for a nightcap, which turned into three or four. The small guest bungalow was chilly and I undressed quickly, eager to get into bed. I pulled back the sheets and instantly jumped backwards as something in the bed moved. The first thought that flashed through my mind was 'Snake!' When I looked again I saw it was just a thin brown envelope. I could hear my heart pounding as I opened it and took out the note inside. The words, printed in bold capitals, just said, 'Asking questions can be dangerous.' That was it, no names, no pack drill, just a simple old-fashioned warning. As far as I could tell there were only three people who could have put it there, and they had all sat down to dinner with me. I doubted anyone else would have taken the trouble to come up the mountain to deliver it. But then you never could tell.

Valentine and Clay had left by the time I went to the house for breakfast. Penny managed a stone-faced expression before telling me they had gone on a charter and wouldn't be back until the following morning, then she went off to her horses.

It wasn't until Sunday served me with bacon and scrambled eggs that I remembered my dinner date that evening, so I left a note for Penny saying I wouldn't be in until late, and wouldn't be dining.

By the time I had left the house my mind was mulling over the secretive charter Valentine and Clay had been discussing the previous evening. It had to be important to risk being shot at – very important. Linking past events together in my mind, my driving concentration lapsed momentarily. Momentarily but just long enough to find myself burning a track down the mountain at Valentine-type speed. The road ahead suddenly twisted sharply to the right, following the contour of the mountain. It left me with a view only usually witnessed from aircraft – an invisible ocean of air. My foot hit the brake pedal a moment later and nearly kicked a hole in the rusting metal floor. No brakes! My stomach rolled up into a tight ball as I wrenched the wheel hard right and the adrenal glands started pumping at somewhere near the speed of sound, the end result being that illusory effect of slow motion.

The pick-up whipped violently and the back end, being light, broke away completely. Opposite lock, now back! I was almost straight and still on the road when I saw the next bend drifting into the windscreen. The gears! The bloody gears! I wrenched the stick out of third and smashed it into first. There was a sickening screech of metal on metal as cogs sought to engage with other cogs, shedding teeth in the process. Then somehow they meshed together. The deceleration was total; I realized that when my ribcage impacted painfully with the steering wheel and my forehead bounced off the windscreen.

Then I was back in control, the gradient less formidable. Jesus, that was close – too close. I headed out to Zomba airport at a sedate ten miles an hour, trying to control the irregular spasms in my legs. It wasn't until I was driving along the flat airport road that I remembered the note. 'Asking questions can be dangerous,' that's what it had said. What's more it seemed they meant it.

The Welsh wizard was beating hell out of a piece of metal when I arrived at the hangar. He stopped and looked at me.

'Hope you're not going to ask if the bloody kite's ready yet?' he said with as much unfriendliness as he could muster.

'No, as a matter of fact I wondered if you could have a look at the brakes on that heap . . . they just failed.'

'You haven't been using that to go up the mountain, have you?'

'A couple of times,' I replied.

'Bloody hell, I've told most everybody about those brakes. Who said you could use it?'

'Lucky Clay,' I said, 'and now you mention it he did tell me that the brakes were unreliable.'

Rees-Williams looked at me with a pained expression, the one that said he did not suffer fools gladly. 'Well, there you are, it's your own bloody fault. Just as well you weren't coming down the mountain at the time. Vehicles are more precious than people out here, you see.'

'I'm sure you're right,' I said sarcastically, 'can you fix it?'

'I'll see to it later, got a fifty-hour check to finish on the Aztec first.'

I went through to the office and the clattering of the electric typewriter.

Sally stopped as I limped in through the door. 'You look terrible,' she said, getting up from her chair.

'That's a nice greeting for first thing on a Monday morning.'

'You know what I mean, you look as though you've seen a ghost.'

I gave a dry, humourless laugh. 'Almost did . . . mine.'

'I'll make you a cup of coffee, you look as though you need it. So, what happened?'

I explained about the brakes failing on the mountain road and then showed her the note I had received the night before.

Her voice was very serious when she said, 'And you think the two are synonymous?'

'I don't know, it's possible . . . anything's possible.'

She handed me the coffee and went back to her chair at the typewriter. 'Do you think it's wise, Stephen . . . ? I mean to pursue this any further, it seems dangerous enough already.'

'Faint heart never won fair lady as they say. Have you got the invoices for the other Dorniers handy?'

She pointed to a number of green-coloured files on her desk. 'But if I'd known . . .' she left the sentence unfinished. The first file was the blockbuster. It told me that all the other Dorniers had been sold to the Israeli Air Force; it also told me that they had been sold for an average loss of 15,000 dollars each. Which meant, with the 20,000-dollar loss on the final aircraft, that Valentine had subsidized the Israelis to the tune of 65,000 US dollars plus of course whatever he had paid out on ferry pilot fees.

The second file was the important one. Important to me anyway. It contained the full delivery details of the last three flights, which meant I had the pilots' names, licence numbers and dates of the ferries.

I turned to Sally. 'All we have to do now is find the diamonds,' I said. 'Can I use the phone? I need to put a call through to London.'

She smiled, 'You're enjoying this, aren't you?'

'Beats flying,' I said and meant it.

The operator said I was very lucky when she called me back five minutes later. She said it normally took up to a couple of hours to get a line to London; I just kept on agreeing with everything she said, eager to get rid of her and be linked up with the British Civil Aviation Authority. Then at last she said she was putting me through. A faraway voice, very bored and very English female, recited the words. 'Civil Aviation Authority, can I help you?' I felt like saying, 'We live in hope,' but then just asked for Mr Trevor Grant, head of FCL5 – the professional flight crew licensing department.

I had served with Trevor in the Air Force, twenty years and a lifetime ago. We had been very close friends in those days and very poor ones, sharing our cigarettes, our beer and even our dress shirts on dining-in nights at the officers' mess. One thing that hadn't changed for me, I was still poor. Trevor had got on as they say, if you consider being a civil servant getting on. That I knew he was now the head of FCL5 could only appear a mystery to anyone outside the flying game. It being such a small closed shop, you end up knowing just about everybody who has travelled or is currently travelling in aluminium tubing. Almost akin to English village life, except your High Street stretches from one world's end to the other.

It took a few clicks and another female voice telling me that I was speaking to FCL5, before I managed to get the man himself. Even then he didn't believe who it was, until I reminded him of the time he had had a flame out in a Hunter, and how I escorted him down 40,000 feet of sky to a dead stick landing at Tangmere. Then he nearly became the old Trevor I had known, the smooth-talking young man in a blue uniform, nearly but not quite. After digging around in a battered box of dusty memories we both knew that; we had little in common any more.

'Anyway Stephen, what can I do for you?'

'I'm trying to get in touch with some ferry pilots I used to know . . . to help me out with a ferrying contract in South Africa. The names,' I quickly checked the files, 'the names are Allen and Stutchbury, I just wondered if you could check their files and see what their home addresses are.' I paused but it was just the buzzing of the line, so I continued, 'I've been trying to trace them but haven't had a lot of joy. Could be dead for all I know.'

'What was that, dead did you say?'

'Just joking, Trevor.'

'Have you got their initials?'

'Allen, G. L. and Stutchbury, C. C.'

'Okay, I've got that . . . look, if you can hang on for about two minutes I'll get my secretary to chase it up.'

'All the time in the world,' I said, then heard the receiver being put down. A few seconds later he was back.

'Hello, hello Stephen, she's just gone off to find the info for you . . . highly irregular of course, but as it's you . . .'

'Very good of you to take the trouble . . . tell me though, if they were dead, would you be aware of it?'

Grant thought for a moment. 'Not necessarily, unless we had been notified by their next of kin, of course. If we hadn't been notified all that we would see would be a failure to renew their medical or their licence, whichever came first.'

The Americans had a different system. I knew because I also held an American licence, and on the back of that licence it stated, 'Certificate should be returned to address below within 30 days of death of airman', which of course was halfway to being ridiculous, especially if the pilot was a loner and especially if he crashed in the middle of some South American jungle whilst doing a bit of illegal drug running. Who the hell was going to return his certificate then?

'Hello Stephen, are you still there?' Grant's voice was becoming crackly.

'Still here, you'll have to speak up though.'

'The information you requested is as follows . . .' I picked up a pen and jotted down the details as they came; by the time he had finished my hand was shaking. I had found the answer I'd been looking for. The one which said I was a dead man.

I thanked Trevor once again and we promised to meet up one fine sunny day in Piccadilly and go for a drink at the Royal Aero Club. We said it, but we both knew it was only talk and that our friendship had ended with the ending of our fighter pilot days.

That was it, the line went dead and I was back to my real world of sweating and the chirruping silence of Africa.

Sally broke that silence; I'd almost forgotten she was there.

'Bad news?'

I looked down at the piece of paper. 'There have been three other ferry flights apart from this one. All bound for Tel Aviv. The first flight, according to this file, was on 16 February 1977; the pilot, a certain John Skinner, was killed north of Luxor when the aircraft he was flying crashed in flames. The flights which followed Skinner's were 4 January 1979 and 1 December 1980; the pilots were Allen and Stutchbury respectively. I've just found out that Allen's licence expired two months after his flight and Stutchbury's three months after his. Apparently neither of them has bothered to renew his medicals since . . . which of course means their licences have now become so much worthless paper.'

Sally gave me a puzzled look. 'So what does that mean . . . just that they've stopped flying?'

'I think it means they're dead,' I said flatly.

'Dead! They didn't say that, did they?'

'Didn't have to. It's all too coincidental. Two pilots, both of whom do a ferry flight for Valentine, then fail to renew their medicals and their licences.'

'You said that the first pilot was killed, how did you find that out?'

'You remember you told me about Bill Kimberley

80

. . . well, I went to see him. He was here when it happened; that's what started me thinking.'

'But you can't be absolutely sure . . . can you?'

'From where I'm standing, yes. Look at it from their point of view. If you're smuggling a fortune in diamonds you've got to be very cautious. Which means that one person letting something slip could end everything. So taking it a step further, you eliminate as you go.'

'But those pilots wouldn't have known anything about the diamonds, surely?'

'Maybe not, but you can never be sure. Not one hundred per cent.'

'So what are you going to do now? What happens if you find them?'

'Hadn't thought about that . . . turn them over to the authorities. It's not so much the reward money, although it would come in handy; it's more a matter of evening up old scores. I don't like being used.'

'I know the feeling,' Sally said bitterly.

Chapter Seven

It was nearly three hours later when I arrived hot and sweaty amidst the hooting car horns of Blantyre. I parked in Lacey's supermarket car park and then followed Sally's instructions; out of the car park, turn left, walk a hundred yards to the traffic lights, left again and it was the first shop on the left.

It had occurred to me over a fresh cup of coffee, laced with a tot of medicinal whisky, that if Valentine had moved a ten-million-dollar haul of diamonds to Tel Aviv using four aircraft, he would more than likely have split the haul into equal parts. If I was going to find the final shipment, I at least needed to know what two and a quarter million dollars' worth of gems would look like – what volume of space they would occupy. With that knowledge I could start a slow methodical search of the Dornier. Which of course introduced further complications. I couldn't very well start poking around the aircraft while it was still in Zomba; somebody would be bound to get suspicious. It seemed the only way would be once the ferry flight was under way. I made a mental note to begin the investigation once I reached Wilson airport, Nairobi. I could even send a telex to Goldstein in Paris, saying I had engine trouble and would be delayed an extra day. That should be enough time to find what I was looking for.

I had explained all of this to Sally, who had then thrown a spanner in the works by asking me what I would do when I found them. I had said something like 'go to the local police', to which she had replied that they were black and as the diamonds had originated from South Africa, which meant apartheid, she reckoned they would keep them anyway and incarcerate me for the duration. It therefore seemed that once I had found the shipment I should fly the Dornier through to Europe and contact Interpol. On the face of it, a pretty straightforward operation; until I remembered all those hours alone at the controls of an aeroplane.

The local jeweller's shop, as Sally had mentioned, was a watch and clock emporium, although it did sport a few cheap rings and necklaces in a thrown-together window display. The interior of the shop was fluorescent-lit and air-conditioned to about the level of an arctic winter, or so it seemed after the eye-aching glare of the outside world. I shivered at the rapid temperature change and made my way to the counter and the heavily built, balding character who was busily rearranging a tray of inexpensive-looking rings.

He stopped when I reached the glass-topped counter and looked up. 'Afternoon sir, something I can do for you?'

'Possibly, I'd like to look at some diamond rings.'

'Amazing,' he said, 'just got a new consignment in today.' His podgy face was all pink and smiling.

'English?' I said.

'As they come,' he replied, 'Old Kent Road. George Reeman's the name.'

I held out my hand. 'Nice to meet you George. Steve Ritchie.'

'Londoner?' he questioned.

'Clapham Common.'

'Near enough, Stevie boy, near enough.'

We talked for a while about home and he told me he had been in Malawi for ten years and that he was managing to scrape a living, then he showed me the rings he had in stock. I followed that up by asking him about diamonds in general and who did the cutting. What followed was a one-sided conversation which drifted on for another twenty minutes; by which time I had found out there are industrial diamonds which tend to be yellowish in colour, and gem quality diamonds which can be clear or tinged with blue. Ascertaining value and the number to make up a two-and-a-quarter-million dollar shipment

83

would therefore seem to hinge on quality. George Reeman's final remark told me that a lot more planning had gone into Valentine's operation than I had at first suspected. The majority of cutters it seemed were Jews, and since the war most of them had returned to Israel. I didn't bother to ask which war, as the question was totally irrelevant. As the newspaper cutting had stated cut and uncut diamonds, Tel Aviv therefore played a key part in the operation.

I stopped at the airport bar before returning to Zomba and managed a Star beer with a whisky chaser, then I set out on the long drive to Sally's house. It was now three thirty in the afternoon and the yesterday promise of fair weather had turned to black thundery skies. The rain started halfway through my journey, sending clouds of steam up from the road ahead. I slowed down and checked the brakes; they were better, but I still didn't trust Rees-Williams's workmanship.

What the hell made me think of Peter Turner I don't know. One minute I was driving along a steamy rain-drenched road towards Zomba, the next I was back about eighteen years to a night in the south of France. It had been a night op. from the Air Force base at Malta to the French military base at Orange. We had stopped off in Sardinia for fuel and then climbed our Hunters back up to forty-odd thousand feet on course for the French airfield. I recalled how bad the thunderstorm activity was that night and how Peter had insisted we divert to Nice. Only problem was we had been stooging around for too long waiting for a break in the weather; so that by the time we descended through some hairy wall-to-wall thunderstorms we were both just about out of fuel.

I lost Peter in the cloud. One moment I was tucked in on his wingtip, descending into the Nice traffic pattern, next moment he was gone. That was when my bingo lights came on – which on a Hunter meant your fuel state was critical. I somehow managed to slide into a tight down-wind leg and arrived on the wet runway with nothing more than a mildish rush of adrenalin. As for Peter, according to the controllers he had climbed back up on top of the weather. Minutes later, with all his fuel spent, the Avon engine flamed out, leaving him with only one course of action . . . his ejector seat. Peter Turner's body was washed up on the beach a few days later.

I'd never understood why he had pulled up out of that weather. I did know he was a fairly heavy drinker though, and if he could get off an op. he would. Now I knew why. I had become another Peter, another pilot afraid of flying. The fear just arrives one bright sunny morning and then like the maggot in the fresh apple it just keeps gnawing away, little by little by little.

I started to wonder who else might have the problem! Airline pilots the world over. Experienced fliers, suddenly, inexplicably struck with a fear of flight. What then? Just call in to see the airline flight manager and say, 'Look old man, I'm afraid of flying and I'd rather stay on the ground. Of course I still need my salary and my pension's due in five years or so. It's the school fees you know, and there's those endless cocktail parties, expensive business . . . you understand?' Like hell, the poor bugger has to live with it. He can't even tell Clarissa, his wife. No, he just keeps bashing away, dreaming of retirement and that paint-peeling old fishing boat down in Penzance. If he's lucky he might even make it. If not, the accident report will state plainly and simply, 'Pilot Error'. Not that the pilot was afraid of flying and had come apart in his head. Just plain old pilot error – covers a lot of ground, that statement.

And what about the poor unfortunates who go down with him? The bucket and spade, kiss me quick brigade; off on their once a year binge to Costa del Paradise. Clinging to their duty free, trusting in air-sickness pills and the steely-eyed ace up front who is more frightened than they are. Christ, what a mess, and nobody is saying a word about it.

I pulled a cigarette out of my shirt pocket and lit it, then I poked my head out of the cab window and peered at the murky scudding rain cloud above. That was what would catch me out on the flight back – weather! If I found myself in that sort of sky I would never survive. A cold shudder ran through my body as I pulled my head back into the dry cab. Someone just walked over your grave, old son.

It was still raining when I arrived at Sally's house; the time was a few minutes past five thirty. I passed her car at a limping run and hurried up the steps to the shelter of the verandah. Then I rang the doorbell and waited. No answer. I opened the outer mesh screen and then the inner door and called, 'Hello in there.' My voice filtered away down the hallway, giving that muffled echo of an empty house. The inside of the place was warm and clammy, with just the steady drumming of rain on the roof to break up the oppressing silence.

I checked all the rooms as I went and ended up in the study, or the room that doubled for one. At first I just saw the cluttered table, then I looked up and beyond. She was standing against the wall, her head hanging loosely on her chest. I moved slowly towards her and saw the end of a steel crossbow bolt protruding below her left breast. She was still wearing the same white dress she had had on that morning, except now it was covered in blood. In the fading afternoon light it looked almost black in colour. I fought back the waves of nausea which threatened to overcome me and gently raised her head. There was more than horror in the wide-open eyes, more than amazement, more than . . . I closed those brown eyes forever then, and tried to remove the bolt from her breast, but it was impossible. It had embedded itself deeply into the wall, leaving Sally North hanging limply like a bloodstained rag doll.

The sickness came over me suddenly. A rushing, burning sickness erupting from my stomach. I only just made the bathroom, kneeling and vomiting until my body was completely empty. Then I staggered into the kitchen and poured myself a large Scotch with shaking hands. It helped, but not enough. I went back to the room and Sally and the disbelief. I had to phone someone, anyone.

That was when my foot hit something solid; I stooped down and found the murder weapon lying almost under the table. It was as I had imagined a crossbow would be. Heavy, lethal and ugly. I didn't know much about them, but enough to remind me that when they were used in the middle ages the bolt, or quarrel, was capable of piercing chain mail and could achieve a range of 1,000 feet. In modern times the weapon had been revived by sportsmen who used it to shoot big game.

I stood up, holding the crossbow in my hands, understanding the look of horror in Sally's eyes as she faced it. Waiting for the steel bolt to smash into her body. I imagined she would have felt little pain, it would have been over in a split second. What I wanted now was the rotten bastard who had killed her. More than anything I vowed to avenge her death.

I was still standing there when I heard footsteps in the hall. That was when panic overtook me and reason deserted my mind. I wheeled round and saw the window; it was half open when the door burst open and three black policemen rushed in.

'Don't move, man!' I turned and found myself looking down the barrel of a submachine gun.

'Get that thing off him,' the same man barked. The tall and gangly one of the three edged over towards me, his eyes big and round and looking about as frightened as I felt. It wasn't until he took it off me that I realized I was still holding the murder weapon. Once he had it, tall and gangly became a little less worried looking, and smashed me in the ribs to prove the point. I doubled up in pain and stayed that way for as long as they would let me. No reason to get up and be hit again.

The other two had found Sally by this time and were involved in a 3,000-word per minute conversation, in a language which could have been Swahili or any of a dozen dialects. Not that it made any difference to me, I couldn't understand a word. Then the head man was back, jabbing my stomach with the barrel of his miniature cannon.

'Why did you kill her, man?' He spat the words out

with enough venom to tell me he wasn't far away from squeezing the trigger.

'I didn't,' I said, 'I just . . .' For that I got the butt across my right cheek. That one really hurt. I felt something floating about inside my mouth as I fought for support against the windowsill. The black face was still smiling as the world came back into focus.

'Now man, we try again uhh?' He was enjoying every minute of this, that was painfully obvious. 'Why did you kill her?'

'I bloody well didn't,' I shouted angrily, spitting out blood and a broken tooth at the same time. That didn't help either, I felt something crash into my skull before the world went peacefully black.

A dull throbbing jack hammer in my head brought me round, that and being dragged unceremoniously into the Zomba police station. The reception there was just as rough. I was slammed up against a wall, while one of the shiny-faced black men emptied my pockets. By that time the blood inside my mouth had congealed and coupled with the painful swelling on the right side of my face meant that I was unable to speak. Not that I particularly wanted to, but if I could just mention I was doing a job for James Valentine I knew the situation stood a good chance of improving.

As my mouth was locked I tried to make the appropriate signs to indicate I wanted a pen and a piece of paper. I might even have got it if the searching officer hadn't put his long fingers into my shirt pocket and produced a diamond solitaire ring. Sally's ring. Jesus Christ, I'd forgotten about that!

That did it, found at the scene of the crime holding the murder weapon and with the victim's blood on my hands- . . . and now the motive. Theft! A sizeable diamond ring, which had to be worth at least 5,000 dollars. The rat-faced desk sergeant barked out an order and I was dragged down an unlit corridor and thrown into a pitch black cell which stank of urine and body sweat.

Following a bout of uncontrollable coughing I managed to drag myself through something which felt like straw, to a wall. I propped myself up against it and tried to work my jaws free. I had to tell them about Valentine, he would secure my release immediately. Except he wouldn't be there, he was away on a charter. Penny would do something though . . . surely.

The sweating started in earnest when I realized Penny Valentine could well be involved. Could be? Had to be? There had been three people at the house last night. Three people apart from myself. It was an odds-on certainty that one of the three had been responsible for leaving the warning note in my bed. What had the note said, something about asking questions can be dangerous? Yes that was it. Then Valentine and Clay leave on a charter operation to somewhere in southern Zimbabwe, which leaves Penny Valentine. Could she have murdered Sally? It didn't make sense. Something else that didn't make sense was how the police just happened to arrive at that precise moment.

I rubbed my hand gingerly over the back of my skull and found the reason for the additional pain in my head. My hair was matted in what could only be blood. My blood. I needed a drink and a cigarette . . . and a one-way ticket on a VC10 to anywhere. Trouble was, I knew I wasn't to get any damned one of them; just the thought in my brain of twenty years in an African jail. It would be at least twenty years, and one lesson you learn in third worlds is that nobody survives that long in a cell. Twenty months maybe . . . but twenty years, no way!

Outside the rain had stopped, leaving a buzzing silence which was interspersed with the sound of my irregular breathing. I sat, sweating and frightened, looking around the blackness, searching for a chink of light – something from which I could get a bearing. But there was nothing. Nothing but a total cloak of hot, smelly, sweating darkness. I couldn't even see my hands. Then I began to feel sick; not in the usual way though, it seemed to be starting in my knees and working gradually up my thighs to my stomach. I pushed my legs out straight in front of me and the feeling passed.

The minutes ticked slowly into hours, or days, or weeks. Each tick sounding like 'Sally', repeating itself over and over and over again. Sally and Victoria station. A door from the past which had opened suddenly and unexpectedly; a chance to go back and try again . . . only now it had been closed forever. The adrenaline eventually trickled to a stop as fatigue took me into a semi-sleep. At one stage, I awoke with a start and found I was crying; burning hot tears flowing endlessly down my cheeks. Then I remembered the dream; the dream where Sally had been murdered with a crossbow. I reached for her in the darkness . . . a twenty-year-old darkness which belonged to a small hotel in a faraway London. I fell sideways, my face ending up on the straw-covered floor. The stench of stale urine brought the bile burning up my throat; forcing open the congealed wound in my mouth. My stomach contracted and urged; hot sickness exploding out of my mouth with the searing heat of a red-hot poker. Then it was over; my stomach an aching empty pit; my throat an acid-burnt, acid-tasting tube that had no part in my body. I gulped in the air. Filthy and germ-laden as it was, it helped. Then the tears started again. The shock was wearing off; and suddenly the implication of what had happened started hitting home. In my head I kept calling her name . . . telling her I loved her.

The voices came out of nowhere, steadily growing louder, only now I could hear footsteps as well. I drew my knees up to my chin . . . the bastards were coming to interrogate me. Or perhaps it was morning and they were going to give me breakfast. I heard the sound of a key grating in a rusty lock and then I was looking directly into the white glare of a torch. My arm went up instinctively across my eyes and then a voice cried, 'Steve'. The perfume and the touch told me it was Penny Valentine and from the tongue lashing she gave the shape holding the torch she sounded a very angry lady.

'Don't just bloody stand there,' she screamed, 'help me get him to his feet.' The figure with the torch did as he was told, only this time the hands were gentle. I was half carried out to the car and lowered expertly into the passenger seat. Penny opened the driver's door and climbed in beside me.

'Are you all right?' she said. 'My God, what did they do to you?'

I didn't speak. I couldn't have even if I had wanted to.

She reached over and squeezed my hand. 'Don't talk now, I'll fix your mouth when we get home.'

Back at the house Penny bathed my head and my mouth, then she gave me three yellow pain-killing tablets and steered me into a pink-tiled bathroom.

'You'll feel better after a soak,' she said, 'and there's a bathrobe hanging on the back of the door . . . if you need me just shout. I'll be through in the kitchen.'

'Thank you,' I said, except it didn't sound anything like that, more the mindless utterance of an imbecile.

I closed the door behind her and went over to the bathroom mirror. I hadn't looked much before, but now with a greenish-black bruise highlighting the swelling on my right cheek, I looked a damn sight worse.

The sweet-smelling bubble bath took away some of the pain and by the time I put on the pale blue robe I had the feeling I would live. I went through to the dining room and found the log fire roaring away, sending flurries of sparks up the chimney. Penny came in shortly, wearing a full-length emerald green housecoat and carrying a glass of milk.

'I don't know if you can manage that, I've put some whisky in with it.'

I took the glass and she sat down beside me on the chesterfield.

'What time is it?' I asked.

'Just after one o'clock,' she said.

'What day?'

She looked at me, then said, 'Monday, well Tuesday now.'

91

'Christ, I thought I'd been in that cell a week.'

'I'm sorry I didn't get there sooner.'

I took a small sip of whisky-milk mixture and winced at the stinging sensation. 'How did you find out?' I asked.

She straightened up, her eyes still held by the attraction of the blazing logs. 'They just phoned to speak to James, I told them he was away . . . then they said Sally North had been murdered and that they had caught the man responsible.' She glanced at me with a small twist of sadness in her face. 'I asked who it was . . . and they gave your name . . . from your driving licence. I came down straight away.'

'Thank God you did,' I said.

'What happened?' she asked calmly.

I ran back over the events of the evening, explaining I had been invited to dinner; the truth could wait. Then arriving and finding her pinned to the wall with the steel bolt from a crossbow. Penny winced at the gruesome details, but I didn't think to spare her. I was still bitter, not about the treatment handed out to me, that was something I could live with; but about Sally's death. About the woman from a past, who had carried the promise of a future.

After a time Penny said, 'What about the ring?'

'Ring?'

'They gave me your personal possessions back at the station, seemed to think the diamond ring belonged to Sally . . . I told them James would sort it out tomorrow.'

'It was Sally's,' I said, rubbing my fingertips over my swollen cheek.

She lifted an eyebrow, asking the question with her eyes.

I said, 'James gave it to her . . . a present. Then apparently he asked for it back.'

'I should have known,' Penny said. There was a quiet anger in her voice. 'And why did you have it?'

'Safe keeping . . . custodian of the crown jewels . . . what the hell does it matter anyway, she's dead. You do understand that, don't you?'

'Yes,' she said tiredly. 'I can't say that I liked her but I am sorry.' She rose gracefully to her feet. 'You'd better have my bed tonight, I'll sleep in my husband's room.'

I was too tired to argue so I followed her down the hallway into a large delicate room of soft pinks. I slipped beneath the sheets and waited a long time for sleep.

Chapter Eight

There was a smell of freshly-ground coffee beans when I awoke and saw the grey light of dawn spilling through a slit in the curtains. There was also a fierce stabbing pain which promised to tear my head from my shoulders. I eased myself very gingerly into an upright position and let the subconscious answer all the questions my conscious mind was asking. At the end of it I was left with a cold and very lonely feeling.

There were two things I could do now: get out, or carry on where I left off. I decided on the latter and swung my legs out of the bed. It was then I realized I was naked. What the hell had I been wearing last night? Bathrobe, blue bathrobe. I looked hopefully around the room, but I couldn't see it anywhere, so I put my legs back into the bed and waited. Someone would be bound to come along sooner or later.

My idea that Penny Valentine had been the murderess now seemed faintly ridiculous. But if not her, who? I had arrived at Sally's house just after five thirty and found her minutes later. Rigor mortis hadn't started at that point, so she hadn't been dead for probably more than two hours. Which would have put the time of the killing at three thirty or later. And why a crossbow? Sure it's quiet, but with the next house more than a hundred yards away and the heavy rainfall to drown out the noise, a gun would have been easier. And why leave the bow at the scene of the crime?

The questions were still milling around in my mind when the door opened and Penny Valentine came in. She was wearing a delicate and expensive-looking white negligee, one of the wrap-around types, tied at the waist.

'You're awake,' she didn't hide the surprise in her voice. 'You looked tired enough last night to sleep for a week.' I tried to speak and found I couldn't.

'It looks worse,' she said, sitting on the side of the bed and inspecting my mouth and cheek. 'Lean forward a little.' I did as I was told, and felt her probing the wound at the back of my head. She took my head gently in her hands and lowered it gently onto the pillow. 'I'd better get something to bathe your mouth, then I'll phone the doctor.'

A few minutes later she had returned with a small bowl of warm disinfected water and a face towel; then prising my lips apart, she dabbed inside my mouth. It hurt, but when she had finished it felt better. 'Now, let me see the head wound,' she said. 'Lean forward.' The fold of her negligee fell away then and I found my face being cradled against her small exposed right breast. I didn't think she even noticed, she was far too preoccupied with her role of nurse.

'Much better,' she said and put my head back on the pillow. 'How does it feel?'

'Painful,' I mumbled. 'Could I have a cigarette?'

She looked at me disapprovingly. 'Perhaps later, we'll see what the doctor says.'

'I think I'll get up,' I said painfully. 'Where's the bathrobe?'

'It had blood on it. I'll get you another one, though. You can go as far as the bathroom and that's all.' Her voice was stern but friendly, not unlike a nursing sister in a hospital.

The doctor came and went sometime during the late morning. He was a red-faced Englishman and wore half-moon spectacles. He poked around inside my mouth, then inspected the cut on the back of my head before pronouncing I would no doubt live. He gave Penny an assortment of bottles and tablets and said I should take things easy for a few days. Cigarettes, he said, were definitely out of the question.

Penny had just brought me some chicken soup when the rains started. She listened to the incessant drumming on the roof for a moment, then said, 'Damn, I suppose

95

that means James and Lucky won't get back today.'

'The police, you mean?'

She nodded. 'They still rely on his judgment,' she added.

I watched her as she paced over to the bathroom window and then back to the bed.

'Did the police say anything to you about arriving at the house when they did?' I asked. 'Seems strange, don't you think?'

Penny sat down on the side of the bed. 'I suppose so . . . no, they didn't say a word, mind you I was too damned angry at the time. I'm afraid they are somewhat overzealous and somewhat limited in their powers of deduction. That's what James always used to say.'

'Probably have taught the Gestapo a thing or two,' I joked.

'You're getting better already, I see.'

'Take more than a couple of knocks on the head . . . does that mean I can have a cigarette now?'

The wide mouth broke into a grin. 'No it does not and what's more you will stay in this bed for the remainder of the day, even if I have to tie you down. You heard what the doctor said.'

'They have been known to be wrong, you know.'

'Not in this house they haven't.' She picked up the tray in one swift movement. 'I'll call in and see you later.'

For the remainder of the afternoon I just lay, restless, unable to sleep. The use of the crossbow still troubled me; it was a heavy, cumbersome sort of weapon, one which would need some degree of physical strength. Lucky Clay would have that sort of strength, so would James Valentine come to that. Who else was there?

A telephone rang jerkily at the far end of the hall, or perhaps it was my nerves pleading for a long stiff Scotch. To hell with it, I'd had enough. I climbed out of bed and put on the white towelling bathrobe which Penny had left; now all I had to do was find the Scotch and the cigarettes and lock myself in the bathroom. I knew Penny Valentine wouldn't approve if she caught me in the act, but what the eye doesn't see, the heart doesn't . . . or however that damned silly saying went. I was halfway to the door when it opened.

'Going somewhere?' Penny Valentine stood, hands on her hips, making horse-riding gear look like the latest Paris fashion.

'I need a drink,' I said gruffly.

'Well, you get back into bed and I'll make you one. Hot milk or tea?'

'How about a small whisky?'

'I'll get Sunday to put some in the tea.'

Having passed the order to her steward, she came back to the bedroom. 'That was James on the telephone,' she said. 'They've arrived in Blantyre. Of course the mountain road's out, but he's driving through to Zomba to see the police.'

'What did he say?'

'Say? Oh, he was absolutely livid, quite rightly so as well. I told him you wouldn't probably be able to do the flight after this . . .'

'I didn't say that,' I mumbled.

'Surely you're not going fly an aeroplane in your condition?'

'Why the hell not, the doc said I'd live, didn't he?'

'Well that's up to you, of course. Personally, I would tell James to go to hell, but then if you've made your mind up . . .'

'I hardly think I can hold James responsible for what happened.'

'But that's my point. You see, he trained these people for years and years. Even now, and he's been out of the force for some time, they ask his advice. And on a case like this . . . murder . . . he will end up doing the entire investigation for them.' She walked across the room and sat down on a pink fluffy stool in front of the dressing table.

I felt like saying you're quite right, book me out on the next flight, but I didn't. Instead I said, 'Have you been riding?'

'In this? Good God no, might do later if it eases up though.'

There was a muffled knock on the door. 'Come in Sunday,' Penny called.

At least the tea had a whisky aroma which halfway helped. I looked across at Penny who was quietly seething about something, perhaps the talk with her husband.

'Would you like me to move back to the bungalow? Feel guilty about pinching your bed.'

She just got up from the stool and marched to the doorway. 'You might as well stay there,' she said, glaring at me. 'Road's out until tomorrow at the earliest.' She slammed the door as she left.

Chapter Nine

'Do you think we could go over it once more, old boy, just to make sure I've got it absolutely right.' Valentine stood before the fireplace, hands clasped behind his back. He had arrived at the house early that morning, concern showing in every line of his face. When he saw the state of my cheek the concern changed to utter disbelief. Now he was standing before me, dressed in a lightweight mid-grey suit, crisp white shirt, and what appeared to be a regimental tie. The black Oxford-style shoes were buffed to a high polish.

I ran back over the story, similar to the one I had given to Penny, except I said the ring had been on Sally's desk at the office and I had picked it up intending to give it to her. Penny gave me a sideways glance when I made that statement, but she remained silent.

'So,' Valentine was saying, 'you came back from Blantyre, stopped at the airfield to see if Sally had finished your typing and found she wasn't there. You then noticed a diamond ring on her desk, the same ring you had noticed on two previous occasions on the third finger of her left hand. You placed the ring in your pocket with the intention of giving it back to her. Once you had done this you took the pick-up and drove to Sally's house.'

'I was going for dinner anyway,' I added.

'Quite, quite.' He thought for moment or two. 'Well, that sounds fine Steve . . . where's the ring now? Better have it, evidence you understand.'

Penny interrupted. 'I've got it,' she said coolly.

'Yes, of course. Well if I can have it old girl, then I'll have to be going. Lots of work to do on this . . . er unfortunate incident.'

When Valentine had departed Penny returned to the drawing room.

'Very diplomatic,' she said icily.

'I don't understand . . .'

'The ring! Not quite the same story you told me.'

'Mrs Valentine, for your information I just happen to be a ferry pilot trying to do a job the best way I know how. Murder, as with family matters concerning another woman, I can well do without . . . eternal triangles, call them what you like, I'd rather not be involved.' I limped out of the house and went to my bungalow to get dressed. I'd had enough of bathrobes to last me a lifetime.

After a shower and a very careful shave, I dressed in a pair of lightweight grey trousers and a red sports shirt; gave my dusty shoes a quick wipe, then gathered up what dirty laundry I could find and went off to persuade Sunday to wash and press it for me.

Then I walked down into the garden and sat by the edge of the swimming pool and had my first cigarette for thirty-six hours. The rains had abated the previous night, now it was sunny and pleasantly warm. Those 5,000 feet made all the difference – down in the lowlands it would be hot and steamy and full of mosquitos.

An aircraft droned high overhead and I found myself looking up, across the cavernous wind-picked sky, beyond the ragged lines of cumulus into the deeper blue of space. But I didn't see it, instead I heard the small frail voice of Isobel, the little girl who was known as Bluebell because the smaller children couldn't pronounce her name, asking Miss Beckerman why Stephen always looked up whenever an aeroplane flew over the orphanage. Miss Beckerman would smile and say because Stephen liked them. Now, all these years later and Stephen is still looking up at them. Only now Stephen hates the sight of them.

I was on my third cigarette when the coffee arrived. It was being carried by Penny Valentine.

'I thought you might like a coffee,' she said. 'I did put some whisky in it.'

I reached up and took it from her. Then we both started to speak at the same time. 'After you,' I said.

'It was nothing, really,' she said in a small quiet voice,

'I thought I should apologize for my behaviour . . . it's just the death of Sally . . . and James . . .'

'It's a bad time for everybody,' I said, 'I understand.'

She shrugged her shoulders in a childlike way, then turned to go. 'If anyone calls, I've just gone down to town. Back at about three.'

'Right. There is something you can do for me, if it's not too much trouble?'

She stopped. 'Yes?'

'Could you get me a carton of cigarettes, filter? Any brand as long as they're mild.'

'Certainly, but on condition you do something for me.'

'And what might that be?'

'Don't call me Mrs Valentine again . . . I don't really mind what else you call me; anything but not that.'

'It's a deal,' I said.

She was smiling when she left.

Clay arrived at the house at lunchtime. I was sitting in the dining room eating a lightly boiled egg and wishing it was a steak, when he bounded through the door.

'Shit! What happened to your face?'

I looked up at his startled blue eyes. 'Didn't Valentine tell you?'

'Tell me what? He said Sally had been murdered and that they'd arrested you . . . then something about Penny getting you out.' He paused just long enough to catch his breath. 'Who did that to you?'

'An overzealous policeman, apparently,' I said.

'Those black bastards should be strung up by their feet, doused in kerosene and burnt alive.' He slammed a huge fist into the palm of his hand. 'Has James been here?'

'Been and gone,' I said. 'I think he's down at the local police station.'

'What did he say about it?'

'Nothing, just looked at me about the same way you're looking now, then took a statement from me and left.'

Clay stormed off to the kitchen. I heard his raised voice, then he came back and dropped heavily into the chair opposite me.

Sunday appeared from the kitchen about three minutes later, carrying a cold meat salad. There was fear written all over his face as he approached Clay and put the plate before him. Once the plate was on the table Clay grabbed him fiercely by the arm and pulled him down to his knees.

'You see your white master!' Clay grabbed Sunday's black wiry hair and yanked his head roughly back until his frightened eyes were looking into mine. 'You see your white master . . . do you see him?'

Sunday's eyes rolled big and wide and his lips twitched silently.

'Speak, you black bastard, do you see your white master?'

'Yes sir, master, I see him sir.'

'You see his face?' Clay shook Sunday's head cruelly from side to side. 'Do you see his face?'

'Yes sir, master, I see his face.'

Clay spun Sunday round and grabbed his throat. The negro's eyes were bulging as Clay increased pressure. 'That was done by a black bastard like you . . . do you understand? If there is ever a next time I will kill you.' There was madness in Clay's eyes as he picked Sunday up by the neck and flung him back across the room. 'Now get out of my sight, you animal.'

Sunday picked himself up slowly. His eyes were full of tears as he dragged his wretched body away to the kitchen.

I just looked at Clay, almost unable to believe what I had seen.

'What the hell goes on,' I said angrily, 'it wasn't his fault.'

'It's all their fault,' he snapped, 'give the bastards their independence and this is what happens.'

'There's good and bad in every race, it's not just reserved for black skins, for Christ's sake.'

'That's where you're wrong, man. As I've said before, your lot are too bloody soft. What you've got to realize is that you don't just take a bunch of primitives out of the dark ages and throw them into the twentieth century . . . it doesn't work. Not as long as the bastards have got holes in their arses . . . it's all too bloody late. They're animals . . . rotten, stinking, dirty animals.' He left the room like a whirlwind. The cold meat was left untouched.

I pushed away the remains of my lunch and lit a cigarette, then silently wished I had never heard of Goldstein, or Valentine, or Clay . . . or aeroplanes. The wishing stopped with Sally, no amount of it would help her any more. I got to my feet and left the cosy little dining room with its worn red brick floor and Welsh dresser stacked with rows of shining plates, and made my way out into the garden.

Valentine arrived back later in the afternoon, looking a few years older than when he left. I drifted into the drawing room to find out the latest news; he just mumbled something about 'Hadn't even dug the grave when I got there . . . God, these people!'

'Grave?' I echoed.

'Buried her this afternoon,' he said quickly and continued making a pink gin.

'I would have liked to have been there,' I said. 'Why the big hurry?'

'No hurry, old boy, normal procedure, it's the heat you see . . . can't keep corpses around too long, unpleasant you know!'

I sat down dejectedly on the chesterfield. 'How's the head now?' Valentine added as an afterthought.

'Rough!'

'In that case you'd better have a whisky, best cure in the world.'

'Find anything out?' I said casually.

Valentine loosened his regimental tie with one hand and surveyed the pink gin with the eye of a connoisseur at the same time. Satisfied that everything was in order he poured me a large Scotch, then came over to join me on the chesterfield.

'Did go over the house as a matter of fact,' he said. 'One or two clues they'd missed, nothing conclusive you understand . . . but at least it's a start.'

'Any idea why he, the murderer that is, would use a crossbow?'

He looked up at me. His green eyes showing mild surprise. 'He, you say; interesting! Can't be sure of that at this stage of the enquiry. Could be a woman, you know.'

'Really, I would have thought the crossbow was a bit of a heavyweight weapon for a woman. Difficult to draw.'

'Possibly,' he commented. 'Which brings us to the second part of your statement. Why a crossbow? Why not a gun or a knife, or even a blow on the head with a heavy object?'

'Any ideas?' I said.

'Plenty of ideas old boy, just a matter of fitting the right one into the puzzle.'

'Any idea on the motive?' I pressed on.

'Difficult one, that. Nothing stolen as far as we can ascertain, which rules out robbery as a motive. Of course it has to be premeditated.'

'Why so?'

'Well, it isn't the sort of weapon you pack in your back pocket is it? No, whoever took the crossbow into the house intended to use it. Would have had to be drawn ready for use you see, no good trying to do it in front of the victim, two-handed job. She could have got away, or at least attacked her assailant, and there was no sign of a struggle, apparently.'

'That's all, then?'

'More or less . . . got the fingerprint boys over from Blantyre of course, we might get something out of that, but I doubt it very much.'

'Gloves, you mean?'

Valentine just nodded.

Lucky Clay arrived shortly afterwards and was halfway through the door when the phone rang. 'I'll get it,' he said and disappeared into the hallway.

'There was something I meant to ask you,' Valentine said absently.

'What was that?'

'Did you by any chance pour a glass of whisky whilst

you were at Sally's house?'

'Come to think of it I did. Didn't mention that before did I, must have slipped my mind . . . it was the shock of finding her, I suppose.'

'Don't worry, just as long as I know. Need to tie up all the loose ends. That's all police work is, you know. Tying up loose ends, eliminating as you go.'

I smiled inwardly. If only he knew I was on a similar trail, and he was at the end of it.

Clay appeared in the doorway. 'Call from Karonga, James, the engineers want to be out at first light tomorrow.'

Valentine finished his drink. 'You'd better go up now then, old boy . . . can't afford to lose that contract.'

Clay looked despondent. 'Yeah, I suppose so,' he muttered.

'I'll see you at the airfield in the morning,' Valentine said, 'you'll be in by seven won't you?'

'Depends on the rains, if it holds off again tomorrow . . . seven. Any change, I'll phone.'

'If you do phone make sure you call the office, I'll be there early.'

Clay just raised his hand in acknowledgment in the same way that Jake Ortega had once done, then hurried away down the verandah.

'While I think of it Steve, I'd better have your licence, I'll call in at the civil aviation office tomorrow afternoon and get your Malawi validation.'

'When do you want it? Now?'

'Please. I'm going back down to Zomba tonight . . . one or two things I need to check at the house.'

Suddenly it had become 'the house', not Sally's house; and the way he had referred to the dead body, not Sally's body. Within a week she would be forgotten, within a year she would never have existed. In his mind maybe, but not in mine. I would never forget.

Ten minutes later, complete with overnight bag, James Valentine had gone. I looked at my watch. Four thirty. Penny had said she would be back at three and I'd run out of cigarettes. I searched through the usual places any house would have but found nothing, so I had another whisky and went back to my bungalow.

When I awoke it was dark. Dark and cold and frightening, just as it had been in the jail cell. I shuddered and reached across for the bedside light. Seven o'clock. I took my headache into the bathroom and splashed some cold water on my face, then I ran a comb through my hair and went over to the house.

Penny was kneeling by the fireplace, throwing logs onto an already blazing fire. She was wearing a silky black knee-length dress. Or what appeared to be knee length; when I first saw it, it had ridden halfway up her shapely stockinged thighs. The shoes were also black and very elegant.

'There you are,' she said. 'I called at the bungalow earlier but you were sound asleep . . . would you like a drink?'

'Thank you . . . did you remember the cigarettes?'

'On the table behind you,' she said, standing up. 'Now where was I . . . ah yes, drink.' She moved gracefully over to the drinks tray on the corner of the sideboard and started clinking glasses.

'Has James been back, by any chance?'

'And Lucky,' I said. 'James has gone back to Zomba, took an overnight bag. Lucky flew out to Karonga to pick up some engineers, returning first thing in the morning.'

Penny handed me my drink. 'The steward's off tonight, so I'm afraid dinner will be a makeshift affair. Always is on Wednesdays.'

'That's all right, still having trouble with eating anyway.'

'Of course . . . how does it feel now?'

'Much better, back to normal before you know it,' I said. I leant back in the chesterfield and felt more relaxed than I had been all day. Penny stood, a matter of feet away, with her back to the fire.

'What did James say?' she enquired.

'Say? Not a lot; just that he'd found a couple of clues at Sally's house. Then he took my licence and log book and said he would get them validated tomorrow.'

'You're going then?'

'That's what I've been paid for.'

She managed a wry little smile, then said, 'James usually gets his way.'

'I take it you would rather I didn't do the trip?' I replied.

'That's not really the point,' she said irritably, 'it's just the principles which are involved. You see James has this God fixation – about only having to clap his hands and everybody comes running. Most of the time that is precisely what happens.' She moved sideways, away from the direct heat of the fire. 'You are obviously aware of his . . . er affair with Sally.'

I finished the sentence for her. 'And you want to get back at him through me, is that it?'

Her big brown eyes looked steadily into mine. 'Putting it bluntly, yes. But as you've already told me, you have no intention of getting mixed up in a family squabble.'

'Well I . . .' I paused long enough to raise a doubt in her mind.

'Or perhaps you have a price after all?' She gave me a knowing smile.

'Everyone has their price,' I said. 'It's a byproduct of age, a realization that you can't buck the system and win. The Americans have a better phrase; they say you can't fight City Hall.'

'And what, pray tell, is your price?'

'I hadn't really thought about it. Surely it can't be that important to you?'

She gave a sigh. 'Oh, it's important all right. He's not worried about Sally North you know, just enjoys being the big white chief, the man who solves all ills. What do you think he would have done if those policemen had killed you? I'll tell you, shall I?' Her eyes lit up in a kind of frenzy. 'He would have given them a lecture on police brutality, then he would have found another pilot to fly his precious little aeroplane to wherever . . . I would just like to see someone tell him to go to hell. Just once in my life.'

'And you think I might do it?'

The frenzy slipped away and she laughed. A low sexy laugh. 'You did say everyone has their price.'

What happened next was a complete surprise, one which I never expected. She reached up behind her neck and undid the hook and eye of her dress, then she twisted her left arm the other way behind her back: I heard the zipper run its full length. With her eyes still holding mine she let the dress slip silently to the floor.

I just sat open-mouthed, looking at the black half-cup bra and flimsy matching panties and suspender belt.

'The rest is up to you,' she said, pulling me onto my feet. Then she guided my left hand to her breast, gently massaging it, to and fro. My right hand she forced down the flatness of her stomach, gasping as it slowly inched lower.

Half an hour later we rolled apart, the savage and near brutal lovemaking finally over. Neither of us made any move to get dressed, we just lay in the warmth of the log fire, totally spent.

'Well?' she said.

'Well what?'

'Did you enjoy it?'

I thought for a moment. 'Not bad . . . for a beginner.'

'Bastard!' she cried and dug me in the ribs.

It was after nine when the phone rang. By that time Penny had rustled up the remains of the lunchtime cold plate and had found a bottle of Graves, suitably chilled. We had eaten on the floor in front of the fire; now we were lying back, me fully dressed, she still in her underwear.

'Damn, I'll get it,' she said, scrambling to her feet.

I had an idea it was James Valentine even before she returned. Just small snatches of conversation I suppose, but more perhaps the tone of her voice. She always spoke to him in a cold unfriendly way.

She came back and sat in front of the fire. 'God, it's cold out there . . . it was James, wanted me to tell you the Dornier is serviceable; he suggests you fly it over to Chileka tomorrow and have the radios checked.'

'What did you say?'

She looked at me, head on one side. 'Even I know your price is more than one quick screw in front of the fire,' she said, 'so I told him you would no doubt be fit enough to do it.' She slid across and put her arms around me. 'However it's a long time until tomorrow and I wouldn't object to paying a second instalment now.' She reached up and bit my left ear, then whispered, 'If you're up to it that is?'

Chapter Ten

The Dornier had been pulled out of the hangar and was pointing purposefully across the green airfield. I started a slow, methodical pre-flight inspection, hoping against hope I would find something drastically wrong, something I could use to cancel the short ten-minute flight to Chileka. Something! Anything!

'It's all there, Mr Ritchie,' the cutting Welsh voice said.

I half turned and found Rees-Williams walking towards me. He was absent-mindedly wiping his hands on a piece of oily rag.

'More than likely,' I replied, 'but you won't mind if I check, will you?'

'Check away,' he said mockingly. 'Of course I've already done it for you – but then I'm just the bloody engineer.'

'And I'm just the bloody pilot who might fall out of the sky if things go wrong.'

'If that aeroplane falls out of the sky boyo, it will be your fault, not my workmanship.'

'Is that all?' I said trying to restrain the anger in my voice.

He dropped his head momentarily; when he looked up the swarthy skin was drawn tight across his cheekbones, the eyes angry and as black as coal. 'Is that all,' he said, mimicking an English accent. 'On the command "dismiss" the airman will execute a smart half turn to the right and march away . . . officers and bloody gentlemen, the silver spoon brigade. I've met your type before Mr Ritchie and d'you know something, you're all a pain in the arse . . . every last one of you.'

'And I've met your type before Williams, chip on the shoulder, world owes you a living, and I'm not interested, so if you've just come over to pick an argument, forget it.'

110

'Pick an argument?' his voice rose as if on a musical scale. 'I haven't the time or the patience to pick an argument with the likes of you. No, it was Mr Valentine, wanted me to tell you to make sure you got the ADF checked out when you got to Chileka; but then being God's gift to the aeroplane world you would have already known that, wouldn't you?'

'Naturally,' I replied. 'Now do me a favour will you?'

His eyes just looked at me questioningly.

'Piss off!'

He took a step towards me, hands clenched tightly at his sides, then stopped. 'I'll have you, Mr Ritchie,' he hissed in a low, dangerous voice, 'you bloody well see if I don't.' Then he turned abruptly on his heel and stalked off into the shadow of the hangar.

I just stood, quietly shaking, as the rage within me subsided. He was a bad lot, that Rees-Williams, a thoroughly bad lot. Not that it should have worried me, except he was the engineer who had fixed the aeroplane I was about to fly, and as he had an obvious dislike of ex-Air Force officers, it left me in a very vulnerable position.

I turned back to the Dornier and my reason for being here. Now came the difficult part, ten minutes alone in the sky with an aeroplane. The realization really hit home when I opened the pilot's hatch and lowered myself into the blue, sweat-stained seat. Ten minutes, just ten minutes. One take-off and one landing, with a bit of straight and level in between . . . easy! The little voice inside my head didn't sound too convinced either.

Things happen in threes, or so the old wives' tale goes. Mine had started at six o'clock that morning, when I awoke in the pink and powder blue bedroom and remembered the previous night. The guilt had started then. The feeling of betraying Sally's memory; the feeling of weakness . . . the weakness of all men. But it was more than that. It was the realization of Sally saying she loved me; and now I wanted to tell her I believed her. Only now was too late.

Penny had turned to me, half asleep, reaching out with her hand. I had slipped quietly out of bed and dressed. The conversation, or what little of it there had been, before I left the house, was stilted and distant. Two strangers meeting in a hotel breakfast room.

I had arrived at the airfield just after nine o'clock. Rees-Williams had looked at my still-swollen face as I crossed the hangar to Valentine's office and had given a self-satisfied smirk before returning to whatever he had been doing.

From what I could make out on the daily flying-hours sheet, Clay had arrived back from Chileka. I had idly checked back through the aircraft movements records to see where they had gone to in Southern Zimbabwe, but the pages were conveniently blank. Another of James Valentine's little secrets. I was still regretting the previous evening with Valentine's wife when Rees-Williams had started his usual antisocial behaviour. Now I had locked myself in an aeroplane cockpit, tightened up the seat harness and had my finger poised over the starboard engine starter button. Things happen in threes . . .

Once the engines were running I released the brakes and slowly started to taxi towards the runway, while inside me the little voice just ran away to hide in the darkest corner.

Power checks complete, I ran through the mnemonic checklist for take-off. TTMPFFGGHH. Even when I had forgotten aeroplanes that would still be there, inscribed on the mind forever. Trim – neutral, Throttle friction – finger tight, Mixtures – rich, Pitch – fully fine, Fuel – on and sufficient, Flaps – fifteen degrees selected, Gauges – engine temps and pressures in the green, Gyros – directional indicator set against standby compass, Hatches – secure, Harness – tight. That was it, one final check of the flying controls – full and free movement.

My right hand closed slowly over the throttles and started easing them forward. Christ no! I slammed the throttles closed and stood on the brakes. My inside was

112

crawling with slimy, ugly creatures, I couldn't do it. I sat for a while sweating and cursing and searching my mind for an excuse. When I didn't find one I reached over to the flight bag on the co-pilot's seat and took out the hip flask. One long swallow of the golden brown liquid burnt the creatures inside my stomach – burnt the bastards alive. Now I had time, not much, but perhaps ten minutes.

The engines snarled and rose to an ear-shattering crescendo as I pushed the throttles all the way forward, then the runway started moving past me; slowly at first, then faster, faster, faster. I eased the control column back and the vibration of wheels running over bumpy grass vanished. I was airborne! My legs were shaking with fear, but I was airborne.

My entire body just sat, tense and afraid, as the little voice of survival ran out of my subconscious and started giving familiar commands to a pair of unwilling hands. Climb power – set; flaps – check your height, 300 feet and climbing, okay, flaps select up; now turn right, gentle rate – one turn, easy, easy, that's good.

The climb continued up the long blueness of sky, then the voice said, level off, lower the nose, power back to cruise setting . . . good, good, now retrim. Little more . . . hold it. Now lift your hands off the controls and make sure the aircraft maintains altitude . . . It does, good.

So far, so good. Another seven or eight minutes; the thought didn't help. I looked at the clock in the top left-hand corner of the instrument panel and watched the sweep hand silently consuming the seconds. Then the little voice was back. Better give Chileka a call.

I dialled up the approach frequency with a shaking hand, then I pressed the mike button. 'Chileka approach, this is Seven Quebec Delta Foxtrot Echo.'

Long moments of nothing, except for the steady blat-blat-blat of the two 380-horsepower Lycomings, which beat a steady path through my headset, sending shock waves to the very bowels of my soul. I tried again and a voice replied instantly.

'Seven Foxtrot Echo this is Chileka, pass your message.'

'Roger, Seven Foxtrot Echo is a Dornier inbound to you from Zomba, level five thousand, estimating you in about seven minutes.'

'Roger Seven Foxtrot Echo, advise when you have the airport in sight. Runway in use three-three.'

'Call you field in sight for runway three three.' I released the transmit button then tried to free my shirt, which was clinging to my back like a wet rag. The aircraft rocked slightly as it passed through an area of light turbulence. I grabbed for the control yoke with both hands. The little voice told me to relax, but all that happened was my hands and legs starting shaking even more, while the sweat dripped steadily from my chin like blood from a dying man.

Then in the distance Chileka's two runways slid into view through the oil-streaked windshield.

I thumbed the transmit button again and told the man we had his airport in sight.

'Roger, you are cleared for visual descent and call the tower now, frequency one one eight point two.'

I nervously clicked the dials around until the correct numbers were staring back at me, then I reduced power and lowered the nose. What now? What now? I waited for the little voice, the voice of experience, the voice which had all the answers. Waited, and waited, and waited . . . but it wasn't there, it had gone. 'Christ!' I yelled, and suddenly my right hand was pushing on the power and the aircraft was rearing up like a startled race horse, reaching for the sanctity of space.

The sunlit sky cartwheeled through the cockpit, sending shadows scurrying across my face; then the nose pitched down, down towards the browns and reds, the occasional greens of the earth below. Now that same earth was cartwheeling; spinning like a giant top; out of control. Things happen in threes! Things . . . happen . . . in . . . threes! Suddenly I was fighting for breath, fighting against the positive g force which slammed me down into the seat . . . into and through the seat. I could even feel the sweat turning into blood; warm, sticky and somehow very final.

Then I saw the flight bag with its scratched black leather and tarnished brass clips. It was still on the co-pilot's seat, pinned like me by some giant invisible force. I pushed my right hand out, reaching, reaching . . . stretching my fingertips further than they had ever been before.

The engines were screaming sickeningly, chasing the howling airflow towards certain destruction as I two-handedly pressed the flask to my lips. Then the little voice was back, looking through my eyes and seeing the ground hurtling up at nearly two hundred miles an hour. Spiral dive to the right it said. Power off, level the wings . . . now start coming back on the control column, gently, gently . . . too much g and you won't have an aeroplane; well you will except it will be in its component parts. Come on, for Jesus Christ's sake . . . pull out!

I eased the control column back and heard the slipstream slowly die. All that remained was the low burbling of the two Lycomings – that and about fifty feet. I opened the throttles to maximum take-off power and started to climb. Thank you God for distilling prayers and miracles in bottles. But even God couldn't stop my legs shaking. Levelling off, I called up Chileka tower and was cleared to land. I ran through the pre-landing mnemonic checklist and started my final approach, while the voice continued with a steady patter of instructions. Even the landing was passable. After coming within fifty feet of death and surviving, I had defeated the enemy – for this flight at least.

I parked at the side of the Air Malawi hangar and left the sighing and pinging of the engines as the hot metal contracted, and made my way into the vast, dark and cool emptiness of the hangar.

After a few enquiries I found the radio engineer crawling around a tired old workhorse of a Douglas

Dakota. He seemed reluctant to take on any more work, especially as he only worked on 'big' aeroplanes. After a while he relented and told me to drop back during the afternoon. He couldn't promise anything, he said, but he'd try.

I limped out of the hangar door and lit a cigarette, then screwing my eyes up against the white glare of the concrete apron, made my way to the first-floor bar in the terminal.

Chapter Eleven

The 500-yard walk didn't do much for my left knee, but the thought of a cold beer kept me going. When I arrived inside the scruffy terminal I realized I had picked a bad day for cold beer, or anything come to that.

Apart from the stale, sour smell of sweat which seemed to permeate the concrete floor and plastered walls, the ground floor of the terminal was seething with passengers; some in shirt sleeves, others with coats draped loosely over tired arms, and as usual in those hot, faraway places, the odd one or two stiff upper lippers battling against the strength-sapping heat in thick tweed jackets and old school ties. There was misery in every bead of sweat as they waited patiently for a heavily accented African voice to announce the departure of Flight BA566 to Dar es Salaam, Cairo and London. English public schools it seemed were still breeding them hard!

When the wishing and the if onlys had died away, and stark reality had explained I was going home a different way, I limped off in the general direction of the upstairs bar. It was equally crowded and almost airless. After five minutes of genteel elbowing and pushing I managed to attract the attention of the African barman.

'Beer,' I shouted above the hubbub of conversation.

He gave me an insolent look, which said he might or he might not, then ambled away up the bar and took a bottle out of a rusty broken-down old fridge. He knocked the top off with a deft right hand chop and then slid the bottle down the wet counter top. I caught it as it toppled through forty-five degrees.

'Three kwacha,' he said shuffling back towards me.

'Have you got a glass?'

'Three kwacha,' he repeated. 'No glasses.'

I sorted out the money from the loose change in my

pocket, then took the cool bottle out to the verandah. All the seats were taken so I hung over the white-painted railing and watched the baggage handlers loading suitcases into the hold of the VC10. It would have been all too easy to quit and buy a ticket for that flight, but I had a promise to keep. Or perhaps it wasn't a promise, perhaps it was a vendetta. To find the killer of Sally North and then the final diamond shipment. The diamond shipment? What the hell was I going to do with it, assuming I found it? Perhaps I should get out, South America, anywhere . . . be a rich man for once? Then again I knew it wouldn't be that easy, there was always a hitch. Mine would be getting caught and spending the rest of my life rotting in a jail cell.

I lit a cigarette and suddenly knew that I would do the right thing – hand the diamonds back to the rightful owners. Miss Beckerman had always taught her little children to believe they would get their reward in heaven. Nice old lady, Miss Beckerman.

I'd finished my beer when the tannoy announced the departure of Flight BA566 and asked all passengers to report to Gate I. I waited a few minutes for the crowd to drift away, then made my way back to the bar and a large whisky to wash away the taste of the beer. Valentine and Clay walked in thirty seconds later.

'You got here okay then?' Valentine said.

'No problems,' I lied, 'it's down at the Air Malawi hangar now, engineer said to call back later this afternoon . . . what are you drinking?'

'Beer will do fine, old boy.'

'Lucky?'

'Same again man, thanks.'

We took our drinks back to the verandah and watched the passengers climbing the steps of the VC10 as the ground engineers started moving away unwanted ground equipment in readiness for start-up.

'While I think of it, old boy,' Valentine started, opening his briefcase and producing a sheaf of telexes, 'your clearances . . . all except Egypt, but that's normal as I said before. Just dash the blighters a bottle of something.' I nodded knowingly and he continued, 'And here's your British licence and your Malawi temporary licence, that will cover you to fly a Malawi-registered aircraft.'

It suddenly clicked in my mind. 'Until I have this in my hand I can't legally fly a Malawi-registered aircraft as commander, is that right?'

'Quite right old boy.'

'Except I've just flown the Dornier down from Zomba,' I said.

Valentine pushed a few wisps of grey hair away from his eyes, 'Er, quite . . . oversight on my part. Still, no harm done, eh?'

'No, I suppose not,' I replied and then thought of the long moments I had spent searching for a reason not to conduct the flight. And I'd had the best one of all. Still, if not today, there would always have been tomorrow.

Clay downed the remains of his beer then looked at his watch. 'You did say you had to be down at the station James, it's nearly one.'

'Already?' he exclaimed. Then, 'You'd better fly back alone. I'll borrow a car or get a lift . . . doubt I'll be through till late.'

Clay said, 'Right you are,' and turned to me. 'What time did you say you were heading back?'

'Don't know exactly, engineer said during the afternoon. Reckoned about three-ish.'

'I'll hang about then, just in case he doesn't fix it. In which case you can come back with me.'

The conversation dried up at that moment as the familiar sound of wind rushing down a drainpipe rose to an ear-piercing whine – the VC10's engines starting up one by one. Within seconds the whine rose to a crackling thunder as the aircraft sought to overcome its own inertia. Then it was rolling, sending swirling clouds of concrete dust down the entire length of the terminal.

We all moved as if of one mind, to the quieter confines of the bar.

'Any progress?' I said to Valentine, as he dusted down the front of his khaki bush shirt.

'The Zomba business you mean?'

'Sally North,' I said.

An uncomfortable expression moved across his face as I mentioned her name. 'Nothing definite, old boy,' he said, recovering very well. 'You know how it is?' He checked his watch. 'Well chaps, must be off, see you later.'

Clay turned to me, 'Beer?' I nodded and he went over to the bar and bought a couple of Stars. Still no glasses; they were littered on the table tops and no one it seemed was in a rush to collect them up for washing.

'Has he found out anything about the murder?' I said, following Clay back to the balcony.

'Wouldn't say if he had, but I've got a feeling he's on to something.'

'Why do you say that?'

'Just a feeling,' Clay replied.

'What do you think about it?'

'The murder, you mean . . . ? I'd say it was some black bastard who reckoned he'd steal something from the house, then killed her accidentally.'

'According to Valentine nothing was stolen,' I said.

'Okay, so he killed her and got frightened, then ran away. Happens, you know.'

It was four hours later when the radio engineer finally finished with the Dornier. Then I found the starboard engine wouldn't start – no fuel pressure. I climbed out of the cockpit a lot happier than when I'd stepped into it and signalled across to Clay, who was sitting in the Baron with engines running. He got the message instantly from the double thumbs down and cut his engines as I went into the hangar to find an engineer. As it was after five o'clock it seemed everyone had finished for the day, that was until I found a wiry-headed man busy making scratching sounds with a chinagraph pencil on a large wall chart.

He carried on writing as I explained my problem, then said they would be able to fix it first thing in the morning, providing of course it wasn't a fuel pump that needed replacing. If it did, they wouldn't be able to help as they didn't hold any spares for Dorniers. I left Valentine's home and office numbers and he told me someone would call during the morning.

Then I walked back across the hangar to Lucky Clay's Baron, remembered my flight bag at the last moment and changed direction for the Dornier.

'What's the problem?' Clay asked as I slid into the co-pilot's seat of his aircraft.

'No fuel pressure, could be the fuel pump.'

'What's happening then?'

'They're going to look at it in the morning and give me a call.'

Clay grunted something back by way of reply and cranked the right engine into life.

The flight back was seven and a half minutes of smooth handling. I remembered Bill Kimberley remarking he had once had the hands of an angel. Well, now I had found another one, a 100 per cent natural. I would have liked to have thought that I had been as good as that once. Good perhaps, but never that good. The landing reminded me of Jake Ortega, one minute you were flying, the next you were down, the point of touchdown being almost impossible to pinpoint.

Once the Baron had been locked and chocked for the night I went into the office with Clay and made a pot of coffee while he completed the aircraft's tech log. Then we sat and discussed the routing I was due to take with the Dornier. As he was familiar with the run up to Nairobi I gleaned some useful tips, ones which might help keep me alive.

We left the office just before sunset, with Clay's white Range Rover soon disappearing into the dusty distance. I just maintained a steady thirty to forty miles an hour and looked forward to the cool, clean air on top of the mountain.

That's how it should have happened, of course. Me arriving at the house about twenty minutes after Clay and pouring myself a large whisky. But it didn't. I had just entered the pine forest when I realized something was wrong. Clay's Range Rover was stopped at a slight angle behind another car. I switched off the engine and went to see what the hold-up was. Obviously the first car had broken down, and as the road was only single track it meant neither Clay nor I could pass until it was rendered serviceable.

I eased around the Range Rover and saw Clay immediately. He was standing half doubled up by the offside front of the broken-down car and even though the light was fading fast I could readily see he was vomiting.

'What's wrong?' I yelled and hurried towards him. It was when I passed the driver's door of what I now recognized as a Peugeot 504, that I knew. I caught my breath and turned away. Holy bloody Christ, what a mess. I turned back slowly, trying to control the muscles in my stomach which were producing a violent urging.

The bolt had passed through the windscreen, shattering it completely, then it had passed straight through the driver's face. The body was slumped back in the seat. What face there had once been was no more, it was almost as if it had disintegrated. All that remained was a bloody mess of flesh and bone and one grotesque eye staring up from the shoulder of a blood-soaked shirt.

Then I looked again. Looked again at the fat sunburnt hands, the hands covered in a million freckles; the khaki bush shirt which was now mostly red, then at the build of the man. I didn't need to check if the eye was green, I knew even then in the fading light of the pine forest that the man was James Valentine.

I limped around to the front of the car and gulped in a few mouthfuls of fresh air. Clay was leaning back against the radiator now, his face ashen, his entire body shaking.

'It's Valentine,' I said quietly.

He just looked beyond me, through me; in his eyes shocked disbelief. After a time he said, 'I know.' I went back to the pick-up, my eyes carefully avoiding the hideous sight of James Valentine, and found the hip flask. Then I went back to Clay and told him to drink. He nearly choked but he kept it down. I emptied the flask and put it into my trouser pocket.

'We'd better get the police,' I said. 'Sooner the better, wouldn't you say?'

Clay shrugged his huge frame and tried to pull himself

together. 'Yeah, right . . . the police. Look, I'll take your pick-up. Back it down the mountain . . . know the road like the back of my hand. I guess you'd better stay here and . . .' the words choked in his throat.

'I'd get moving, while you've still got some daylight.'

'Yeah . . . sure.' Clay moved slowly down the passenger side of the car, his movements almost those of a drunken man.

The pick-up's engine caught at the second time of asking, then there was just the faint whine of reverse gear as Clay backed down the sloping road. I listened long after the sound had gone, and darkness had descended like a cloak of black velvet over the forest.

I would have probably stood rooted to the spot until Clay returned with the police if it hadn't been for the coughing. You expect sounds at night in a forest, but not a person coughing. Or perhaps I hadn't heard it, perhaps I had imagined it! I strained my ears and waited, but the only sound was the constant series of soft, high-pitched trills of a thousand ground crickets. Funny how your mind blocks out a constant background noise; I hadn't even heard the crickets before. Now it was all I could hear. What was funnier still, was the way the adrenal glands pump out fear; especially on dark nights in African forests. But more than fear, there was also a heightened perception – an awareness. The information leaflet in the VC10; the one I had been reading on the flight out from London, suddenly came to mind. Baboons! I had read something about baboons living in the hills in Malawi. Why the hell was that so important?

The answer came from nowhere, dredged up from the murky depths of a subconscious mind which must have read or heard at one time that leopards eat baboons. And leopards cough!

I was in Clay's Range Rover within seconds, furiously winding the driver's window closed. Then I switched on the headlights, started the engine and began blasting away on the horn. If it was a leopard out there the noise would have frightened him away. I lit a cigarette with shaking hands and looked around; the feeling of not being alone was very strong. Perhaps the killer was still here?

Valentine couldn't have been dead very long. How long? And why was he here at all? He did say he wouldn't be back until later . . . unless of course he had found the final clue and was hurrying back. But if that had been the case he would surely have had an army of policemen with him.

The engine started running rough, too much fuel, so I blipped the accelerator a couple of times and blasted away on the horn just for good measure. Leopards and crossbow killers . . . what the hell was happening? What the hell was . . . The answers clicked into place with a metallic clunk in my mind.

Valentine had gone to southern Zimbabwe with Clay to pick up the final package of submarine goods. The ideal place to keep them stashed away. Independent Africa, where whites are *persona non grata*. The South African police were obviously still keeping an eye on all the ports and airfields, even as far north as Malawi. But they wouldn't get a look-in anywhere in Zimbabwe.

Having slipped across the border, on the pretext of doing a local flight, you returned to Malawi and the 'government transaction' of ferrying out a Dornier. Which explained why the Dornier had been unserviceable for so long. Valentine had been unable to collect the goods because his other pilot had been killed at Tete. In fact he'd said something like that to Clay one evening. The fact that the Dornier was now unserviceable through fuel pressure problems, was just one of those things. I had all the clearances in my flight bag . . . and the diamonds were obviously secreted somewhere in the aircraft.

It all seemed logical except for one isolated fact. Valentine was now dead, which seemed to indicate someone else knew about the diamonds. Another fact which seemed totally logical.

Thirty minutes later I found out how illogical my logical thinking really was.

I was on my third cigarette when the car headlights blazed into my rearview mirror. I cut the engine and climbed out of the Range Rover as two black policemen rushed past me towards the Peugeot.

'You okay, man?' Clay seemed to have recovered after the journey.

'Just about. Thought I heard a leopard earlier, so I got in your Rover and started making a hell of a noise.'

'Good thinking, man. It would have got the scent of blood and come down to have a look.'

'They don't attack people though, do they?' I said.

'Not normally, but if they get the scent of blood you never know.'

More policemen arrived in a second car, pouring out before it had stopped. They rushed past us. Clay watched them for a moment then turned back to me. 'Bloody bad news!'

'What?'

'They know who the killer is.'

'Who?'

'Taffy . . . Rees-Williams!'

The hair seemed to lift on the back of my neck. 'Rees-Williams? Who told you that?'

Clay leaned back against the Range Rover, his face half hidden in the shadow. The other half was caught in the headlight glare of the first police car. There seemed to be a nervous twitch near his right eye as he spoke. 'These buggers did,' he said in a forced whisper. 'What's more I wouldn't want to be in his shoes when they get their black hands on him.'

I didn't need to ask Clay to elaborate on that. From my own treatment it seemed reasonable to assume they would shoot first and ask questions later.

'What evidence have they got?' I said, searching through my pockets for a cigarette.

Clay frowned. 'Enough, from what they told me. Not that they'd need much. Valentine was a respected man, you see, almost like a father to them . . . I think they'd even forgotten he was white.'

'I thought they were sympathetic to the whites?'

Clay gave a low cynical laugh. 'Don't ever believe that, man, they're about as warmhearted as a wounded lion on the game trail . . . pounce at the first excuse.'

I turned to the frenzied activity around the Peugeot. The police now had Valentine's body laid out on the track in front of the car, while other officers were making a slow methodical inspection of the surrounding area. The police sergeant, whom I recognized from the Zomba station, strutted down the track towards me.

'Captain Ritchie,' he said coldly, 'I believe you found the body!' I had expected him to add the word 'again', but he didn't, he just waited for my reply.

'No, not this time, Mr Clay here found him.'

'No matter, we have the man . . . would you help us to move some of the pine logs back in the forest . . . we can then lift the Peugeot to one side and reopen the road.'

'What then, Sergeant?'

'You and Mr Clay will come to the police station to make a statement.'

'Have you phoned Mrs Valentine?' I asked, following him back to the now-covered body of Valentine.

'Inspector Ogobushi has gone up the other road. Now if you can help my men, Captain.'

'Mister will do fine,' I said.

He stopped and gave me a quizzical stare, 'You are an aircraft captain . . . isn't that right?'

'Yes.'

'So I will call you Captain. Rank is rank, Captain.'

And black is black, and white is white, I thought. Thought but didn't say; I doubted the police sergeant had heard of shades of grey. Instead I joined Clay for half an hour's sweated labour in the sergeant's temporary road widening project.

By the time we arrived at the police station it was nearly ten o'clock. The sergeant had called in at the house on our way up and down the mountain. Clay and I had waited in the Range Rover with a surly-looking young police officer for company. Now we were sitting in an untidy little office answering a barrage of questions. Although the answers didn't vary the sergeant still managed to indicate by his manner and tone of voice that Clay and I were far from being free of suspicion. Then he took two pieces of foolscap paper from a desk drawer.

'Perhaps you will both write down exactly what you have told me.' He slid the papers across the top of the desk.

The very next moment all hell broke loose when a young wild-eyed policeman came rushing in, shouting in his native tongue. The sergeant was out of his char in an instant, rushing towards the door.

'What the hell was all that about?' I asked, turning to Clay.

'Been down to pick up Rees-Williams apparently . . . he got away.' There was a hint of anger in his voice when he added, 'They think they've winged him, though.'

'Do you think he'l make it?'

Clay shrugged disinterestedly. 'Depends on how bad he was hit, if he was hit at all, that is. Serves the bastard right but I still don't like bloody blacks hunting whites . . . I just don't bloody like it.'

By the time the sergeant had returned we had both written out our statements. He picked them up and with little more than a cursory glance tossed them into a already full filing tray.

'You will both be returning to Mr Valentine's house?' The question was more of a command.

Clay said, 'That's right.'

'Good, that is all . . . for now.'

We walked to the door. 'Goodnight then Sergeant,' I said.

The sergeant jerked his head upright and looked directly at us. 'Goodnight Captain . . . Mr Clay.'

Clay turned, unhappiness written all over his face. 'Night.'

We arrived at the house just over half an hour later, Clay having chastized me on the way for being so courteous to blacks. I'd argued that it seemed good sound psychology to keep them sweet, but Clay wouldn't have any of it.

Our differences were temporarily forgotten when we went into the drawing room and found red-eyed Penny sitting alone in front of a blazing log fire. The inspector had left.

'You okay, Pen?' Clay asked. 'Can I get you a drink?'

She looked up at him. 'No thanks, not at the moment.'

'Steve?'

'Scotch,' I said, and sat next to Penny on the chesterfield. 'Sorry about all this,' I said to her, 'must have been quite a shock.'

She lifted her eyes to mine. 'I just can't believe it,' she

whispered. 'I just can't believe it.'

Clay came over and joined us, handing me a large whisky and taking his over to the chair at the side of the fireplace.

'Thought you were a beer man?' I said.

'After tonight, man, I doubt there's a drink in the world that's strong enough to help me get over that.'

'You have been told it was Rees-Williams,' Penny said quietly, looking first at Clay, then at me. We both nodded.

She continued, 'The inspector told me that James had given Rees-Williams his notice last month; something to do with Sally North.'

I looked up sharply. 'Sally? What's that supposed to mean?'

'It seemed faintly ridiculous to me,' Penny replied. 'The inspector said that Rees-Williams had been pestering her, and she told James about it. James, it seems, had spoken to Rees-Williams about the matter, but it seemed to no avail . . . so James fired him. He would have completed his month't notice this week.'

'And they reckon Williams killed them both because of that?' I said disbelievingly.

'Not altogether, the inspector did mention some letters, love letters, which had been found at the house. Apparently they dated back to the time he was going out with her. I think he summed it up as a crime of passion, or words to that effect.'

'Going out with her! What, Rees-Williams and Sally?'

Penny said, 'When she first started working for James. Apparently she had a few dates with the Welshman.'

Sally hadn't mentioned anything to me; but then why would she have? I said, 'But surely that's all circumstantial?'

Clay gave one of his ironical laughs. 'They'll hang you for less than that out here.'

'Oh there was one other thing,' Penny said. 'Rees-Williams was a member of the Blantyre expats' club, he did a lot of archery. The inspector mentioned he was something of a specialist with a crossbow.'

'Which means he's also crazy,' Clay said. 'He must have wanted to get caught.'

'If he'd wanted to get caught why the hell did he escape?' I exclaimed.

'Escape!' Penny said in amazement.

'We just heard at the police station, they went to arrest him and he got away. That doesn't sound like a man who wanted to get caught, does it?'

The amazement had died from Penny's eyes when she said, 'No, I suppose not. It was just that the inspector indicated they already had him in custody.'

'You know what they're like!' Clay said knowingly.

We sat until the early hours, talking about Africa and how it was all changing. I didn't really agree with Clay's point of view but I still remained drinking whisky and letting the warmth of the log fire instil tiredness into my body. I needed all the help I could get if I was going to sleep at all that night.

We broke up the wake at about two o'clock with Penny mentioning the funeral would be tomorrow afternoon, then looking at her watch she corrected the statement to 'this' afternoon, and would we both accompany her.

I'd just reached my bungalow and had started undressing for bed when I heard the heavy roll of thunder. Not long after that the rain started. But then it always rains for funerals it seems.

Chapter Twelve

I awoke early and went over to the window to draw the curtains. Outside it was one of those English cobweb mornings thick with mist, except it wasn't mist, it was low cloud capping the top of the mountain. It was like England though, very autumnal, very still. Whenever I was abroad it was the one picture I carried. Isolated in a country cottage with a cheerful log fire blazing from the hearth, while outside, the rolling fog was innocently stealing the roads, the hedgerows, the hills, the fields and the rivers; leaving you and your cottage like a solitary ship on the vastness of some great ocean.

Standing at that moment it felt as though I had been in Africa forever, and England, like the picture, was nothing more than a blurred and faded memory. I silently cursed my sentimentality and lit a cigarette, then went through to the bathroom.

Half an hour later I was thoroughly scrubbed and thoroughly awake. I polished my black shoes to somewhere near the perfection James Valentine would have approved of, brushed some life into my grey suit and unpacked a new white aircrew shirt from my holdall. As black ties are a normal part of a pilot's uniform, as are black socks, it seemed I had come well prepared.

I hadn't worn the suit since my arrival a week earlier and it generally felt one size too big; which corresponded with Jack Sullivan's parting words. 'Try to lose a bit of weight.' I'd done that all right, not that I ever wanted my pilot's licence back, but I could do without the high blood pressure. Having combed my hair with more than the usual care and taken a last glance at the too-old mask of scars and neglect, I went out into the morning.

Normally it would have felt good, but my mind was too full of problems and doubts to allow that kind of feeling. I found Penny in the dining room, alone. Her eyes were puffy, through lack of sleep.

'You look awful,' I said, then bit my lip and added, 'you know what I mean, tired . . . drawn.'

She looked up from her untouched plate of scrambled egg, 'And you look too damn good for so early in the morning.'

'Don't worry, it doesn't happen very often.'

She poured me a coffee as I sat down opposite her. 'Do you know something Steve, I'm still trying to understand the inspector's reasoning.'

'I thought we covered all that ground last night,' I said.

'Perhaps. But if James knew it was Rees-Williams he would have surely gone to the airfield or Rees-Williams's house to question him.'

'I suppose so.'

'So how do you explain he was killed in the pine forest?'

'I don't know, perhaps he was coming back here first to collect something . . . or perhaps he didn't know it was Rees-Williams and had called it a day.'

'Impossible,' she said, 'the inspector said they already had the man, Rees-Williams. So James must have told him that much at least.'

I hadn't had time to think about it before, or perhaps I had tried to push it out of my mind but now looking back at the evidence it seemed distinctly odd. I tried to put myself in Valentine's shoes and approach the investigation from that angle. It still didn't work. Then I got to wondering why Sally hadn't mentioned Rees-Williams had pestered her and Valentine had given him notice. Although that could at least explain the Welshman's obtuse behaviour.

After breakfast I returned to the bungalow and went through the telex clearances for the Dornier ferry; anything to take my mind off the gruesome business of murder. As Valentine had said it was all there – except for the Egyptian clearances. There was also a copy of a telex message to Max Goldstein in Paris. It read simply, 'Dornier 7Q-DFE e.t.d. Zomba Saturday 29 November stop. *Mazel und broche* – Valentine.'

Saturday! That was tomorrow. And what was *mazel und broche*? I went back to the house, arriving as the phone jangled noisily into life. It was for me. An engineer

131

who introduced himself as Bob Eades. He said he'd found a wire adrift on the Dornier's fuel pump and had resoldered it; adding I could pick up the machine any time I liked. I thanked him and went into the drawing room and poured myself a small whisky. The thought of being up there again put the fear of God into me.

Clay wandered in some time later, dressed in a neat single-breasted charcoal grey suit and looking as much the Greek God as ever. 'Hate bloody funerals,' he said, pacing up and down the Persian carpet.

'Can't say I particularly enjoy them,' I said.

Clay stopped pacing. 'Do you play chess?'

'Once in a while.'

We spent the remainder of the morning trying to concentrate on opening gambits, middle and end games; both failing miserably by leaving glaring openings that even a six-year-old would have capitalized on.

The cemetery was small but well cared for and backed onto the Anglican church, an unimposing wooden structure which was painted a pale cream colour. The open tower on the roof housed the single bell which tolled mournfully across the lowlands. What struck me as impressive was the number of mourners who, even at such short notice, had somehow arrived out of nowhere with what seemed like hundreds of wreaths. The beautifully ornate coffin had been borne solemnly by six hatless police officers, before being gently lowered into the freshly dug grave. Now the round-shouldered old vicar was giving the last rites. The bell had since stopped and all that could be heard was his high-pitched voice, lifting from time to time above the warm wind which carried the scudding clouds southwards.

'Ashes to ashes, dust to dust . . .' the hollow patter of a handful of soil falling on the coffin sounded louder than any bell. It was the final act . . . or nearly. An immaculately turned out police inspector suddenly snapped to attention and took one precise military step forward. Then he barked out the order to shoulder arms and six rifles slammed smartly into six shoulders.

'Fire!' The command was lost as the volley of rifles

132

cracked in unison over the churchyard. All that was left was a moment's drifting smoke, ringing ears, and the acrid smell of cordite. The rain which had threatened throughout the day started shortly afterwards, sending the mourners hurrying for shelter. I looked round, searching for Clay, and saw him and Penny talking to the inspector. They were huddled together under a large black umbrella. I moved towards them.

Clay said, 'There you are, man, you'd better take the car; we're going down to the station with the inspector.'

The inspector looked at me, uncertainty in his eyes. 'You are Captain Ritchie?'

'That's right, Inspector,' I held out my hand but he ignored it and turned back to Penny Valentine.

'We will go to my car then Mrs Valentine . . . Mr Clay.'

Clay pushed the car keys into my still outstretched hand, waited until the other two had moved sufficiently far away to be out of earshot, then said, 'You'll never learn, man!'

I stood and watched him go as the heavy rain soaked quickly through my suit, my shirt and onto my skin, then I limped down the muddy path to the Range Rover. By the time I reached the mountain track, the rain had eased to little more than a drizzle, although the low cloud still clung to the upper half of the mountain, reducing forward visibility to a matter of yards. By the time I entered the pine forest my speed was down to a walking pace. The windscreen wipers clunked dully back and forth as I moved cautiously on. It was safe enough now, but once I left the forest I would be back to sheer drops bordering the twisting, slippery road. Although I was concentrating on the red track directly ahead, my eyes picked up the almost imperceptible movement in the trees immediately. My foot instinctively slackened on the accelerator as I glanced to the right. I was too late! The driver's door was suddenly flung wide open and I found myself staring down the barrel of a flat black revolver.

'Stop!' the voice screamed. I let out the clutch and the vehicle jerked, stalled and was silent. I was looking at the bedraggled figure of Rees-Williams, his hair hanging black and lank across his unshaven face. The dark hunted eyes stared unblinkingly as a slow wicked smile spread to his lips. 'So it's you Mr Ritchie, there's a bit of luck, isn't it?' He paused then took a few steps back. 'Out . . . move!' I climbed down slowly. 'This way,' he snarled, waving the gun in the direction I should walk.

We went deep into the forest and came to a makeshift shelter; a result of falling pine needles forming a thatch across the low branches of one of the trees. At the entrance of the shelter a few charred sticks; the remnants of a fire. 'Sit there!' Rees-Williams commanded, pointing to a spot by the trunk of the tree. I sat in the damp pine needles and waited. 'Yes, I'm glad it's you Mr Ritchie . . . very glad.' He went to squat down opposite me and accidentally knocked his left arm. He grimaced in pain and swore softly. It was then I noticed the tear in the sleeve of his dark blue windcheater. I couldn't see any blood, but as the material was dark in colour it would be difficult to tell.

'I'd get a doctor to look at that,' I suggested.

'A bloody comedian as well!' he said sarcastically.

'Comedian be damned . . . you'll never get away with it you know!'

'That's just the bloody point Mr Ritchie, I've got nothing I want to get away with.'

'What the hell are you talking about?' I said. 'You killed Sally . . . and Valentine. Isn't that enough?'

Rees-Williams's face suffused with anger. 'That is where you're wrong. I didn't kill anybody.'

'Which explains why you escaped from the police and are now on the run, I suppose. Hardly the actions of an innocent man.'

Rees-Williams gave me a hard stare. 'Have you got a cigarette?'

'Yes.'

'Light one for me,' he ordered. 'And don't try anything or I'll blow your bloody head off.' I lit the cigarette with a shaking hand. 'Now throw it down there.' I did as I was told and he stooped carefully to pick it up. 'So as I was saying,' he continued, 'I didn't kill anyone . . . I've been framed.'

I stared at the man, who had the look of a hunted

animal. If I could keep him talking for long enough, Clay would arrive, and what was more he would be in a police car. 'And why should I believe that? Ever since I've been here you've gone out of your way to play the arch-bastard . . . or was that just because Valentine had given you notice to quit?'

Rees-Williams laughed cynically. 'Christ, you don't think that that made any difference to me do you?' The humour had faded from his voice when he added, 'I'll tell you, why shouldn't I? Twenty years ago I left Halton. Now you'd know that Halton teaches the cream of aircraft engineering apprentices, wouldn't you? So after three years of hard slog I passed out as a junior technician. Then I took my corporal techs board and got through that. You see Mr Ritchie, having clawed my way up from a poor mining family that wasn't halfway bad going for a boy from the Rhonda.' He took another drag on his cigarette. His voice became softer. 'No, that wasn't bad going at all; if only my Dad had been there to see it . . . I reckon he would have said that. But he wasn't, you see. He was dead; buried under the black, wet, slimy earth . . . the place the poor bugger had spent most of his life. Silicosis it was . . . you wouldn't know about that would you? Coal dust man, you see it gets into the lungs . . . restricts the breathing. Slowly, ever so slowly until in the end the breathing stops. Not a nice way to die Mr Ritchie, not a nice way at all.'

'I can understand that,' I said quietly.

'Understand!' he cried. 'Understand! Like bloody hell you understand. I understand, I was there. Born into it I was . . . but I escaped. It was hard work but I made it. You see I'd planned a career in the Air Force . . . it was my life. Then I ended up on a bomber station. That was when some snotty-nosed little pilot officer reported me for not saluting him inside a technical area. I mean, he didn't seem to mind that station standing orders said that airmen didn't have to salute inside certain defined technical areas or they'd be saluting all day instead of getting on with their work. Anyway this little runt kept on my back after that; right up to the point that I was told if there were any more complaints I'd be in the guardroom.

Then one day out at his aircraft he had another go at me. I decided it was better to walk away than argue; and that was when he follows me and hits me across the face. Of course I saw red and gave him a bloody good hiding. As the only witness was his navigator that was it. Court bloody martial. Two months inside Colchester and end of career.' He paused long enough for it all to sink in. 'And that, Mr Ritchie, is why I don't like Air Force officers past, present or future.'

'Fair enough,' I said. 'But you started being funny long before you knew I'd been in the Air Force.'

'Oh I knew all right; got a nose for that sort of thing . . . Clay's the same!'

'Lucky Clay?'

'Who else. Ex-Rhodesian Air Force. But the bastards paid him back in spades.' A satisfied smile spread across his face.

'What do you mean?'

'Come off it boyo, you know all about that . . . stalling for time is it? Waiting for the cavalry to come along and rescue you.'

'You said you'd been framed. By whom?'

'I'm not really sure. But I'll tell you something for nothing, when I do find out I'll rip their arms from their bodies . . . you see if I don't.'

'Why not go to the police and tell them all this?'

'A white man go to black police! Even you should know by now what the bastards are like. I mean they pulled you in over Sally's murder, didn't they? And I hear if it wasn't for Penny . . . Mrs Valentine, you'd still be in the jug.'

'I realize that . . . but you could still try.'

'No way,' he said with finality. 'No, the only way is to get across the border and catch a flight back to Europe . . . and that's where you come in!'

'Me! What can I do?'

'Take me to Nairobi.'

'Impossible!'

'Like hell it's impossible; you're taking the Dornier that way aren't you?'

'Yes . . . but I have to stop at Karonga; there'll be customs.'

136

'I'll take my chances,' he said.

'It still won't work,' I replied.

'If it doesn't boyo, you're a dead man . . . think on that.'

'Do you mind if I have a cigarette?'

'Go ahead, and while you're at it light another for me.'

'Just as a matter of interest,' I said. 'How did you manage to escape from the police?'

He exhaled a trail of blue-grey smoke through his nose and mouth. 'Bit of luck really; I'd just got back from work when they arrived. They questioned my houseboy first – Joseph. Said they'd come to get me for the murder of James Valentine. Course they were talking to the wrong boyo . . . old Joseph's as bent as a seven-dollar bill; been in the slammer a couple of times himself, and he hates the bastards as much as me. So Joseph tells them I've gone up the road to a friend's house for a drink . . . then he comes and tells me. I was pulling out of the driveway when they came running back and started shooting . . .'

'How bad is it . . . the arm?'

'Just a flesh wound . . . second bit of luck really.' His voice had become almost gentle. This was the real Rees-Williams. The one behind the mask.

'You didn't kill Valentine did you . . . or Sally?'

His face was bleak when he said, 'Don't tr~~u~~ ~~t~~he old soldier Mr Ritchie; I've been around too lo~~ng~~

'No old soldier,' I said. 'You really di~~d~~ ~~kill them did~~ you?'

'Why do you say that?' ~~cro~~ssbow.'

'Because you're an expert w~~ith a~~

'Who the hell told you t~~hat?~~

'Police mentioned it ~~. . . kill them you wouldn't have~~

'So?' ~~a wea~~pon; one which would immedi-

'So, if you w~~ould b~~e caught, of course. And as you used such a~~ . . . w~~ others as prime suspects . . . not

ately iso~~lated . . . un~~derstanding dawned in the Welshman's

unle~~ss . . .~~ you're saying you believe me. How can I

137

trust you not to turn me in at the first opportunity you get?'

'You can't, but if it's any consolation your poor mining family upbringing in the Rhonda sounds a damn sight better than my fifteen years in an orphanage.'

The deep veneer of cynicism nearly cracked then, nearly but not quite. 'Save the violins boyo, I'm not interested.' He said it as though he didn't believe it himself.

'What now?' I said.

'When are you planning to leave?'

'I was supposed to depart tomorrow . . . Saturday, but the plane's still in Chileka. I thought I'd pick it up and move it back to Zomba in the morning and set out early Sunday.'

'Sounds okay to me.'

'What are you going to do in the meantime?'

'Easy,' he said, 'you're going to take me up the mountain. Valentine's got a woodshed up there. I'll hide in it until Sunday . . . and just in case you're thinking of contacting the police just remember I've got a gun and it's loaded, and before they get me I'll make damn sure I get you or Clay or even Penny Valentine. You do understand that, don't you?'

'I get the message,' I replied. 'Now I think we'd better get moving; Clay and Penny went from the funeral to the police station and I'm betting they'll be along any minute.'

Rees-Wil. believe a word just gave me a look that said he didn't and rose unsteadily to his feet.

Chapter Thirteen

'What did you mean about Clay being paid back in spades?' I said, maintaining a steady five miles an hour up the fogbound mountain.

'You don't know?' Rees-Williams said surprisedly.

'I'd hardly ask if I did.'

'Long story really,' he replied. 'All started when Clay went to fly for Smith's Air Force, when it was Southern Rhodesia. Anyway he was poling Hunters round the sky, ground attack stuff on the rebels in Zambia and wherever. Well, after the war he went back to his farm in Zambia. Apparently, so the story goes, his cookboy came to him one day and told him to sack the gardener . . . different tribe you see, didn't like him. Instead Clay sacked the cookboy for being insolent. So the cookboy goes down the road to the rebel headquarters and tells the chief that Clay had been flying for Smith and that he had seen him going past in a Hunter . . . so the rebels went after Clay. He just managed to get away in that Baron of his, lost the farm though, the lot.' Rees-Williams gave a low satisfied chuckle at the thought, then added, 'Funnier than that though, the cookboy didn't really know Clay had flown for Smith, just his way of evening the ~~~~ore. And you asked me why I hadn't turned myself ~ to the police . . . Jesus Christ. You just take that ~nd ~he cookboy goes to the rebel chief, the big boss m~dome and oxygen mask a Hunter. So there's Clay~nd he comes steaming in at on, with just his eyes ~i~oing over five hundred knots about two hundred ~ same time. And this African is and firing cann~~g and says to himself – "Ah, that is just standin~ the rebel chief believes every word of Bwana C~wly into the long drive with a few ideas it. Th~ny mind. But they would have to wait. First I

139

had to get Rees-Williams to the woodshed and then see if I could find him some food and a bandage for his damaged arm.

Half an hour was all it took. By that time I had checked that Sunday was in the servants' quarters, then taken half a loaf of bread, a lump of reasonable-looking cheese, six fresh oranges and a bottle of milk. I'd just reached the woodshed when I heard a car approaching down the long driveway.

'Take this quickly,' I said, scrambling over a pile of dry logs.

'What is it?'

'Car! . . . Look, I'll get back after dark. Bring some water and a bandage for the arm.'

'You'd better bring a blanket as well.'

I started piling the logs back before making my way out of the open-fronted shed.

'One thing, Mr Ritchie!'

'What's that?' I said tiredly.

'No funny business . . . I meant what I said earlier.' Although I couldn't see his face at the back of the shed I knew the threat in his voice was very real.

The car was nearing the house as I pressed myself against the inner wall of the shed. Thank God for the fog, at least when they passed I could slip away to the bungalow undetected. The drive ran directly past the woodshed then went down a slight incline to the carport next to the house. The distance between me and that carport was no more than twenty feet.

The police car appeared ghostlike out of the mist and for a moment I thought the sl__ they had seen me, but the car continued down the sl__ they had seen me, but the car a halt. I counted to th brakes squeaking as it came to drive and into a cluster o d slipped quietly over the towards the bungalow. _ipani bushes which led

I changed quickly into some suit on a hanger and threw e_ thes, hung my wet bottom of the wardrobe, then lit _ else into the blank piece of paper from my flight _e. I took a edge of the bed. I started writing dow__t on the unanswered questions, loose ends Valentin__ so far

140

and he had been absolutely right. The list numbered eight. Eight questions to which I needed to find answers. There would be more of course, of that I was certain.

Satisfied my detective work was now taking shape in a more organized manner I folded the paper and slipped it into my shirt pocket, then left the bungalow and made my way to the house. The police car was still parked under the carport as I made my way up the three wooden steps to the verandah, which meant I would probably be answering questions instead of asking them.

I checked my watch as I entered the drawing room. Five thirty. Mustn't forget Rees-Williams! Penny looked up at me with uncertainty as I entered the room. She was sitting in the chair by the fire. Clay was opposite, lounging back in the chesterfield, and the immaculately turned out inspector from the funeral was standing with his back to the fire. His hands were clasped behind his back, something he had no doubt picked up from Valentine.

Human beings at the best of times are complicated creatures. We all, it seems, have an uncanny knack of knowing something isn't quite right. For feeling tension in the atmosphere of a room even though we haven't been forewarned of its presence. And this was one of those moments; one which needed a knife to cut through the heavy air of unrest.

'Ah! Captain Ritchie, I'm glad you have joined us,' the inspector's voice had that ring of superiority. 'There are one or two questions I would like to ask you.'

I walked straight at him, flicked my cigarette into the blazing fire and said. 'Go ahead Inspector, I'm listening.'

'Perhaps you would like a seat?'

Clever bit of strategy that, always talk down to people. Psychological advantage.

'Seat? Not necessary old man, after spending your life in the military you get used to standing.' I pulled myself up to my full height, our eyes were level. 'Now you were saying, questions?' The laid-on English accent and the attacking manner caught him off guard.

'You are a military man then?' he said uncertainly.

'Ex-military, Inspector. Royal Air Force. And you?'

His eyes wavered for a moment. 'I am a policeman

Captain, plain and simple.'

'Plain and simple, Inspector? I think you are being too modest; you are Inspector Ogobushi aren't you?'

'That is correct.'

'Thought so, yes, James – God rest his soul – was only saying to me last week how effective the force was these days. Even mentioned your name, said you were one of the top men.'

The inspector's chest puffed out noticeably, his ebony face glowing with satisfaction. 'He was a good man Mr Valentine, a very good man.'

'Yes Inspector,' I said sadly, 'but I'm sure you will keep up the tradition in the finest manner.'

'We do our best, Captain.'

'Now Inspector, what were the questions?'

'Ah yes, the questions,' he thought for a moment. 'It was concerning a certain diamond ring which belonged to Miss North.'

'I explained all about that to James Valentine,' I said hastily.

'Yes Captain, I know that, but perhaps you could tell me what happened to the ring?'

'Happened?' I glanced quickly across to Penny but she avoided my eyes. I ran through the story of Valentine arriving back and taking the ring as evidence.

The inspector was pensive for a few moments. 'Yes . . . yes. We believe he still had the ring with him when he was murdered.'

'In which case Rees-Williams probably has it,' I replied.

'Possibly,' he said.

'I take it you haven't caught him yet?'

'Just a matter of time Captain, we will catch him.'

'I hope so Inspector, he seems a very dangerous man.'

'When you were guarding Mr Valentine's car, Captain, at the time Mr Clay came down to the police station, did you . . . er enter that car for any reason?'

'It's all in my statement Inspector, you'll see from that.'

'I have already seen it, so you are saying you did not.'

'If you are trying to ask if I stole the diamond from the dead body of James Valentine, Inspector, the answer is I did not. You may take my fingerprints if you wish and then check the Peugeot.'

'That is not necessary, Captain. There is one other question. When are you leaving?'

'Sunday morning,' I said.

'From Zomba?'

'That's right, Zomba to Karonga.'

'You will have no objections if my men search the aircraft before it leaves?'

I felt a shudder pass through my body, but at least my voice sounded casual enough as I said, 'My pleasure Inspector, my pleasure.'

'Well, I think that is all for now, Captain, Mrs Valentine, Mr Clay.' He made a small formal bow to each of us and walked towards the door.

Penny rose from her chair. 'I'll see you to your car, Inspector.'

He just nodded solemnly and they both went out through the door.

'Cagey so and so isn't he?' I said, turning to Clay.

'You're learning though man, liked the way you handled that.'

'Maybe,' I said, 'but I don't think he's as dumb as he looks.'

I went over to the sideboard and poured a whisky. 'Did he ask you about that diamond ring as well?'

'In a roundabout sort of way, even asked Penny, which I thought was a bloody cheek.'

'Loose ends,' I said quietly.

'What was that?'

'Nothing, just talking to myself. That's what happens when you start ferrying aircraft for a living. Empty skies, noisy engines and no one to talk to, so you start talking to yourself.'

Clay gave a noncommittal grunt. 'Are you going to let him search your aircraft?'

'Why not . . . nothing to hide,' I lied.

'Not the point,' he said. 'He's got no bloody right.'

'Except he's a police inspector with the right-coloured skin,' I added.

Clay laughed. 'As I said, you're learning.'

Penny came back into the room looking more relaxed

since the death of her husband.

'A drink would be in order after that,' she said.

I picked up the whisky decanter. 'One of these do?'

'Please,' she replied, walking over to the fire.

'While I think of it,' I said, 'could you send a telex to Max Goldstein in Paris tomorrow morning and say I will be leaving a day late? I suppose you'll want to mention something about James as well.'

Penny said, 'If I can work the telex machine.' Then to Lucky, 'Perhaps you'll drive me down.'

'Sure.' Half turning on the chesterfield he said to me, 'You picking up the Dornier tomorrow?'

'In the morning I suppose.'

'In that case we'll all go down tomorrow, then I can fly you over to Chileka . . . otherwise you'll have to leave the pick-up there.'

'Hadn't thought of that, thanks.' I passed Penny her drink and sat down by Clay. Outside it was already dark and I had to get a blanket and some bandages to Rees-Williams. I decided to give it another ten minutes, then make an excuse about going back to the bungalow to check on my flight planning before dinner.

The screaming started five minutes later. At first it sounded like a wild animal caught by a predator. We all sat rooted in shock as the realization of something more horrendous sank in – the screams were human.

Sunday, who must have been preparing dinner in the kitchen, came running into the room waving a lethal-looking carving knife.

'Big cat, Master,' he cried, looking at Clay. 'Big cat in the woodshed.'

'Jesus,' I said, leaping to my feet.

Clay was suddenly at the door, grabbing the knife out of Sunday's hand. 'Penny, you stay here and keep the door closed . . . Steve, come with me.' I rushed after him. 'Are the keys still in the Rover?'

'Yes,' I said, the dull realization sinking in. Rees-Williams's arm . . . the scent of blood!

Clay leapt off the verandah steps and across to the Range Rover which was parked in the wide carport.

'Get in,' he yelled.

I ran around the front of the vehicle and had just made the passenger seat when Clay let in the clutch and sent the Rover hurtling back. He screamed above the revving engine, 'Make sure your window's closed.'

I checked. It was. Then we were rocketing past the woodshed. Clay slammed on the brakes and the Rover skidded violently; in the same action he engaged first gear, and with the headlights blazing we moved forward until the interior of the shed was visible.

The sight was more than horrific. Much, much more. The leopard was more than ten feet long from head to tail, typically yellowish and spotted with dark rosettes. It was crouching over the body of Rees-Williams.

'Get away, you bastard,' Clay screamed, at the same time blasting on the horn.

The leopard didn't move, its green eyes seemed transfixed by the headlights. 'I'm going to ram it!' Clay yelled.

'You'll never make it, the shed isn't wide enough.'

Clay didn't reply, he just trod hard on the accelerator and let out the clutch. That was when the leopard's head went down and it picked up what appeared to be a piece of rag. It looked up as the Range Rover smashed into the side of the shed and the roof collapsed at a crazy angle.

The leopard sprang immediately, straight at the windscreen. That was when I saw the piece of rag was in fact an arm. Rees-Williams's arm. My hand went up to my face in a reactive gesture of defence as the big cat thudded against the windscreen, then rattled over the top of the vehicle, before disappearing into the dark and misty night.

Clay was out first, pushing back the sagging roof. I followed him through the driver's door. The blood was still pumping out of the exposed shoulder joint by the time we got to Rees-Williams, although it was getting slower all the time. I ripped my shirt off, screwed it up tight and pressed it against the gory wound.

'Get a doctor!' I shouted.

Clay was holding Rees-Williams's right wrist. 'Too late man, the pulse has stopped.'

'Get a bloody doctor, there's always a chance.'

'Have you seen what you're kneeling in?' Clay exclaimed. 'He's lost more than half his blood already.'

'I don't care, get a doctor!' I screamed.

Clay got up reluctantly and made his way back out of the partially demolished shed. I kept up the pressure until my arms hurt with strain – even though I knew he was dead. I should have known! I should have remembered! The leopard in the forest, when I had been waiting for Clay to return with the police. The scent of blood! And Rees-Williams had been wounded. Christ! why hadn't I remembered?

Clay was back minutes later, sending timber flying in all directions.

'Doc's on his way . . . and I told Penny to phone the police. Saved them a job anyway.' He dropped down beside me and looked at the badly clawed face of the Welshman. 'The crazy, mad bastard, why the hell did he come up here?'

'Good question,' I said. 'Take over, will you?'

'What for, he's dead.'

I looked at the face, marble white in the headlights. Yes, he was dead. I dropped the blood-soaked shirt and stumbled back against a pile of logs. The smell of cut pine should have masked every other smell in that shed, but it didn't. The blood of the Welshman saw to that.

The doctor and the police arrived forty-five minutes later. By that time I had returned to the bungalow, taken a hot shower and changed. Now I was sitting with a large whisky waiting for the questions to start all over again.

Chapter Fourteen

It was precisely midnight when Inspector Ogobushi left and drove down the mist-covered mountain. During the preceding four hours he had taken over the dining room, cleared the table except for a carafe of water and one glass and a notebook and pen, then questioned Clay and myself. I was last to go in and got the distinct impression he would have liked me shot. He kept up the rapid-fire questions, probing cleverly from every angle, but as I stuck to my guns there was nothing he could do. It was his final remark which told me all I wanted to know. He had first asked if I intended returning to Malawi and when I replied that I didn't think so, he said, 'Good!' Then he said, 'I can't be sure what it is about you, Captain, but ever since you have been here there has been very great trouble; in my tribe we would say you carry the mark of death . . . might I therefore suggest it would be unwise of you to return to my country?'

That was it, end of questions. Now just after midnight Clay and I sat by an almost lifeless fire having one for the road. With the inspector's departure Penny had gone straight to bed, saying she had a raging headache and that she had had enough of killing to last her a lifetime. As for me I'd even considered telling the inspector the whole gruesome story, but the thought of that tiny, dark, evil-smelling cell in the Zomba police station made me hold my tongue. Not that I wanted to fly the Dornier, but if I was going to die, I could think of worse places than aeroplanes. One at least, and that was the Zomba jail.

I went back to the bungalow and added another two questions to my list. Now it numbered ten. The first on the list was, 'Where do you stow two and a quarter million dollars' worth of diamonds on a Dornier?' Tomorrow I would find out.

Saturday morning dawned blue and cloudless and ran according to plan right up to Chileka airport. Then Clay returned to Zomba in his Baron and left me standing outside the Air Malawi hangar. The fear had been building up all morning, as it did with every day and every week and every year. One day it would be altogether uncontrollable, altogether deadly. Just like the rest of the people in the world who had their own morbid dread of open spaces, enclosed spaces, water, fire, heights . . . the stammerer who is thrust before a thousand people and asked to read out a speech, the build-up is always the worst. The hot flushes, the inner torment, the muscular spasms. My fear was no different, except I was trying to face it, to overcome it – if only for a short time – to live with it. How the hell do you live with fear?

I picked up my flight bag and walked over to the Dornier. First things first. I completed a thorough external inspection of the aircraft; looking inside fuel tanks, inside engine cowlings, removing access panels under the wings which were normally taken off by engineers to check control runs or electrical wiring. Nothing showed up, so I moved to the inside of the aircraft. Under seats, behind seats, zips in head-linings, under the carpets, more engineers' access panels. At the end of one and a half hours I had the distinct feeling the diamonds were not on board. Then I remembered the radio bay down in the tail section; so I climbed out of the rear passenger door and pulled the release knob for the aft baggage hatch. Taking the torch out of my flight bag I crawled headfirst into the stifling darkness, making a ninety degree turn to the right – into the tail section. The torch beam picked out looms of white electrical wiring nestling snugly along the zinc chromated interior of the aircraft's skin. Radio equipment, inverters, silica gel tube, two voltage regulators, more radio gear. After thirty minutes of sweating in that black hole, removing anything which could be removed and then replacing it, I had had enough.

I dropped wearily back to the concrete and gulped in the humid clammy air; then I picked up my flight bag and headed for the terminal. The fridge had broken down since my last visit, but the warm beer made life slightly more bearable. I went out to the balcony and lit a cigarette. Where the hell would Valentine have stowed the diamonds? They had to be on board . . . or did they? I had been instructed to clear customs at Karonga, at the north end of Lake Malawi. That had been Valentine's first change in my original routing. So why not slip the package on board at that point? It wasn't much to go on, in fact it wasn't anything to go on. But what was left? I flicked the cigarette into a graceful parabolic arc and watched it disappear towards the concrete apron below. The rule book said you do not do things like that, especially around aircraft movement areas . . . fire hazard. And being a professional pilot I should have known better. I put it down to nervous reaction. Aircraft and airports, it seemed, affected me that way.

The flight back to Zomba was the usual nightmare, except this time the whisky flask was close at hand. That and my usual litany of prayers to a long suffering God. The landing was nearly a disaster. Three ugly, brutal bounces which shook the airframe to the point of tearing it apart. I taxied up to the hangar and cut the engines; then sat with the dying whine of gyros. And to think I had once loved that sound. But then any marriage would be wearing thin after twenty-three years . . . long after the thrills had ceased to exist.

'How did it go?' Clay asked as I limped into the office.

'Like oiled silk,' I lied.

Penny turned from the telex machine and managed a luke-warm smile. 'Just received a message from Max Goldstein in Paris,' she said. 'He asked that you contact him as per letter of instruction.'

'Is that all?' I replied.

'That's all.'

The remainder of the day passed quietly, with Clay beating me in three consecutive games of chess. Following dinner I went to the bungalow and packed my bags for the long haul north; then I went over to the window and stared up at the big clean moon shining out of a distant sky . . . Somewhere in my dreams was an old English cottage with a fire blazing cheerfully in the hearth. But like Sally, it seemed forever out of reach.

Chapter Fifteen

The inspector was waiting when I arrived at the airfield with Clay. 'Good morning Captain . . . it is a nice day for your flight, I think.'

I looked up at the dawn sky towards the mountain ridge. It appeared completely cloudless. 'Possibly,' I replied.

'I will try then to detain you as short a time as possible. Perhaps you could open the aircraft and allow my men to have a look.'

'If you tell me what it is you're looking for perhaps I can be of more help.'

'Merely a routine check Captain, nothing more, nothing less.' His eyes said otherwise. When I'd unlocked the aircraft, three of his men started crawling all over it. I walked back to the hangar entrance and lit a cigarette. Clay had disappeared into the office, leaving the inspector standing by his car.

'Inspector,' I said, moving towards him. 'There is a question which has been puzzling me . . . why did your men arrive at Sally North's house when they did?'

He eyed me cautiously. 'A telephone call, Captain – an anonymous telephone call.'

'Oh,' I said. 'Still, you've sorted it all out now, haven't you?'

'Perhaps!' His eyes swung across to the Dornier. 'It seems my men have finished, Captain . . . I think you can leave now.'

'Yes, I suppose so.'

'A safe journey,' he said and climbed into his car.

Minutes later I was securely strapped into the sweat-stained seat. The engines coughed and then caught, sending clouds of billowing white smoke back over the tailplane. I let the engines warm up for three minutes then released the brakes and moved slowly away from the hangar. Clay was standing by the Range Rover, his hand half raised in farewell. Then I was bumping out over the grass towards the runway.

Checks complete and a last long swallow from the hip flask and I was ready to go. I waited longer than normal as the pictures flashed through my mind. Pictures of Valentine in the pine forest, never knowing what hit him; Rees-Williams who had never been given a fair crack of the whip, finally being savaged by a killer leopard. And Sally. Dear, sweet Sally; who had magically reappeared from a long ago and far away Victoria station. The only woman I had ever loved, the only woman to whom I had ever belonged . . . and now she was gone. The knot of fear turned slowly to pain deep inside my stomach.

This was always the bad part, when the psychological implications exploded inside of you. Up until this moment it had been a paperwork exercise, a distant unloved thought – something you could always reject. There had always been the VC10 flight home . . . but not any more. This time they have caught you, locked you up in a perspex prison, which with one wrong move would become a perspex coffin. The inner voice of experience was back as I opened the throttles and felt the aircraft coming to life in my hands. The green runway accelerated past me and then dropped quickly away. I synchronized the engines to climb-power setting and fumbled through my pockets for a cigarette.

The air was calm as I crossed the eastern ridge of the mountain at 6,000 feet. From here to Karonga the track was 356 degrees magnetic and the distance 344 nautical miles; which at 120 knots meant approximately three hours. A long time for things to go wrong. Then I remembered the list and took it out of my shirt pocket and scored a line through one of the ten questions. An anonymous telephone call, the inspector had said; which of course raised another question. Who made it? What the hell, that was his business now. Now I was free of Zomba – forever.

Levelling off at 11,000 feet I pulled out a topographical map and let my finger follow the double-arrowed track from Zomba plateau, past Liwonde, abeam Monkey Bay and then plain sailing. Follow the western shoreline of Lake Malawi until thirty miles south of the mountains which lead into Tanzania; and down on the left is Karonga. On a clear day that is. My sky was looking anything but.

I dialled up Blantyre Information on the radio and passed them the details. En route Karonga, flight level one one oh – the trade name for eleven thousand feet; Victor Mike Charlie – phonetic language for visual meteorological conditions; and e.t.a. Karonga. They came back asking me to report abeam Kimbiri Point. I'd never heard of it but I said 'Roger' and consulted the map. I found it in the southwest corner of the lake, east of Salima. Then I went back to just sitting and praying.

The trouble started an hour later. I was approaching battlements of towering cumulus which I estimated were at least 15,000 feet and growing. I turned ninety degrees to the left and flew along the length of the seething mass. There had to be a way around it. The adrenalin was running as freely as the sweat as the turbulence reached out and rocked the wings with a malevolent violence. After ten minutes I knew I would never get around it; and at the rate it was growing I'd never get over the top. I reduced power and turned back towards the lake. At 700 feet I was below the base of the cloud. Once I reached the lake I turned back onto my original heading and followed the lake's shoreline.

A long way away to my right, and partially obscured through light veils of rain, was Mozambique – forbidden territory. Over to the left Zambia – no clearances for that place either. A simple matter of staying in the middle, where the weather was rapidly going downhill in a big way. The turbulence beneath the cloud was, in pilots' terminology, 'slight'. In my book it was 'severe'. I looked down at the surface of the lake and saw the white horses breaking in a southerly direction, which meant the wind was a norther, which meant I had a bloody headwind. Which meant longer in the air. Damn . . . damn . . . damn!

I had forgotten about Blantyre Information so it was a surprise to hear an Uncle Tom's Cabin voice calling 'Seven Foxtrot Echo'. I mumbled, 'Go ahead.' My hands were too full of aeroplane and my brain of survival to worry about radios. The voice asked me for a position report; I said something like Kimbiri Point and the man was happy. The background static was a mixture of frying bacon and hissing steam, and I knew when he asked me to report 'operations normal' in thirty minutes' time I would be out of radio range. If I climbed to a higher level I wouldn't – but if I climbed to a higher level I would be in the cloud. And if I went in there I was a dead man.

My finger was still crawling along the map, marking my position, when it stopped at a tiny lakeshore village called Bandawe. From there the coastline, according to the map, swung out into my path, becoming mountainous terrain. Only problem was I could see no further than half a mile past the village. The rain was getting worse. I settled into a holding pattern over a scattering of ragged palms, white sand and thatched native dwellings. After twenty minutes I was getting dizzy. Perhaps I should go back. Back to Zomba, back to anywhere that had an airstrip. A place I could land and shake a fist at the elements.

I shook myself. I had to get to Karonga, I couldn't go back. I talked myself and the Dornier down to an estimated 300 feet and picked up the original heading for Karonga. Seconds later I entered the waterfall of grey driving rain. Too high! Too bloody high! The lake surface disappeared in the water-smoke of the storm. Christ! I slammed the power on and hauled the Dornier round in a steep right-hand turn and headed back to the patch of sand and palms.

The nagging fear kept on telling me I couldn't do it, whilst the distant voice of experience said I could. I took the hip flask from my flight bag and found the courage I needed. Then I pushed the nose down until I was no more than fifty feet above the boiling, angry lake. The voice of experience told me it was easy, told me to keep the high ground a matter of inches from the left wingtip and the lake surface below. If you get too close to the high ground it said, you'll lose your left wingtip . . . and a plane . . . and a life!

By this time the Dornier's two hatches, which served as pilot and co-pilot entrance doors, were leaking badly, causing steady streams of water to run down the instrument panel and into the radios. The plane was bucking and swinging violently. I gave a quick nervous glance at the airspeed indicator – 115 knots. Back to the outside. A black wall was moving left to right; black, slippery, wet, shining granite . . . a moving mountain! Except it wasn't the mountain that was moving; I was flying into it. I jerked the machine thirty degrees to the right and then I was lost. A jab of left rudder brought the mountain back. Jesus God I needed a drink . . . and a third hand.

Out of the corner of my eye I noticed the ADF needle, my only navigational aid, pointing uselessly towards the east. It should have been indicating somewhere ahead, towards the Karonga beacon; unless the mountains were bending the radio waves . . . or water had got in the set. The sweat was sticky on my face as I watched the craggy blackness sliding down the left wingtip. One bad gust and it would be the end of everything.

Now the visibility was dropping towards zero, which meant I had to do some quick thinking. Only way out was to turn right, towards the centre of the lake, then head south – back to the clearer weather. I eased the power back until the speed was steady at 90 knots. Then I tried to remember flying fighters. Things used to happen about five times faster in those days. The clipped voice of fighter controllers vectoring you to a practice intercept on an imaginary enemy. Going through the gate to buster power. Shooting the bastard down . . . in your mind at least. Now I was here . . . at the bottom of the pile. What the hell had gone wrong! What the hell . . . The seconds dragged into minutes. Long sweating agonizing minutes, as I poured all my mental and physical strength into staying a few feet off the side of the mountain. I was on the verge of giving up . . . of throwing my arms across my face and admitting defeat when it began to grow very slightly lighter. The ADF needle was still not doing what it was supposed to, but now the visibility was returning. I was through! Ten minutes later I called Karonga and advised them I had their airport in sight.

'Cleared to land runway one seven,' the controller's

voice said in that slow African articulate way.

I slid in to a bumpy landing, but it didn't matter, I was down. Down and alive. I taxied slowly through the pools of standing water towards the long wooden hut of a terminal building. Any thoughts of diamonds, murder or nine unanswered questions were pushed deep into my subconscious. What was important now was how to survive the remainder of this trip!

Two Africans appeared from the fuel compound and made their way towards me. 'Morning Captain sir, you want fuel?' the first man asked.

'Up to the top,' I replied and waited until they had pulled up a rusting step-ladder. When I was sure they knew what they were doing I picked up my flight bag and limped over to the control tower.

'You going far sir?' the controller asked, sliding a blank flight plan form across the desk.

'Nairobi, Wilson,' I said, lighting a cigarette.

He gave me a look which made Nairobi sound like the end of the world.

'How's the weather over the Livingstone range?'

'You'll have to ask the met. man sir, that's down the stairs first door on the left.'

I pushed the completed form back. 'Thanks.'

'Have a safe flight, Captain.'

'I'll try,' I said and went down the narrow staircase.

The met. man as it turned out was too well informed. He thought it might be solid cloud cover all the way, with the tops of the cloud about 8,000 feet. As for the Nairobi weather he hadn't got a clue. But if I would like to wait he would try to send a telex message. I told him to forget it. I had to keep going before the courage ran out.

The two refuellers found me in the passenger lounge; a junk-shop assortment of ten tables and thirty rickety chairs. The customs officer had wanted the usual paper-work; but wasn't interested in looking over the aircraft. Perhaps it was the refuellers? Perhaps they had been paid to slip a waterproof bag into the tanks. Having taken the details from the Shell carnet, the refueller pushed the triplicated form over to me. I signed and was given the pink copy. That was all. Time to go. Except I still didn't know if the diamonds were on the aircraft. The other problem was that the ADF was unserviceable.

I lit another cigarette and ran over all the places I had searched. Exterior, interior, radio bay in the tail. Where else? There wasn't anywhere else! I went out to the aircraft and decided to see if I could get the ADF working. Perhaps a connection had come adrift, or water had got into the loop aerial! Or perhaps I was just looking for an excuse to stay on the ground.

Overlooking the obvious is something we all do. And it was something which Valentine had obviously banked on. It wasn't until I crawled down into the tail section to check the loop aerial for water contamination that I realized how clever he had been. The diamonds were literally staring me in the face. Admittedly they were inside a long hollow transparent plastic tube with breather holes at each end; but in the torch light you couldn't miss the glittering clearness and the occasional twinkle of blue. The label on the tube said, 'Silica Gel – NATO STOCK No. 4440/99/224/6995.' The manufacturer, J. Crosfield & Sons Limited, Warrington, England. And all military planes that I knew of had silica gel containers in the radio bays. Being a porous crystal it absorbs moisture, and as radios are prone to suffer if exposed to moisture – presto!

I prised the plastic container out of its two spring metal clips and removed one of the ends. Then, carefully placing the torch on the top of a radio transmitter box I emptied part of the contents into the palm of my hand. They were cut and polished, every last one of them . . . and very, very beautiful. Silica gel I recalled had more the appearance of opaque sea ice. What I was holding was the real thing. I carefully returned them one by one into the container. Except for one. And that one was about three times as big as the one on Sally's solitaire ring had been. I slipped it into my shirt pocket and carefully buttoned down the flap. Then I went about checking out the ADF. Everything seemed about normal so I crawled backwards out of the radio bay. What the hell, I'd get it fixed in Nairobi. I patted my shirt pocket. After all I was a rich man . . . now.

Lady Luck smiled on me after takeoff, offering me a temporary break in the overcast. The shaking and sweating were still there, however, when I levelled off at 10,000 feet and set up the engines to give me fifty-five per cent cruise power. According to the book that meant I had six and a half hours' fuel endurance. My flight-planned time to Wilson airport, Nairobi, was five and a half hours. Without the ADF it was a matter of flying set headings for set times and hoping at the end of it all you descend over Nairobi. If the winds aloft were to change from those forecast I could end up descending into nowhere and finding myself hopelessly lost. I pulled the hip flask out of my flight bag and took a long pull. Then I stared down at the solid layer of rumpled white cloud below. It stretched on forever, somehow warning me that if I didn't get my dead reckoning navigation one hundred per cent correct I was in big trouble . . . rich man or not.

Chapter Sixteen

It was nearly four hours later when the cloud started to break up. Not very much, but enough for me to catch an occasional glimpse of the red and brown earth below. I checked my flight log and then the map. According to that I was somewhere over the Mangati Plains, with Lake Sereri about forty miles ahead. One way to find out for sure was to go down and have a look. As it happened that was one of my worst decisions of the day.

I spiralled down through a ragged hole in the cloud and suddenly found myself being thrown all over the sky as vast invisible thermals belched sickeningly up from the scorched plains below. The sweating started up with a vengeance as I fought with every ounce of my strength to maintain a straight path. The enormity of it when I finally dropped beneath the cloud base was nothing short of agoraphobic. What seemed like a million miles of nothingness. The stark frightening horror of the dawn of creation. A place you could sit down and die and never be found. A place with no people. And I had thought the sky was lonely!

I managed to level off at 5,000 feet and pressed on. The sweating and the continual fighting with the controls were rapidly wearing me down; but I had to find the lake before I dared climb back to the smoother air above the clouds. Until I found that lake I was lost.

Five minutes later I saw the farm – the bush station – and what was even better it had an east–west runway running alongside of it. I decided to land there and rest up until the morning; the air would be smoother then. I gritted my teeth and fought back the burning-hot bile which was creeping steadily up my throat. It wasn't until I was directly overhead the farm that I realized it was deserted. A derelict leftover ruin from the days when this

158

country had been known as Tanganyika and the Germans had run it with their typical Teutonic efficiency. Now they had gone, independence was here, and everything was going back to bush, in the same way it had been for a million years before the Germans came. The runway was broken up; weeds and shrubs forcing up through the concrete; dust-clouded wind banging the broken shutters on the main house. It was a place where people and aeroplanes had once been and might never be again. Perhaps Clay had been right after all. Perhaps the blacks had never caught up with the twentieth century, perhaps they never would!

I swung the Dornier back onto the heading for the lake and started praying. Not the pat little prayers recited on Sunday mornings from ornate prayer books, these were real prayers. Man to man argument. I knew he was there and he knew I was here; and at the end of the day we were bartering for my life. Fifteen minutes later he proved my point and slid the lake into the frame of windscreen. I said, 'Thank you for the bone, you old bastard,' and drifted slowly over the three-mile-long lake. It should have helped of course; knowing that I was on track. But it didn't . . . I still had another 200 miles to go before I reached Wilson. I pushed the throttles forward and heard the deep-throated snarl of the Lycomings and the scream of the Hartzell propellers as the tips went nearly supersonic. Then I was climbing up the long delirious blue towards the smoother air.

I was at 11,000 feet when the trouble started. The cloud tops were building rapidly . . . I had to stay on top . . . I had to. I kept the climb-power on and eased the nose up; oxygen or not I was going over the top. I must have been abeam Mount Kilimanjaro when I realized I wasn't going to make it. The altimeter indicated 17,000 feet, and the Dornier and my lungs didn't want to go on. The clouds ahead did. That was when I started flying up and down the towering line looking for a way through. Then I remembered the radio, I selected the Wilson frequency and immediately heard an English voice reporting finals for runway zero seven. I didn't hear the controller reply but as soon as the next aircraft had stopped transmitting I gave them a call. No reply. I tried to contact one of the aircraft in the circuit . . . still nothing. Then it all went quiet. A distant phrase from a long-forgotten instructor flashed through my mind – duct propagation of radio waves, freak weather conditions carrying very high frequency transmissions further than is theoretically possible. In other words we were too far out. Too far! Now I had to go back down to the turbulence; there was no other way. I went for my hip flask and found it empty; that was the last of it. No more whisky until I arrived in Nairobi. If I ever arrived in Nairobi!

I descended slowly, back to the rolling plains which were darkening with the solid cloud cover and the approaching sunset. I set up the original heading and started shouting. Shouting out loud that I could do it. Shouting out that nothing would stop me. Shouting to some far away God that he wasn't having me yet. The shouting stopped when I saw the band of charcoal blackness in the distance. A darker band separating earth from sky. Rain! Lucky Clay had mentioned that mid-November to mid-December was the period of short rains around Nairobi. The jagged flash of lightning which ripped through the sky confirmed it. Getting low on fuel and thunderstorms did nothing to control the shaking. I tried the radio again . . . silence! And suddenly a million voices were screaming at me, asking me the same question over and over again. What now? What now? What now? What now? I rubbed my eyes and tried to think, tried to put it all together in my mind. The information was dragged bit by bit from a partially paralysed subconscious. Wilson airport . . . over 5,000 feet above sea level . . . your altimeter reading 7,500 . . . current ground separation 2,500 feet . . . danger factor – lot of high peaks in this area . . . fuel remaining less than one hour . . . no apparent ground features tie in with map . . . conclusion LOST!

The rain started six minutes and thirty seconds later. I knew that because I was counting the seconds to being down on the ground. At first it was a gentle patter, then the drops became larger and louder, entirely obliterating my forward vision. I knew then I wasn't going to make it; not today, not this lifetime, not any lifetime. The farm strip flashed into the failing survival programme of my brain. If I went back could I find it? Did I have enough fuel? Would it be dark before I got there? Too many imponderables . . . too bloody many! I started turning anyway. Why I don't know. To get away from the rain perhaps, so that at least when I crashed I would see it all. The radio crackled faintly . . . then again . . . I was still turning when I heard the voice say 'Seven Foxtrot Echo, do you read?' I mouthed the words silently; it was then I realized it was me. He was talking to me.

I banked the plane back in the general direction of Wilson and thumbed the radio transmit button. 'Wilson radio, this is Seven Foxtrot Echo reading you fives, how me?'

There was a scratchy carrier wave sound, 'Seven Foxtrot Echo, reading you strength three to four . . . what is your position? I say again what is your position?'

I laughed; the insane laugh of a madman. My position? Bloody comedian! I pulled myself together. I was low down, say 2,500 feet above ground level and we were talking. Red lights started coming on in my brain again, like a central alert system in an airliner . . . flashing reds and bells warbling in your headset. I took a stab at the truth. 'Er, Wilson Fox Echo approximately twenty miles out, over.'

Another pause, then, 'Roger Foxtrot Echo, have you now twenty-seven miles southeast of the airport . . . are you familiar with the entry lane?'

'Negative.'

'Roger Foxtrot Echo, turn left now on to a heading of two seven zero degrees.'

I eased the Dornier around in a gentle turn. 'Turning onto two seven zero. Fox Echo.'

'Roger sir . . . limited radar coverage I'm afraid, excessive rain clutter in that area.'

161

I sat gripping the control yoke, concentrating on maintaining the heading. Not far now; not far! Ahead of the nose lightning flashes ran raggedly to earth. My thumb moved to the transmit button . . . too late! We hit what appeared to be a brick wall. The Dornier commenced to dive, roll and shake apart all at the same time. The instrument panel a frantic blur of movement; the instruments almost unreadable. Turning left . . . turning left . . . I forced the control column to the right to compensate, at the same time noticing the instruments were indicating I was still straight and level. Vertigo . . . rotational sickness . . . the leans . . . it didn't matter what name it went under it was still a masterpiece of confusion. Trickery and deception; inner ear sending false impulses to a tired brain; the tired brain sending corrective commands to a pair of frightened but willing hands . . . except the commands were the wrong ones!

The sweat was running into my eyes; stinging pain and blurred vision. Fly the bloody instruments. From the artificial horizon pick up a scan. Forget the outside world, just fly the instruments.

The controller said, 'Seven Foxtrot Echo, turn right now, onto a heading of three five zero.'

My mouth had dried up completely when I croaked, 'Roger.'

The turn made it worse; the leans taking a more commanding hold. What was happening? Where the hell was I? Rain, lightning, thunder . . . now hail! The deafening machine-gun rat-a-tat-tat of hail drumming on aluminium. The noise drowned out the engines – as though the engines had stopped!

'Seven Foxtrot Echo . . . what is your heading?' There was something approaching anxiety in the controller's voice.

I looked at the directional gyro. I was still on a westerly heading. I yanked the controls hard right and rolled out on three five zero. Another mistake! When suffering from vertigo keep all control movements small. I passed back the new heading information.

The flickering blue and green flames caught me unawares. I felt my heart physically bounce off the wall of my chest as it missed a beat. I looked again at the windscreen . . . at the flame dancing around the edges. St Elmo's fire! . . . that's all. Forget it! Just keep going, for Christ's sake keep going . . . how far now? . . . I pressed the transmit button. 'Wilson Fox Echo, range check.'

'Nine miles . . . positioning you right base for runway zero seven . . . QNH one zero two one.'

'Copied . . . how's your weather?'

'Surface wind zero nine zero at eighteen knots gusting twenty-eight. Eight oktas fifteen hundred feet; visibility about one mile out of heavy showers. We have standing water on runway zero seven; be advised braking action poor. QNH one zero two one.'

'Weather copied, QNH one zero two one.' I glanced out of the side of the cockpit and saw what appeared to be a fence and a long bush road. I eased the nose down.

Four minutes later the runway, glistening wet, slid into view.

'Fox Echo has the runway.'

'Cleared to land Foxtrot Echo . . . braking action poor.'

I lowered the flap and let the speed get too low. Another mistake! You need more power at high-level airfields. The Dornier stopped flying about ten feet off the deck. The landing was heavy, sending water drumming up against the underside of the fuselage. Then it was over. We were down. I looked up at the sky; expecting to see a break in the weather and a benevolent God smiling through, but all I saw was black storm clouds boiling angrily. The loveless gates of hell!

I taxied in following the controller's instructions and parked next to a dirty-brown-coloured Beaver near the customs shack. The engines died simultaneously, sending a gentle shudder through the airframe. I snapped all the switches off, unhooked my harness and climbed out into the warm Kenya rain. The airport was deserted; not a soul in sight as I limped the fifty yards to the control tower. By the time I reached the green-painted door I was soaked to the skin, but it didn't matter a damn. I was still alive and what was more to the point I had the diamonds.

The air traffic controller was a thickset individual with an ugly, lived-in face. 'Lucky to get in when you did,' he said matter of factly, 'seems to be getting worse.'

I stared out through the large plate-glass window. The end of the runway had disappeared. 'I take it you got my earlier transmissions?'

He looked at me and shook his head. 'No . . . had your flight plan though, and as you were running late thought I'd give you a call.'

An uncontrollable spasm ran though my body when I realized the only reason I was here at all was down to luck. Luck plain and simple. He had decided to give me a call because I was running late. Five minutes later and I would have been out of range heading back towards a derelict farm strip.

'Thanks,' I said quietly.

'All part of the service . . . how far you going?'

'Cyprus.'

'Ferry pilot are you?'

'I've been called worse,' I laughed.

He gave me a crooked smile. 'Thought you probably were. No one else seems to fly in this sort of weather, but then I suppose you've seen worse!'

'Once in a while.'

'Funnily enough there's another ferry guy on the way in from Dar.'

'Know his name by any chance?'

'Half a tick.' He shuffled through an untidy pile of papers. 'Yes, here we are . . . he's flying a twin Commander. Name's Rafferty.'

'What time's he due in?'

'According to his plan in about one hour from now.'

'Thanks . . . see you again.'

'Sure thing.'

We wouldn't of course, but we said it anyway. I went out of the door and down the dark staircase. Once I had completed the arrival formalities I would wait for the smooth-talking Irishman.

Chapter Seventeen

The Shell refuelling truck rolled up as I approached the Dornier so I told the driver to fill it up and made my way to customs. The duty officer was asleep, having probably decided that no one would be flying on such a day. He stirred uncomfortably, rubbed the sleep from his eyes, and hauled himself out of his chair. 'You just going somewhere?' he yawned.

'No, just arrived from Karonga.' I pushed a damp copy of my inbound general declaration under his nose.

He took the form and scanned it carefully. When his eyes arrived at the bottom right-hand corner and the official Malawi customs stamp he gave a grunt of approval and tossed it into an overflowing in-tray.

'How long you staying?'

'Until the morning, then I'll be heading for the Sudan . . . Juba.'

He went over to the window, hitching his trousers up as he walked. 'Which is your aircraft?'

'The blue and white Dornier . . . next to the Beaver.'

'You'll have to move it from there,' he mumbled, dragging his feet back to the chair. 'That is the customs area.' He didn't say another word, just dropped heavily into the soft-cushioned leather armchair and closed his eyes.

Back at the aircraft I completed the paperwork for the fuel uplift, and once the Shell truck had departed removed the silica gel tube from the radio bay. Radio engineers checking out ADF systems might notice silica gel which isn't really silica gel. I placed the tube in my flight bag and hurried through the steady rain towards the Safari Air Services building.

The plush passenger lounge was deserted except for a youngish girl in reception who was carefully painting her nails.

'Not a very nice day,' I said, leaning across the counter.

She stopped painting and looked up. Scrawny, African, with a mop of frizzled wiry hair. The big wide eyes were quite vacant.

I tried again: 'The weather . . . not very nice!'

A kind of understanding dawned as her mouth broke into a grin showing uneven, nicotine-stained teeth. 'You American?' she said.

'Nearly . . . English!'

'English,' she said. 'You are a pilot?'

'Yes.'

'You have cigarettes?'

I reached down into my flight bag and handed her a couple of packets of Lucky Strikes. She smiled hugely.

'Any chance of a cup of coffee?' I asked.

'I will make you coffee, Captain. You sit over there.' She pointed towards a selection of easy chairs.

'I also need a radio engineer,' I added. 'Where is the radio workshop?'

'I will make the phone call for you, Captain : . . you take seat.'

Five minutes later, complete with coffee, cigarette and a comfortable chair I was quietly counting my blessings at being on the ground, and trying to forget about the remainder of the trip, when the radio man arrived. I explained the problem, then limped over to the big picture window and pointed out the aircraft.

'If it's fixable,' he said, 'I'll fix it.'

From the questions he had asked, and his easy usage of technical jargon, I had no doubt he would.

Rafferty landed at six o'clock. By then the storm had passed and the aeroplane world was back in action with engines running up and various types taxiing down past the Flying Doctor's hangar, or the other way towards the threshold of runway 07. I went outside to the mono-chrome scene of little lakes winding off to distant lines of parked aircraft; and the Aero Commander which had stopped opposite my Dornier. The air was warm and muggy, wisps of steam rising lazily from the tarmac.

I was passing the Dornier as the engineer wriggled out of the hatch. 'Any joy?' I asked.

'Okay, I think . . . just need to check it.' He took a handkerchief from his pocket and cleaned the lenses of his hornrimmed spectacles. Having done that he climbed up into the cockpit and flicked a few switches on.

'Should be all right now,' he said, lowering himself back to the tarmac. 'I've had to jury rig a wire from the sensing aerial to the indicator. Might tell your engineers that when you get to where you're going . . . not the approved way of doing things of course, but it'll get you there.'

'Unusual sort of snag . . . I mean, open-circuited wiring!'

He scratched his chin thoughtfully. 'Could say that . . . yes, it's invariably the indicator or the aerial system . . . still you know what aeroplanes are like?'

'Like women, you mean.'

'You've noticed as well,' he laughed, and started collecting his tools together.

'How much do I owe you by the way?'

'Not me unfortunately, the company. Drop in at the office. I'll get Miss World to make you out a receipt.'

'Miss World?'

'The fuzzy-wuzzy in reception . . . you should go through to the stores; they've got Bo Derek.'

'Sounds fascinating,' I said.

He picked up his toolbag. 'Helps to stay sane . . . have a good flight.'

As I was running out of original answers to that remark I nodded dumbly.

Rafferty was giving instructions to the refueller when I arrived. 'Holy Mother of Mercy,' he exclaimed turning round. 'And what would you be doing in my neck of the woods?'

The reference was quite normal for a ferry pilot who is usually seen on the North Atlantic run, intermittently propping up bars at the Loftleider hotel in Reykjavik; the

Arctic Hotel in Narssarssuak; and the Albatross in Gander. Where Rafferty was different from the rest of us was that he had his own company; named appropriately Raffair; and had made enough money from wheeling and dealing in Africa to be able to buy and sell his own aircraft. That he was the company salesman, chairman of the board, company pilot, clerk and tea boy, didn't matter. He was totally independent.

'Thought I'd come and see how the rich half live,' I said.

'What are you ferrying?'

I pointed to the Dornier. 'Taking it through to Cyprus.'

His dark suntanned face set in an easy smile. 'Ah to be sure, after the Lord Mayor's Show . . . one day you're up with the angels in a beautiful jet prop job, the next . . . I hope they're paying you well?'

Now it was my turn to smile. 'Well enough,' I said.

He said, 'I take it you're staying overnight?'

'That's the general idea. Haven't sorted out a hotel yet, though. Where do you normally hole up?'

His eyes twinkled. 'Leave it to your old friend Rafferty. There are only two hotels in this town where they serve Irish whiskey . . . not forgetting the colleens as well.'

Fifteen minutes later, having moved the Dornier from the customs bay and replaced the silica gel tube in the radio bay, I locked up the aircraft and went back to Safari Air. I had considered keeping the diamonds with me; but the strong possibility of being mugged by some down on his luck African made the aircraft the safer bet. It was dark by the time the taxi pulled out of the airport and joined the steady flow of traffic into Nairobi. Rafferty was still smiling about the cost of the repair on the Dornier's ADF. All 115 US dollars' worth.

'And I thought gold was a good investment,' he said lightheartedly. 'Must make a note to tell my accountant to investigate the electrical cable market.'

But then that was Rafferty. Always finding humour where none existed. He doubtless considered the world had been arranged on 1 April, and was therefore one

169

great big practical joke. And until someone proved conclusively to the contrary, Rafferty would still be laughing at the futility of it all. To look at he could have passed as Mediterranean stock; his darkly handsome features and jet-black hair lending themselves more to an Italian than an Irishman. He was of average height and build; with brown, perpetually smiling eyes. But it was the voice which captivated. Soft, smooth and charmingly Irish.

'How's business with you these days?' I said, offering him a cigarette.

'Can't complain,' he said. 'Just managed to screw a guy in Dar-es-Salaam on that Commander.'

I gave him a light. 'What happened?'

He laughed. 'You know I've been trying the "your price is twice too much" line for years; never thinking it would ever come off. But this time that's exactly what happened. I've even got it insured at wholesale book value . . . and I end up buying it for half that . . . can't be bad, can it?'

'I suppose you're selling it back in England!'

'Hell no. That's the second part of the secret when buying in stock. You only buy what the market will stand in the dear old USA; and only then at dealer wholesale. Then you ferry it straight through to the States and sell it through the trade. Fast turnover . . . small profit . . . and all that privileged information will cost you a large one at the hotel.'

We ended up at the Serena and agreed to meet in the bar in half an hour. Following a shower and a passable shave I changed into my light grey trousers and a blue short-sleeved shirt. Then I took the diamond from the pocket of the other shirt and lay back on the bed looking at it. Cut and polished and very beautiful. And to think I had perhaps another hundred of similar quality hidden on the Dornier.

Quite inexplicably my entire life changed at that moment. Forty years of rules and regulations and moralistic claptrap went out of the window along with the noblesse oblige a commission in the Royal Air Force had instilled into my every fibre. It was then I knew the diamonds were not going to be handed over to anyone. Because now for the first time in my life I was rich . . . filthy rich! I need never work again; and at forty years of age with no job, no flying licence and no future prospects it was a lifeline to survival. If I didn't grab it with both hands I would drown in Rafferty's April Fools' Day world.

I found Rafferty in the bar; glancing out of the shadows with a debonair weariness of knowing all the ropes. 'What are you having?'

'Too late,' he said indicating the glasses, 'but the next round's trebles.'

I picked up the glass. 'Cheers.'

'Not much of a toast,' he smiled. 'But the night is yet young.'

'Tell me,' I said. 'You travel all over Africa; have you ever heard the expression *mazel und broche*?'

Rafferty thought for a moment. 'In a word yes, but I seem to recall it being used in a specific context.' He swilled the whisky around in his glass and thought some more. 'No good . . . anyway it means "luck and blessing".'

'Is that all?'

'Unless you can tell me what it's to do with; that might trigger the reason for it being used.'

'Not important,' I said and called the barman over.

My list of questions, for what good they were worth, was now reduced to eight. The telex between Valentine and Goldstein had carried that phrase. One that now seemed totally unsignificant. I paid the barman for the fresh whisky supply and turned to Rafferty. His attention had been drawn to a gorgeous-looking redhead who had arrived with three men. Aircrew types! She was probably a stew. She looked casually around the room until her eyes found the corner of the bar . . . and the Irishman. Then she said something to one of the men and walked towards us.

'Rafferty,' she said. 'Where did you come from?'

Rafferty kissed the offered lips and took her hands in

his. 'I was going from Cork to Dublin . . . but being such a terrible navigator . . .' She laughed. 'May I introduce an old friend of mine; taught the Wright Brothers all they ever knew . . . Steve Ritchie, Ann Balmer. Ann's with British Airways.'

She extricated her right hand and held it out. 'Any friend of this Irish rogue,' she said warmly.

Rafferty laughed out loud and snapped his fingers at the barman. 'Dry martini Samuel, and two more of the usual.' The black face beamed and hurried away to fix the drinks. 'So, my lovely girl,' he said turning back to Ann, 'have you eaten yet and if not where are you taking me?'

Her blue eyes gave Rafferty a searching look. 'No I haven't . . . and you're taking me.'

I was having the distinct feeling of interrupting a very private twosome, when a pretty brunette sidled up. Ann introduced her as Vicki while Rafferty set up another round of drinks.

'Why don't we all go out for dinner?' Ann said suddenly.

Rafferty just smiled and Vicki gave me a look which said she would rather not. Her character however was not as strong as the lady with the red hair, and after the next drink we all tumbled into a taxi, with Rafferty calling out the instructions.

After a circuit of the lesser-known bars we ended up in an Indian restaurant ordering chicken vindaloo. By that time the icy Vicki had warmed ever so little and was telling me all about her fiancé, an electrical wholesaler in Hounslow, and that she was packing up flying at the end of the year.

It should have ended at that point, with the four of us catching a midnight taxi back to the hotel, and me saying a polite goodnight to Vicki whilst Rafferty pursued other activities with his doting companion. But it didn't.

Ann decided she would like to see Rafferty's latest aeroplane, and Rafferty being Rafferty and all obliging, ordered the taxi driver to make a detour via the airport.

'Of course it's not just selling aeroplanes,' Rafferty was

172

saying quietly to Ann. 'Did this lovely deal over in Nigeria at a place called Maidugri . . .' I half listened as he continued explaining how he had found a white-haired old character who dealt in forged sovereigns, and how he had sold Rafferty a vast number of half sovereigns at exactly half the price of full sovereigns. Rafferty rocked with laughter at the thought. 'Only thing is my love, half sovereigns are worth more than the full ones . . .'

Ann snuggled up closely to her rogue of an Irishman and started whispering things in his ear, while Vicki and I tried to keep a number of respectable inches between us, which on the back seat of a taxi with four people was not easy.

The taxi driver swung the old Mercedes into the airport entrance with an easy grace and braked to a stop. 'This is as far as I go sir,' he said, addressing Rafferty.

'That's fine,' Rafferty said. 'Wait here for five minutes, then you can take us to the Serena.'

The air was very still and very warm as we made our way between the hangars towards the apron. Up above, the sky was clear and a full moon shone down giving everything it touched that clean metallic look.

I saw the runway lights as we cleared the hangars. Two rows of white twinkling lights.

'Didn't know they did night flying this late,' I said.

'Don't normally,' Rafferty replied. 'Must be a medivac job from the Flying Doctor's place.' Then to Ann, 'There it is, my girl.' He pointed towards the Aero Commander. 'A real aeroplane, not like the things you work on.'

She gave an alcoholic giggle. 'I don't think my captain would approve of that statement,' she said.

'And that's the sadness of it all, my beauty, he's forgotten what real flying is all about.'

When we reached the aircraft I left Rafferty and the two girls looking around the plush interior and went over to the starboard wingtip and lit a cigarette. I had seen enough aircraft interiors to last me longer than forever, and at this moment all I wanted was a comfortable bed and a good night's sleep.

173

The image was shattered in that very second as an aircraft engine barked into life. But it wasn't just an aircraft engine, it was a halfway familiar sound, something I knew. I turned and stared into the velvet night, towards the Dornier which was parked about a hundred yards away. That was when the second engine coughed and caught and the moonlight captured the swirling grey smoke in the propeller slipstream. It was the Dornier! Somebody was stealing the bloody Dornier!

I ran that hundred yards faster than I had ever done before, possibly even faster than in the days when my left knee was perfectly normal. By the time I reached it, it was moving out towards the dim blue lights of the taxiway. I was too late, it was pulling away, but the thought of the diamonds kept me going and with a final desperate lunge I grabbed the handhold and pulled myself up onto the wing root which held the port engine to the lower side of the fuselage. Less than eight feet in front of me the three-bladed propeller blasted cold air directly into my face, taking my breath away completely. Inch by painful inch I clawed my way towards the cockpit. My eyes were smarting from the petrol-oil mixture of the slipstream as I tried to make out the dimly lit shape over the controls.

I was almost there when a second figure started waving frantically towards me. Then the hunched figure half turned and opened the storm window on the left side of the cockpit, at the same time swinging the aircraft slightly right to follow the taxiway. The moon caught his face then, startled and close and dangerous; it also glinted off the gun which was now protruding from the window.

I released my hold as two faint cracks sounded above the Lycomings' roar. My knees hit the tarmac first, followed by my arms and head. I instinctively rolled to the left as the tailwheel passed within an arm's length of my face.

All that was left was the receding engine noise and the dying breeze from the propellers . . . and the face in the moonlight. The face of Lucius Clay.

Chapter Eighteen

Rafferty arrived as I was dragging myself up from the tarmac.

'Sweet Jesus,' he said, 'what the hell's going on . . . wasn't that your plane?'

'Was!' I replied. 'Some rotten, thieving bastard has just stolen it.'

Rafferty turned on his heel. 'The tower, I'll try to get them to stop it . . .'

I grabbed his shoulder. 'Forget it, it's more complicated than that.'

'What the hell do you mean? Someone has just pinched your aeroplane, isn't that enough? I mean how much more complicated can you get?'

'Can you send the girls back to the hotel in the taxi . . . ? I'll explain it to you then.'

Rafferty shrugged. 'There'll be the matter of compensation of course!'

'Compensation!'

'My love life,' he said, 'and I have the feeling that Miss Balmer will not be overjoyed at the prospect of an empty bed.' He was laughing quietly to himself as he walked away.

I turned towards the runway as the Dornier's engines rose to a deafening roar. So it had been Clay all along. Or at least Clay and an accomplice. The pieces began to fit. Clay had lost his farm to the rebels and had then gone to work for Valentine, where he had accidentally stumbled on the diamond smuggling. Probably in the same way I had done. Then he and an accomplice had cleverly designed a plot to get rid of Valentine; at least with him out of the way they wouldn't need to keep looking over their shoulders every day of their lives.

I looked up and watched the white tail light of the

Dornier moving slowly westwards towards the higher ground. Then the light disappeared and was shortly replaced by a green navigation light. Starboard wingtip, he had turned onto a northerly heading into the Rift Valley. Within a day Lucius 'Lucky' Clay would have vanished from the face of the earth and the diamonds with him.

We were sitting under the wing of the Aero Commander in the warm night air. Rafferty still hadn't spoken, but he was thinking hard. I had told him about the diamonds and about Valentine and the killings; and finally how Lucky Clay had arrived and taken the aeroplane.

'One thing that puzzles me,' Rafferty said. 'Why would your man Clay wait until now to take the diamonds, why not back in Malawi?'

'As I told you he used to fly for the Rhodesian Air Force, probably blacklisted by the rebels, so he thought it would be safer to wait until the shipment was out of the country. Personally I think the Malawi police were doubtful about him, perhaps they were watching him, waiting for him to make a move. I had the feeling they knew about the diamonds!'

Rafferty looked serious for one of the few times in his life. 'Sure, that would be it. Malawi black police sympathizing with the black rebels and waiting for the first opportunity to arrest him or ship him back to where he came from. Next question, Stevie boy, why would he take the Dornier, why not just the diamonds?'

'Hell, I don't know. If he arrived in his Baron, it would have been a damn sight quicker to have taken that.'

Rafferty started laughing. Quietly at first, then louder. 'Mother of Mercy, isn't he the sly one.'

'Why do you say that?'

'You obviously had diplomatic clearances for your flight!'

'Yes.'

'What was your routing?'

'After Nairobi, Juba, Khartoum, Luxor and then

through to Larnaca.'

'There you are you see . . . and I'm thinking he will follow the same route.'

'Almost plausible,' I said. 'But what about me?'

'What about you?'

'What happens when I report the aircraft stolen?'

'Ahh! but he's ahead of you there. Firstly this is Africa; internal communications work about one per cent of the time, and only then if you're lucky. Secondly, even if some official was notified in Khartoum, and he decided to get off his fat bum to go and investigate – which is highly unlikely – Clay would know he could easily bribe the man to let him through.'

I looked across at Rafferty. 'Feel like going flying?'

'When?'

'Now!' I took the diamond out of my shirt pocket. 'Payment if you help me get the rest of the shipment back.'

Rafferty let out a low whistle. 'It's a lovely, lovely world, Stevie boy . . . and getting lovelier by the minute.'

Having persuaded the controller to keep the airport open another hour, we eventually flagged down a car on the airport road and gave a surprised African twenty dollars to take us to the Serena.

'You don't seem at all surprised,' I said to Rafferty as the car sped down the wide streets.

'Surprised about what?'

'Diamonds, smuggling, that sort of thing.'

Rafferty gave me a knowing wink. 'Been doing it myself for years,' he said. 'Not on such a grand scale of course . . . but it's the way Africa ticks.'

'And would I be right in thinking that you just happen to know a man who would buy a selection of diamonds?'

'Everything except drugs and white slavery,' he laughed. 'Now what are the details on this flight?'

'What's the range on your Commander?'

'As it's practically full of ferry tanks, about fifteen hundred miles.'

'So we can make Khartoum nonstop?'

'No problem.'

'Good. Because Clay will have to stop at Juba to refuel; which means we can be waiting for him when he arrives in Khartoum.'

Less than an hour later, having checked out of the hotel, caught a taxi to the airport and filed a flight plan, we were picking our way down the dimly-lit taxiway. The whisky had long since worn off, but I'd purchased half a dozen bottles from the hotel when I was paying for the bed I'd never slept in.

Rafferty pushed the two throttles slowly forward and we accelerated down the runway. Seconds later he selected undercarriage up and we rushed into the dark night. The moon was now hidden by bands of high cirrus, which in turn meant we could see less of the mountainous terrain which we had to fly through. Rafferty pushed the airway charts onto my lap. 'Welcome on board, not every day I have a navigator.'

By the time we had levelled off at 11,000 feet Rafferty was turning north into the Rift Valley. I glanced down at the chart on my knee. It stated that the sector safe altitude in this area was 15.3. Which meant 15,300 feet.

'Have you got oxygen on board?' I asked.

'No . . . never touch the stuff. Why do you ask?'

'Well . . . the sector safe is fifteen three, and as we're down at eleven . . . I don't like the idea of four thousand-odd feet of mountain sticking up in front of me.'

Rafferty reached out and retuned the ADF. The needle moved sluggishly round and pointed directly ahead. 'See that?' he said.

'Yeah.'

'Nakuru beacon . . . the story goes that if we maintain this heading of three two four, we should pass between the Nyandaran Range and the Mau Escarpment. Once we hit Nakuru we come right on to about three five five degrees for Lodwar. After that it's all downhill. Of course there's always a nice little sting in the tail . . . like if some genius has moved the mountains; or if the Nakuru beacon

178

is emitting erroneous signals . . . in that happy event you need never worry about anything again.'

I didn't say anything in reply. Nothing seemed appropriate. Instead I stared nervously down at the airways chart and checked the distance to Nakuru . . . forty miles. Forty miles at 180 knots; which added up to thirteen minutes of sweating and praying and dying . . . over and over and over again.

We passed over the Nakuru beacon on schedule. From here the terrain to Lodwar was less formidable. But Lodwar was still another 208 miles on into the night. The tension remained. I reached back and took a bottle from my flight bag. I'd lasted as long as I wanted to. 'Want a drink?' I said to Rafferty.

'And why the hell not; the worst is over after all . . . it wouldn't be Irish by any chance?' He took the bottle. 'No. Somehow I didn't think it would . . . still beggars can't be choosers.' He took a long pull and handed back the bottle.

'Something I was going to ask you,' I said, wiping my mouth with the back of my hand. 'Have you any idea how much that diamond is worth?'

'I could hazard a guess, but that's all it would be,' he replied. 'Assuming the particular stone in question is top quality clarity, colour and cut. And assuming I'm right in thinking it's at least eight to ten carat. I'd say the going rate would be in the order of sixty-five thousand.'

'Dollars?'

'Pounds . . . English pounds.'

'Christ, as much as that?'

'Except,' Rafferty added, 'as you will have to sell them through the back door you can only count on half of that.'

And there were about a hundred more, maybe not as big, but still a lot of diamonds. Which could mean as much as five million dollars' worth or more.

'Something else Rafferty?'

'I'm listening.'

'The original theft eight years ago said a total of ten

million dollars' worth of cut and uncut gems had been stolen. Now if the haul was shipped out in four equal parts that means this shipment is worth two and a half million dollars, right?'

'Wrong!'

'What do you mean wrong?'

'Well you would be aware that cut and polished stones are more valuable than uncut wouldn't you?'

'Yes.'

'Right. The next part is a little tricky if you don't know a thing about them. Diamonds you see are like finger-prints, totally unique. Therefore it would be my guess that the man concerned would have left the cut ones until last, which means that your little package is perhaps worth more than the rest were put together. Also prices will have changed a lot over the last eight years.'

It was after we had passed Lodwar and I had had the time to think about it that I put the proposition to Rafferty.

'Half? You're crazy.'

'Not at all, I know next to nothing about the bloody things. So if you're going to help me get them back we go fifty fifty.'

Rafferty smiled. 'It's a deal Stevie boy, it's a deal.'

We arrived at Khartoum at 7.30, having picked up a slight headwind somewhere along the way. Or as Rafferty had aptly put it, 'It's all uphill, what do you expect?'

The visibility was about two miles in blowing sand as Rafferty reported over the green belt on finals for runway 35 and the Commander rocked its way down through the early-morning turbulence.

After landing, the ground controller sent us to the light-aircraft park which was to the north of the Shell fuel compound and about six hundred yards from the terminal building.

The morning was already breathless with the tempera-ture climbing into the eighties and the air was alive with fat white-bodied flies.

'The distance from here to the terminal increases

through the morning; by lunchtime it's more like a mile,' Rafferty said as we walked across the sandy wasteland to the Shell compound.

'God, and I used to think it was bad in the Philippines,' I replied, wiping the sweat from my forehead.

Rafferty just laughed and went through the tall wire gates towards the office. I followed him up the steps into the darkened room.

'Abdul my old friend, how are the six wives?'

A fat man rose from his desk and thrust out a podgy hand.

'Captain Rafferty, *salaam alaikoom.*'

'*Alaikoom salaam,*' Rafferty replied. 'This is my friend Captain Ritchie.'

Abdul gave me a warm, soft handshake. 'Welcome, Captain Ritchie. Please gentlemen, be seated . . . you will take tea of course?'

Rafferty said, 'Of course.'

Abdul went to the door and shouted loudly in Arabic, then waddled back to his chair.

By now my eyes were becoming accustomed to the semi-darkness of the office. It was large and dirty and very untidy. In one corner a broken-down old camp bed was covered by a dirty white sheet, while further along the same wall an air-conditioning unit was rattling noisily as it attempted to keep the room temperature to a more livable level than the glaring white outdoors. Elsewhere around the room were chairs and tables, some broken, some intact, but all dusty and dirty. The windows, of which I counted six, were all covered by plastic venetian blinds and all carried the odd one or two heat-warped slats through which bright slanting sunlight spilled unevenly around the room.

A small boy appeared and poured out the tea, then with a bow he hurried away. 'So Abdul, you old rogue, you still haven't told me . . . how are the six wives?'

Abdul clasped his podgy hands together and gave a look of sadness and happiness all rolled into one. 'Captain Rafferty, you know I am only a poor man, how

181

would such a man afford six wives?'

Rafferty laughed and picked up his flight bag and put it on his knee. 'I know, Abdul my friend . . . but you are a good man.'

Abdul smiled and watched Rafferty's hands delve into the bag. 'Two bottles of Bushmills, four hundred cigarettes . . . and for your wife French perfume.' Rafferty deposited the gifts amidst the jumble of paperwork on Abdul's desk.

'My friend, you are too kind . . . how can I ever repay you?'

Rafferty laughed off the question. 'That's what friends are for, Abdul.'

'Some more tea?' the fat Arab said, picking up the ancient metal teapot. He started pouring. 'Perhaps you and Captain Ritchie would be my guests and come to my humble house this night and take food?'

Rafferty feigned great sadness. 'Abdul, I am eternally sorry; but we have to leave soon . . . perhaps to Luxor. Next time though . . . next time.'

'So be it,' Abdul said with equal sadness. 'But next time you will stay. You also Captain Ritchie. Whenever you are in Khartoum my house is your house.'

'Thank you Abdul, you are very kind.' Then to Rafferty, 'I'd better get over to the terminal and check on the Dornier.'

'Right you are,' he said. 'I'll sort out the fuel and meet you in fifteen minutes . . . say in the duty-free shop at the front of the terminal.'

Outside the heat hit me . . . it was like opening an oven door. The glaring sun bounced back off the prestressed white concrete of the main apron, hurting my eyes. All around the quiet thunder of jet a.p.u.'s which maintained air conditioning inside the airliners when the engines were not running; that and forklift trucks buzzing back and forth with the day's freight. But the flies were the worst, clamouring to land on exposed skin with what felt like cold feet and ignoring all attempts to be brushed away.

The inside of the terminal was cooler, and after climbing endless stone stairs and searching down gloomy unlit corridors in which lingered the stench of urine and spicy food, I found the glass door leading to the flight clearance office. Apart from an American pilot who was arguing unsuccessfully about a routing to Jeddah, the place was deserted. I lit a cigarette and waited for the sweating red-faced Yank to depart, then asked the slightly built Arab if he had a flight plan on the Dornier.

'He's probably inbound from Juba,' I added.

The Arab nodded and shuffled through the inevitable pile of papers. 'We have nothing,' he said.

'You've got the registration right . . . seven QDFE.'

'Seven Quebec Delta Foxtrot Echo; yes I know. But there is nothing from Juba.'

'Can you check with Juba?' I asked.

'That is not possible, we have no communication today.'

I counted to ten and let the moment pass. If he had no communication he would hardly have a flight plan! 'Perhaps you could check with the tower. They may be in radio contact!'

'A moment.' He went over to the other side of the room, the flip-flops on his feet slapping loudly on the stone floor as he walked. He picked up the black telephone. After thirty seconds of arm-waving and shouting excitedly into the mouthpiece he replaced the receiver and came noisily back towards me.

'They have nothing,' he said with finality.

I turned and went out of the door.

Rafferty was sitting at one of the tables opposite the duty-free shop, quietly smoking a cigarette and watching the African labour through the open arch-shaped window.

'And our lot complain,' he mused as I joined him. 'I'd give them all half a day in those conditions, and that's a fact.' He turned and passed me a cigarette. 'Bad news, I take it!'

'To be more precise . . . no news. No flight plan, no radio contact, no nothing.'

Rafferty took an airways chart from his flight bag and spread it neatly on the table. 'Let's take a look see now. What range did you say you had on that Dornier?'

'At one twenty knots I'd reckon on no more than eight hundred miles to dry tanks.'

'Right. So starting at Juba he could have gone to El Fasher which is about five hundred miles west of here . . . and from there he could have headed north to Kufra in Tripoli and then on to Benghazi. The only other alternative, assuming he's heading for the Med, would be back across to Addis, then up the east side. Asmara, Port Sudan and Luxor.'

'But the Dornier hasn't got clearances for those places!'

'Maybe not, but he could be relying on the old bribery and corruption routine,' Rafferty said. 'Although it's still my bet he'll pass this way. After all it is the shortest and the easiest way out . . . and it is a slow old aeroplane.'

'Agreed, but if it was me I'd be avoiding the big airports if possible.'

Rafferty wasn't listening, not to me at least. He climbed quickly to his feet and moved over to the white stone window. 'There's your answer,' he said pointing up into the sand haze of sky.

I heard the sound long before I picked out the faint, dark outline of the Dornier. He was high, possibly as much as ten thousand feet, and he was heading due north. 'Looks as though you were right,' Rafferty said, grabbing his flight bag. 'You get out to the aircraft and start the engines . . . the fuelling should be finished by now. I'll run up to the clearance office and see if I can find out where he's going.' He stopped halfway across the mosaic floor. 'Of course has it ever occurred to you that there could be more than one Dornier in the Sudan?'

'Maybe . . . I'll see you at the plane.'

By the time I reached the Aero Commander I was sweating through every pore in my body. Sweating, heart thumping, and lightheaded. It wasn't until I had dragged myself into the crucifying heat of the aircraft's cockpit and started searching for halfway familiar switches that I realized what I was doing. Not you, Ritchie . . . not you! It's nearly livable if someone else is playing silly buggers and cranking up aeroplanes . . . but not you! My hand pulled back from the magneto switches and reached for the bottle. The instant cure for all of life's ills.

The right engine had just burst into life when Rafferty appeared at the door. 'Move over, I've got it.' He slid into the left seat.

'That was bloody quick.'

His glistening face broke into a smile as his hands primed and started the left engine. 'As though the devil himself was at my heels,' he said. 'Cost you another hundred dollars by the way.'

'What?'

'Instant takeoff clearance . . . they're holding a Tradewinds seven oh seven in the stack and anything else that wants to land, at that.'

'I'm impressed.'

'Not what the Tradewinds guy said . . . he's squealing like a stuck pig.'

'Where we going by the way?'

'Karima, Stevie boy . . . Karima!' Rafferty released the brakes and gunned the Commander into a screeching right turn down the taxiway. I slipped on the spare headset as he thumbed the transmit button.

'Khartoum, Mike Mike Romeo's with you, just coming out of the light aircraft park.'

'Roger Double Mike Romeo, you are cleared to enter and take off, runway one seven . . . switch to tower when ready.'

'We'll do that sir, thanks for your help.'

'A pleasure, Captain.'

Rafferty flicked the various switches round to tower frequency.

I said, 'I thought they were using runway three-five!'

'They are. Something else you get for your hundred dollars . . . the nearest runway.' He pressed the transmit button. 'Tower Mike Mike Romeo's with you, entering runway one seven.'

The thickly accented Arabic voice said, 'Cleared to go, Mike Mike Romeo.'

'Is that you, Muhammed?'

'*Aywa*, Captain Rafferty.'

'You got the . . .'

'*Shukran*, Captain.'

'*Afwan sadeek* . . . see you next time perhaps!'

'A safe journey, Captain. Allah go with you.'

'Wrong faith, Muhammed, but thanks anyway.' Rafferty kicked the rudder straight and pushed the throttles smoothly forward. Fifteen seconds later the Commander rotated towards the sky. Rafferty reported airborne and was immediately cleared to en route frequency. He reached forward and switched the radio off before settling back comfortably into his seat.

'Yet another escape story for the little blue book,' he said drily.

'Something less than last night at least.'

'You're right there. That was a major bloody epic. Stage ten at MGM, angels, heavenly choir . . . the works.'

'But you've done it before of course?'

'Daylight only Stevie boy, never in the dark.'

'Christ! Now you tell me.'

Rafferty laughed. 'No need to concern yourself; I had all the gen from a missionary pilot. And as he had local experience and God on his side . . .'

I lit a cigarette with shaking hands. 'You seem to know a lot of people in Khartoum,' I said.

'Years of patient practice,' he replied, adjusting the power settings. 'That and a never ending supply of booze and cigarettes.'

'Works though.'

'Christ yes. Legalized corruption; can't beat it.'

'Where did you say we were going?'

'Karima; about one eighty miles north of here. There's an NDB there and a short bush strip on the side of the Nile.'

'Did they tell you that in flight clearance?'

'No. Just said that the pilot of the Dornier was diverting there. Then I remembered a crop-spraying type name of Jess Markham telling me they had a fuel dump up there.'

'Did you get the registration . . . of the Dornier?'

'No, but he's out of Juba and I'm betting there's not a lot of Dorniers doing that particular route today.'

'I suppose that information came out of the hundred dollars as well?'

'I'll say one thing for you, Stevie; for an Englishman you're quick on the uptake.' He cranked the trim wheel forward and levelled off at 6,000 feet. 'That should do for now. Bit bumpy, but we stand a fair chance of overhauling him.'

I took the airways chart from Rafferty's knee and did a rough distance calculation from Juba to Karima. 'I make the distance Juba to Karima eight hundred and forty miles, which means he must have picked up a tailwind.'

'Either that or he's flying on the fumes,' Rafferty said. 'Though I still don't understand why he didn't land at Khartoum.'

'As I said before, playing safe. Also he can be in and out of there a damn sight quicker than Khartoum . . . plus the fact he doesn't have to file a flight plan. Which means Clay and the diamonds conveniently disappear.'

Rafferty checked his watch. 'We've been airborne exactly fourteen minutes, which leaves about another forty to Karima. As he'll have his speed right back to conserve fuel I reckon we'll pass underneath him in the last ten minutes.'

'So hopefully we'll land first!'

'And have the drop on him, you mean?'

'Sounds about right.'

Rafferty smiled tiredly. 'I take it you have a plan after all this?'

'Not much of one, but it might work.'

'What if it doesn't?'

'I should think we'd both be past caring.'

Twenty-nine minutes later we made visual contact with the Dornier. It didn't have to be that way; the aircraft could just as easily have been a few miles or more off the direct track between Khartoum and Karima. With any lesser pilot than Clay it probably would have been; and then those few miles would have swallowed the Dornier up in the haze. I'd banked on Clay's predictability and so far he was running to form. He was still high; staying in the thinner air until the last possible moment, running the engines at the weakest mixture he could; taking the aircraft to its optimum range performance.

'Start descending now,' I said to Rafferty. We were about a mile astern and 4,000 feet below. 'All the way to the deck; I'd rather he didn't see us.'

Rafferty lowered the nose and retrimmed the Commander into a steepish dive; engines and slipstream howled in unison as the thermal turbulence from the orange desert beneath rattled every rivet in the aircraft's structure. I instinctively pulled my seat harness tight. Tight, until the shoulder straps bit painfully into my shoulders. Then I clenched my fists and watched the ground growing in detail at nearly four miles a minute.

At 500 feet Rafferty eased the nose up and adjusted the power. The slipstream returned to its normal steady hiss. The visibility was less than one mile.

'Must be approaching the Nile,' Rafferty yelled. 'Higher humidity!'

'Which side is the strip?'

'North. The river runs northeast to southwest at this point . . . there!' Rafferty shouted excitedly. 'Palms!'

I saw them as he spoke. Tall, scattered clumps of palm trees pointing ragged-topped towards the sky. Rafferty started reducing power as they flashed quickly beneath and the muddy waters of the Nile reflected the hazy sheen of sun.

'Keep a look-out your side,' he ordered, snapping the undercarriage selector lever down.

I wiped the sweat out of my eyes and nervously licked the salt off my dry lips as the Commander continued its descent. A lateen-rigged boat was being loaded on the north bank. I counted three white-clad natives humping baskets down the narrow shore as we swayed the bordering palms with our prop-wash. Then we were past, turning left to follow the shoreline.

'Got it!' Rafferty exclaimed, slamming the flap lever down.

I looked up and ahead and my heart stopped. It was impossibly short. A few hundred yards of rough strip hacked out between the towering palms.

'We'll never make it . . . it's too bloody short!'

Rafferty laughed and pushed the nose even lower. We needed every single inch of that makeshift runway, every single precious inch, and even then we stood a fair chance of overrunning into the tangle of trees at the far end.

Chapter Nineteen

The final solitary act of commitment cloaked the chaos. Rafferty's commitment to land on a runway which was totally unsuitable; my chaos of fear. A chaos of irregular heartbeats, ripping flesh, breaking bones and endless silent screams. The aircraft hit hard – a carrier landing – pounding hell out of the undercarriage. Then the Irishman was standing on the brakes as we skidded and slithered towards the end of the clearing. I was still pushing my body through the back of the seat when we juddered to a stop. The distance remaining was a matter of yards. I looked at Rafferty, sweat dripping from my chin. 'I now see why you didn't get into Aer Lingus, they probably thought it'd be nicer to have a fleet of unbroken aeroplanes . . . anyway you mad bastard, how the hell do we get out of here?'

Rafferty laughed, pulled a handkerchief from his pocket and wiped his face and neck. 'We don't,' he replied. 'Not unless we extend the runway.' He swung the aircraft round and taxied back up the strip. At the halfway point it widened out. We parked by a small derelict mud-walled building, the surface of which was lined with a thousand cracks.

'Better get moving,' Rafferty said, cutting the engines. 'They'll be here any minute.'

'Where's the fuel?'

'Probably back at the village. Wouldn't leave anything here, some thieving bastard would steal it . . . somebody will be down shortly, will have heard the plane.'

I opened the rear passenger door and climbed out into the sauna bath heat and stench of rotting vegetation. Rafferty was already out of the pilot's door and unfastening the cowling on the starboard engine when the familiar synchronized snarl of the Dornier grew imperceptibly out of the southern sky. I moved quickly into a thick clump of palms about thirty yards from the Commander's left wingtip. Hopefully Clay would park the Dornier in the space between me and Rafferty. All I had to do then was wait for Rafferty to distract Clay and his accomplice before gaining access to the radio bay. If the diamonds had been removed and hidden elsewhere we would be faced with another problem. But although Clay was armed I had the element of surprise on my side. Fighter pilots used to be taught that sort of thing; and, I reasoned, if those tactics worked satisfactorily in the air they would also work on the ground. Rafferty's story was that he had been en route to Luxor when he had developed excessive vibration in the starboard engine. Being familiar with the Karima airstrip he had decided to land there and try to rectify the problem.

The Dornier's engines cut back to idle power as Clay started his descent. Less than a minute later the aircraft glided in to a silky three pointer and stopped in half the distance available. Good short-field performer the Dornier; and with Clay at the controls it looked even more impressive.

I suppose I had known all along; or if not known at least guessed. But even that deep subconscious revelation did nothing to absorb the dull shock which reverberated through my aching empty stomach. The shock of seeing Penny Valentine climbing out of the co-pilot's hatch of the Dornier. So it had been her and Clay all along and if Rees-Williams had been telling the truth . . .

Clay had followed that instinctive action of all pilots and swung the Dornier back towards the airstrip – neatly lined up along the Commander. Tidy people, pilots – always like to park wingtip to wingtip pointing the same way. I watched as he and Penny Valentine walked to the blind side of the Commander, then moved quickly and silently across the clear ground to the Dornier's radio access bay. I'd just reached the aircraft when I remembered the release catch. I had to open the passenger door first. A cold sweat crawled across my scalp when I realized the keys were in my flight bag. I reached for the handle and said, 'Please God!'

It was open. I crawled slowly into the darkness; only this time I didn't need a torch. I knew exactly where to feel. My left hand found the silica gel tube at the first attempt. I gave a small sigh of relief and began shuffling slowly backwards. All that remained was to close the door and get back to the cover of the palm trees. It was an odds-on certainty that Clay wouldn't check the radio bay again before he departed. He had no reason. I smiled to myself. By the time he found out they were missing we would be a long way away; and better still he would never know who had stolen them. The smile was still on my face as my feet touched the ground. It died when I turned and came face to face with Clay.

'The ferry pilot himself,' he said grimly. He raised his right hand and motioned me towards Rafferty. The black snubnosed revolver looked very convincing.

'How did you know I was in there?' I said.

'Control cables,' he said with a satisfied smile. 'I'd just sent Penny off to the village to find the fuel guy and happened to notice the rudder twitch. As there's no wind, it seemed an unlikely situation.'

I turned to Rafferty. He lifted his hands in a gesture of hopelessness. 'Sorry, Stevie boy . . .'

'Forget it,' I said. Then to Clay, 'What now?'

'Firstly I'll take the diamonds back,' I moved forward; he smiled. 'Not that way man, they stopped running banana boats a long time ago. No, what we do is put them on the ground, slowly and carefully.' I did as instructed. 'Good . . . now you and your friend back up . . . hands on your head.' He reached down and picked up the silica gel tube. His eyes never left us for a moment.

'So,' I said, 'you've got the diamonds . . . how about us?'

He glanced quickly past the mud-walled building to the dusty track which must have led to the village. 'Penny should be back shortly. You can both get in your aircraft in the meantime . . . once we've fuelled the Dornier I'll tie you up and make sure your plane never flies again . . . then we leave.'

I looked at him in surprise. 'You mean you're not intending to use that miniature cannon?'

'Kill you, you mean. Christ man, I'm only interested in the diamonds . . . I don't kill people.'

'How about ground-attack sorties on rebels?'

His face hardened. 'Who the hell told you about that?'

'Rees-Williams,' I said. 'Told me everything. How you flew for Smith's Air Force. Hunters wasn't it?'

Clay nodded.

'What mark?' I said.

'Sixes . . . you?'

'Amongst others,' I said. 'So do I take it that the old fighter pilot's creed still holds good and we don't kill each other unless we use Aden cannons?'

'Sod that,' Clay sneered. 'That's got nothing to do with it. I flew Hunters to get back at the black bastards who were taking my family's hard work.'

'It is their country!'

'Jesus fucking Christ Ritchie, you still don't understand, do you? It's my country as much as theirs. My father and his father before him slaved day and night to make something of it . . . which is more than those black buggers did in a thousand years . . .'

'Point conceded,' I said. 'But why Sally North and James Valentine?'

The wild blue eyes opened wide. 'What do you mean?'

'Why did you kill them?'

The gun levelled at my face. 'What the bloody hell . . .' He stopped in mid-sentence, his eyes looking beyond me.

Penny Valentine was wearing a white jump-suit, complete with a dozen or so zips. Even in the humid, sticky heat she was looking remarkably cool. The Arab who was leading the flea-bitten old mule was leathery-skinned, with closely cropped grey hair. He was dressed in a tattered sweat-stained *galobea*, which might once have been white; but that would have been a long time ago.

The Arab followed Penny into the clearing and stopped his mule. Penny winced noticeably when she saw me; then she put on her hard-faced bitch appearance and came over to Clay. 'His name's Youssef Ghorab,' she said. 'He's got two drums of fuel only. One hundred and ten gallons.'

'That'll do,' Clay said. 'Can you show him where to put it; fill the inners first.'

'What about these two?' she said icily, looking at Rafferty and me.

'I'll keep them in the Commander until the Arab's gone.'

'Do you mind if I have a drink?' I said to Clay. Rafferty and I were sitting in the front seats of the Aero Commander, slowly burning up in a hundred degrees.

'I'll get it,' he said. 'Where is it?'

'In the flight bag . . . Scotch.'

He passed the bottle forward and I took a long swallow before passing it to Rafferty. 'This, by the way, is Rafferty.' Then to Rafferty. 'His name's Clay.'

'I won't say pleased to meet you Mr Clay, but you'd understand that wouldn't you?'

Clay shrugged. 'You ex-Air Force too?'

'Nothing as grand I'm afraid. No, I'm just a simple Irishman trying to make an honest living.'

'Like stealing diamonds, you mean,' Clay said sarcastically.

'Ah, but you've got a sharp tongue, Mr Clay and that's a fact. I mean do I look like the type who would do such a thing?'

Clay ignored the remark and turned to me. 'How did you know I was coming here?'

I said, 'We were waiting for you in Khartoum . . . we saw you overfly.'

'But how did you know about Karima?'

'You informed control, remember?'

'And they told you?'

'Not me. Rafferty. And only then after he'd greased a few palms ... anyway that's water under the bridge. What about Sally and Valentine?'

Clay raised what I now recognized as a Smith and Wesson 0.38. 'Look Ritchie,' he snapped, 'you know as well as I do what happened!'

'Except Rees-Williams maintained he didn't do it. In fact he said he'd been framed.'

'You're talking in riddles, man ... when did he tell you that?'

I took a deep breath and started. From the time Rees-Williams had stopped me in the forest, until the leopard had ripped him apart in the woodshed. Through it all Clay listened silently; his only action being to wipe the sweat from his forehead from time to time. His lightweight khaki drill uniform of short-sleeved shirt and matching trousers had lost its crisp smartness and was now heavily stained with dark patches of perspiration. But at least he looked wide awake and well fed. I had been on the go since leaving Zomba and thirty hours or more without sleep were catching up with me. The stabbing pangs of hunger and the oppressive heat added to the misery. I found myself thinking about the hotel room back in Nairobi. Cold showers, clean freshly-laundered clothes, a T-bone steak and a bottle. And finally a bed. A bed most of all. Soft and springy; I could almost hear the quiet rustle as the white sheets were folded back ... feel my head sinking into the downy pillow.

'Are you listening, man?' Clay was talking.

'What? What did you say?'

'I said that's the sort of story he would tell you. He had to try to get away didn't he?'

'What chance would he have had if he'd given himself up? Would he have got a fair trial?'

'With those black bastards,' Clay said cynically.

'Exactly ... that's what Rees-Williams reckoned. He knew he wouldn't get a fair crack of the whip; so he decided to get to hell out of it. And I'll tell you something else ... you'd do the same.'

Clay looked at me, then at his watch, and then through the window at the Arab who was slowly transferring the contents of the drums into the wings of the Dornier.

'It doesn't change a damn thing,' he said eventually. 'I had nothing to do with it.'

Clay grabbed my shoulder and jerked me round angrily. 'Be careful, man. I've been patient up to now, but if you start on her . . .'

I said wearily, 'You're right Lucky; it's none of my business . . . if it wasn't for that one flaw . . .'

'What flaw?'

'You remember you found Valentine's car in the pine forest?'

'Yes.'

'Well doesn't it strike you as odd that if Valentine had been after Rees-Williams he would have gone straight to the airport or his house? Why up the mountain? But you're right, the case's closed . . . post mortems are hardly going to help anyone now, are they?'

Clay rubbed the light stubble on his chin with the barrel of his gun. His blue eyes were troubled and thoughtful, but he didn't speak.

It took another hour and the remains of the whisky bottle before the Arab had completed the refuelling. Then he came over with Penny to the Commander. She opened the passenger door.

'He wants dollars,' she said.

'How much?' Clay replied.

'Five hundred!'

'Five hundred!' Clay exploded. 'The robbing bastard. Tell him . . . no, on second thoughts you come in here Pen and keep the gun on these two. I'll sort him out.'

Penny, still looking cool and composed, slid into the rear seat as Clay stormed out to talk to the Arab.

'Nice to see you again, Mrs Valentine,' I said.

She lifted the gun fractionally. 'Shut up,' she hissed. The ladylike quality of her voice had disappeared. Now she sounded like the hard-faced scheming bitch she really was. I had no doubts in my mind she would stop at nothing to get what she wanted. I turned my head away and joined Rafferty in watching the argument which had now progressed to the nose of the aircraft. The crusty old Arab was standing in a tired manner listening to Clay who was ranting and raving with all the finesse of a madman. Maybe I didn't know Africa, but I knew third worlds. I also knew and believed in the saying, When in Rome . . . Clay however was hooked on the nineteenth-century belief that a white skin was the answer to everything. The argument continued.

Chapter Twenty

The Arab had a look of low cunning on his face. His people, after all's said and done, had been in the market place a lot longer than Clay's; and Youssef Ghorab knew it. It was some time before Clay capitulated, and only then perhaps because of time. He had places to go, and with less than six hours of daylight remaining he would want to get the tired old Dornier back in the sky, putting time and space between us. I watched as he counted out five one-hundred-dollar bills into the Arab's palm; then he turned sharply on his heel and hurried back towards the passenger door.

'Bloody bastard,' he muttered, leaning into the aircraft. 'Bloody, bloody bastard.' He reached towards Penny and picked up the silica gel tube. 'I'm going to put these back in the radio bay . . . bring those two outside.'

Penny smiled and turned to me. 'You heard,' she snapped. 'Out.'

By the time we were out of the aircraft Clay was back.

'What are we going to do with them?' Penny said.

Clay shrugged. 'Tie them up, then I'll fix their plane. That should give us all the time we need.'

'What about the Arab?' she asked.

'No problem, I told him they had plenty of fuel and were repairing an engine . . . he won't bother to come back and check.'

Penny raised her left hand to her cheek and brushed away a wisp of damp hair. Normally it wouldn't have meant a thing. Normally it would have been nothing more than an unconscious movement, one that people make every day of their lives. Today, it seemed, was far from being normal. Perhaps it was vanity that had made her do it. Or then again it could have been plain old-fashioned reluctance to keep beauty and wealth hidden away.

Whatever the reason it didn't really matter, because now I knew. Now I was certain.

'They could still inform the police,' Penny said after a moment's thought.

Clay's eyes swung round to me. His face was bleak. 'But I won't,' I said. 'And Aden cannons were a long time ago . . . for me at least.' I looked across to Rafferty. 'Your secret's safe with him as well . . . which just leaves your conscience.'

'What do you mean my conscience?' Clay snapped.

'Sally and James Valentine, and in a way Rees-Williams. High price to pay for a few cut and polished stones, wouldn't you say?'

Clay turned pale. His body shook as he fought to control his anger. 'It's a pity you're not black,' he said menacingly. 'Because if you were I'd kill you right here and now. As for the bloody Zomba business I've already told you . . .'

I interrupted, 'You've already told me you know nothing about it. On the other hand if you ask Mrs Valentine I'm sure she'll explain all.'

Clay's control gave out at that point as he lunged forward grabbing me by the throat. 'The ring!' I croaked. 'Ask her . . . about the ring . . . Sally's.'

The powerful hands released their grip as he turned back to Penny. She looked suddenly hunted, off guard. Her left hand moved guiltily behind her back. There was a moment of complete silence; then Clay said, 'You?'

She looked at him with contempt. 'Yes me. What the hell does it matter now? We've got what we wanted, haven't we?'

'But why? We'd have got them without killing.'

She gave a small ironical laugh. 'And do you honestly believe that James would have let it rest at that?' Her voice rose to a shriek. 'Do you? Do you?'

Clay didn't answer. His face looked strangely tired and old. Older than his years. His big-man image faded like wax in a flame.

Penny continued, 'He made me suffer for years, and do

199

you know why? Because I am what I am . . . a half caste . . . but I got him. Once I found out about the diamonds, he was trapped. All I needed was the way out.'

'But what did Sally North have to do with it?' I said angrily.

'What do you think . . . she was white, she was having an affair with my husband, for whatever good he was; he was still my husband. Then I found out she knew about the diamonds . . . she'd been asking too many questions.'

'And Rees-Williams proved a gullible scapegoat; someone you could implicate and who would carry the can for you.'

'He was just a simple fool.' She spat the words out.

'And an expert with a crossbow! Which no doubt gave you the idea in the first place . . . I suppose he even gave you lessons on how to use it?'

'My, my, aren't we the little detective. As I said he was a simple fool. Once I'd decided on the plan it was easy to get him to demonstrate the crossbow. Then I took two of his collection and practised every day in the forest.'

'I imagine you paid him between the sheets as well,' I said cuttingly.

Clay suddenly came back to life, his eyes lighting up with the same fine madness I had seen during his unprovoked attack on Sunday. The back of his left hand smashed into the side of my face, sending me sprawling to the ground.

'You're a bloody fool, Clay,' I said staggering to my feet. 'She's just using you. She even went to bed with me.'

He grabbed my shirt and pulled my face close to his. 'If you're lying, Ritchie, I'll tear you apart with my bare hands.' The threat was little more than a whisper through clenched teeth. The wild rage in his eyes told me he meant it.

'Now you!' he yelled turning back to Penny. 'Is it true?'

Penny backed away. She was still holding the gun at her side.

'Well . . . is it?'

'It was nothing,' she said quietly. 'Just sex . . . I don't

200

have to answer to you or any other man.' She raised the gun to waist level as if for protection, but she was too late. Clay was upon her instantly, his huge fists clubbing her into insensibility as they fell to the ground. The shot was a dull, muffled explosion which echoed and died in the palm trees on the other side of the airstrip.

Rafferty, who had been standing quietly watching the drama unfold, reached them first. Clay rolled back, holding the gun. 'Get away,' he snarled. 'Both of you.' Penny lay quite still, hands clasped into her stomach and the rapidly spreading crimson stain.

'Better get help from the village,' Rafferty suggested.

'Shut up,' Clay yelled. 'You'll both stay here until I'm airborne. Then you can do what the hell you like.' He waved the gun threateningly. 'Now give me the keys to the Commander.'

Rafferty took them from his pocket and tossed them across.

Clay barked, 'Inside . . . move!'

We climbed into the aircraft and Clay locked the pilot and passenger doors. He threw the keys into the trees and started running towards the Dornier.

'Emergency exit,' Rafferty said, climbing over the seats. It took seconds to remove the Perspex cover guarding the red handle and even less to release the handle. I went out first as the Dornier's engines shattered the afternoon stillness. I reached Penny and knelt down, taking her head in my lap. Her eyes opened slowly, pain contorting her face into an ugly mask. 'Where . . . is he?'

'Lucky?'

'Yes . . . where is he?'

'Gone,' I replied.

Her head turned agonizingly towards the fast-taxiing Dornier; then slowly back to me. There were tears in her eyes when she whispered, 'I did . . . I did . . . love him you know.' A gentle breeze, possibly from the Dornier's propellers, rippled through the trees. And that was when she died – like a candle flame in a draughty room . . . gutted, spent, lifeless. I lowered her head gently to the ground and closed the unseeing eyes.

The Dornier's engines rose to full power as I got to my feet. The aircraft accelerated rapidly; flaps down at about twenty degrees. It was a little more than halfway down the short strip when Clay hauled it towards the sky. The perfect short-field takeoff, best angle of climb, the lot. And he had probably never read the aircraft's flight manual. Just one of those one in a million pilots who instinctively knows when it's right. One of those rarities who belonged to the sky as much as the birds.

The propellers were still screaming at nearly the speed of sound when there was a momentary silence, followed by a surging of power. The sort of sound every ferry pilot knows when he runs a fuel tank dry before transferring to the next tank. But this sounded worse. The engines were backfiring, belching, spitting . . . and then they died. Simultaneously! The Dornier hung for a split second before Clay took recovery action; ramming the stick forward in an attempt to beat the stall. He might even have made it if it hadn't been for the tall palms which caught his right wingtip. Twenty feet higher and he could have dead-sticked down to the river on the other side of the trees. As it was he didn't have a chance. The aircraft cartwheeled sickeningly down; metal tearing trees; trees tearing metal. Then silence . . . a tall cathedral quiet.

We both stood, brains numbed by the crash. Staring in silent horror at something that shouldn't have happened. Pilots live with crash sequences running through their minds. Every flight could be their last. Every flight could lead to a thousand different ways of dying. Could . . . but never does. Not to them at least. They will always be around; kicking the tyres on early morning pre-flight inspections, chatting up the latest stewardess, or the latest sexy-voiced lady controller, or running youthfully on to their next affair. Crashes didn't happen to pilots; especially when other pilots were looking on.

We were running and shouting towards the wreckage. 'You get Clay,' I yelled, 'I'll get the diamonds.'

It was easier said than done. The aircraft had plummeted down between the trees, buckling up as it fell, and the baggage door was jammed solid. I moved around towards the cockpit and Rafferty who was kicking hell out of the pilot's hatch in an attempt to free it. When he did, and when he lifted the opaque crazed Perspex, we both recoiled in horror.

Clay had only fastened his lapstrap for take off and that had been enough to jack-knife his head into the instrument panel and his ribcage into the control column. The face, or what little of it remained, was a bloody mask of featureless flesh. A few broken white sticks, tinged with occasional red, stuck out through the back of his shirt. Except they weren't sticks, they were part of his ribcage.

'God have mercy on your soul, Mr Clay,' Rafferty said softly.

I turned away and went back to the baggage door. I was still hammering away when the Irishman grabbed me by the shoulder.

'Too late, the engine the other side's burning.' Even as he spoke I heard the sullen crackling of flames.

'Help me,' I yelled, tugging at the door.

He hesitated, then started pulling with me. Slowly, inch by inevitable inch it groaned open. The flames were now more than a crackle; they were a roaring inferno. At any second it could blow. A hundred and ten gallons of high explosive which would scatter Rafferty and me a million different ways to hell. I hauled myself into the smoke-filled tail section and clawed my way towards the radio bay. It was hot, unbearably and unbelievably hot. I felt my throat scorching as my hand closed on the silica gel tube. Back . . . back . . . back . . . which bloody way was out? Suddenly I was blind, and burning and choking and vomiting. Jesus bloody Christ . . . I was dying! My ankles were trapped; something had fallen across them. I tried to pull away, but the harder I pulled the more difficult it became. I wanted to call out for help, but there was no air. No air to shout. No air to breathe. Great steel bands tightened convulsively around my chest, squeezing, paralysing, destroying . . . then I was falling. Falling and spinning, spinning and falling like a dead autumn leaf into a long dark waterless well. Far beyond the darkness and the pain, a white shining light.

The first thing I saw was an aeroplane. It was nothing more than a hazy, rippled outline, but it was an aeroplane.

'Where am I?' My voice was a small, far-away croak.

'If it's heaven you're thinking, you'll be disappointed.'

I turned my head towards the voice and waited as the face came slowly into focus.

'Drink some of this,' Rafferty said and pressed the whisky bottle to my lips.

The burning liquid caught in my throat and I rolled over, vomiting in the sandy earth by my mouth. 'What . . . what . . . you trying to do . . . kill me?'

The Irishman laughed and pulled me up into a sitting position. 'Not a lot wrong with you, you old bugger,' he laughed.

'What happened?'

'What happened? Oh not a lot, you just climbed into a burning aircraft and when I grabbed your ankles to pull you back out you started fighting like a madman. Then as luck would have it you passed out.'

It all came back in a roaring flood; memories and recent events tripping over themselves in their hurry to be recognized. A classroom of little children, all eager to tell their story first.

'What about the Dornier?'

'Gone,' he said. 'A bloody great, hollow, rending carrumph . . .'

'When did it go up?'

'Just now, as you were coming round. I thought you'd heard it; talk about a sound to wake the dead.'

'Any villagers here yet?' I asked.

'No, but it won't be long.'

'What about Penny?'

Rafferty glanced up towards the bush track leading to the village. 'Too late to do anything now, Stevie boy, they'll be here any minute. I did think about dragging her body down to the wreckage, but with all that petrol about to blow . . .'

'Petrol! That's it, help me up.'

The world seemed to rock from side to side, but after the first few faltering steps it began to improve.

'Where did the Arab put the empty drums?'

'Over there, by the building.'

As Youssef Ghorab had used a wobble pump to transfer the fuel from the drums, it meant a few pints had been left behind in each.

'Tip this one over,' I said to Rafferty. 'Hold it! The bloody diamonds, what happened to them?'

Rafferty looked up at the sky. 'With that kind of explosion I'd say scattered to the four corners of the earth.'

A feeling of sickness spread up into my throat, then Rafferty laughed and said. 'And they would have been if you hadn't hung on to them as I pulled you out of the wreck.'

I put my face in my hands and rubbed away the tiredness. That and the knowledge of being a rich man again was the only tonic I needed.

'Where are they?' I said.

'In the Commander, tucked away in a safe place. Nice feeling, wouldn't you say?'

'The best to date,' I replied. 'Now, tip the drum over; carefully, I just want a small sample in my hands.'

The bluey green avgas trickled into my cupped palms and with it fat globules of clearer fluid. Water!

'It's contaminated, look at this.'

Rafferty looked. 'The stupid bastard didn't use a filter.'

'And Clay didn't check his drains,' I said. I didn't have to say any more. We both knew. Water has a higher specific gravity than avgas, therefore it goes straight to the bottom of the tank. The Dornier would have had enough of the original fuel in the lines to effect a normal start-up, and as he had taxied out and taken off within seconds the fuel in the lines would have been enough. Ten seconds after the Dornier had lifted off the contaminated fuel would have reached the engines, being atomized into a fuel/air mixture for distribution to the various cylinders. Except it wasn't just fuel being mixed with the air, it was fuel and water. And as nobody has yet found a way to turn water into a combustible material . . .

Youssef Ghorab arrived driving his mule and cart and leading a selection of villagers, ranging from scruffy barefooted children to old men with dried-up faces. They reached the clearing and stopped, their eyes drawn to the column of thick black smoke crawling sluggishly into the quiet sky. Clay's sky. He was still the best pilot I'd ever known and I still believed he could have taught the birds a thing or two. That birds rarely crash had nothing to do with it, because birds do not have to rely on man-made machinery to achieve flight. Clay did, and it was that machinery which in the end had let him down. Yes, it was still Clay's sky, and more than ever now.

The village people, having got over the initial shock, were now gathered in conspiratory huddles talking excitedly, eyes darting suspiciously from the wreck to Penny's body and finally to us. Rafferty went on the offensive immediately, striding purposefully towards Youssef Ghorab and catching him by the shoulder. A look of bewilderment flickered through the Arab's eyes as he was gently steered towards the two empty fuel drums.

Rafferty said, '*Mayya fi al benzine!*'

'*Mish mumkin,*' Ghorab replied.

'Like hell it's impossible,' Rafferty said. Then to me, 'Tip that drum over.'

I tipped the drum and Rafferty caught a sample of fuel in his hands. Then he thrust his hands close to Ghorab's face.

'*Mayya . . . ki teer mayya.*'

Understanding slowly dawned in the Arab's eyes as they turned from the water-contaminated fuel to the pall of black smoke at the end of the strip.

'*Robbama ehna otlab al bolis?*' Rafferty said.

Ghorab looked puzzled, or perhaps he didn't fully understand Irish-accented Arabic.

'*Bolis, bolis!*' Rafferty repeated.

'No police . . . not good,' Ghorab said.

'You old sod,' Rafferty laughed, 'you speak English.'

'A leel . . . little English, *effendi*. Not good.'

'Good enough. I am Rafferty, this is Ritchie.' He pointed to me.

'*Tasharrafna*,' he held out a bony hand. 'I am Youssef Ghorab.'

'We know that, my fine friend; now we have some business to talk. You send the other people away, yes?'

Ghorab nodded and went across to the gathering of villagers.

'What are you going to do?' I asked.

Rafferty smiled. 'How about our silence in return for their cooperation?'

'Keep going,' I said.

'Well our cagey old friend is soon going to find out that Penny didn't die in the crash, I mean dying old aeroplanes don't shoot bullets. Right?'

'Right.'

'So he gets rid of the body and waits until we've departed before contacting the authorities in Khartoum. Which puts the crash down to pilot error or whatever else they want to call it.'

'You've forgotten one thing,' I said. 'He's an Arab and whatever he agrees to now he's just as likely to change his mind when we've gone, because by then he will have been able to get rid of the drums . . . which means we have nothing on him. Just our word against his, and we are not of the faith.'

'Where did you learn all that?'

'When I was working for the Queen, spent nine months in Sharjah in the Gulf. Okay, maybe they're a different breed of Arab down this way, but that doesn't alter their basic makeup. We are still infidels.'

'So what do you suggest?'

'I'm too bloody tired and hungry to suggest anything at

the moment, but that's only half of the problem. We still have to get that Commander out of here and with only three hundred or so yards of runway available . . .'

'I've been thinking about that,' Rafferty said. 'I reckon if we strip all the excess weight out of her and take off as much fuel as possible we can just about do it. Then again I could always get Youssef and a few of his mates to cut down a few palm trees.'

I shook my head. 'No, we'll have to leave the trees, might look suspicious if the authorities come up from Khartoum. Who knew we were coming here by the way?'

'Just Muhammad in the control tower.'

'Will he talk?'

'Maybe, maybe not.'

The lust for diamonds and wealth was still there; as it had been in the hotel room in Nairobi when I realized I intended to keep them. Only now the dream was turning into a nightmare; a nightmare of death and broken bodies and more intangibles than I had ever imagined. I remembered Sally asking me if it was wise to get involved . . . No Sall, it wasn't. And if I had listened to you in the first place . . . if I'd listened!

After much discussion, Youssef Ghorab returned. The village people were drifting away reluctantly, casting backward glances as they went. Ghorab waited until they had disappeared around a bend in the track, then said to both of us, 'We talk business now!' In his eyes was the same look of low cunning I had witnessed when he was bartering with Clay.

He may have been a rheumy-eyed old relic with one foot in the grave, but something told me that I would need to watch this man. Very, very carefully.

Chapter Twenty-One

The sun was low by the time we reached the village; the Nile an implacable lava flow of deepest red. A felucca drifted silently towards the riverbank as the boatman expertly hauled down the solitary white sail.

The village itself consisted of a winding sandy street lined with single-storey buildings amongst which were a few walled groves of orange trees and date palms. At the end of the street and glowing pink in the evening light was the inevitable mosque, its minaret waiting patiently for the Muezzin to call the faithful to prayer.

As I had suspected Youssef Ghorab was as crafty as a cartload of monkeys. Using Arabic interspersed with the occasional bout of broken Engish he had conducted the business for us. He was sad that the *kabir ragil* – the big man – with the golden hair had died, and even more pained in his heart that Allah had seen fit to change the petrol to water.

Nice touch that, Allah carries the can for everything in the Arab world. The expression on his face had hardened when he looked towards the body of Penny Valentine. Because she hadn't been in purdah and therefore of the wrong caste, her way of death was 'just'. That's what Ghorab had said anyway. The last part about her death being 'just' was said with a knowing smile. A smile which spoke of bullets and possible murder. And as Allah was responsible for the death of Lucky Clay, Ghorab had obviously decided he was now in a strong bargaining position.

The talk dragged on for an hour, in the Arab tradition of circles. It is improper and unethical to go straight to the heart of the matter. Instead you discuss the weather, the fishing, the different types of boat on the Nile, slowly building up to the big question. Finally, through tiredness more than anything, I short-circuited tradition and said, 'How much?'

Ghorab feigned surprise for a respectable number of seconds, then rubbing his fingers and thumb together he said in mild astonishment, '*Feloos?*'

'Yes, money. How much?'

'I am a simple man, *effendi*, also very poor . . . any gift you bestow on such a wretched servant will be greatly blessed by Allah.'

I smiled to myself at the carefully worded reply. If I offered too little I would greatly offend Allah; if I offered too much Allah would be bounteous in his blessing. I turned to Rafferty.

'Five,' he murmured.

'Dollars?'

He nodded.

'Five hundred dollars,' I said.

Youssef Ghorab's face went quite vacant, as if he had suddenly lost control of his tongue, and his command of the English language likewise.

Rafferty said, '*Khomsomiyya* dollar!'

The Arab's watery eyes flickered from the Irishman to me and back again.

'*Alff* dollar,' he replied.

Rafferty gave a humourless laugh. 'Bastard wants a thousand.'

'I haven't got a bloody thousand,' I snapped.

Rafferty just winked and launched into a fast and furious session of bartering. Ten minutes later the price was fixed at seven hundred and fifty. The figure also included a room for the night, food, and someone to stand guard over the aircraft until dawn. Once we had departed Ghorab was to send a message downriver to Khartoum informing them of the crash. He was to say there were two people on board, a man and a woman and that the plane had exploded on impact. As for the Aero Commander, Rafferty and myself, he and the other villagers had never set eyes on us.

Ghorab had accepted the terms with languid hand-waving and an often repeated '*Ana afham*' – I understand; whilst his eyes greedily watched Rafferty counting out the money from a sizeable bank roll.

Even in death it seemed Penny Valentine was proving to be an expensive lady, although I wouldn't have minded if I had thought I could trust the Arab. But I knew I couldn't. Even if I persuaded him to swear on a stack of Korans six feet high, there was always a way out. Allah was all-forgiving and all-understanding, something akin to the Catholic confessional, only tenfold.

That was when I crushed out the half-smoked cigarette, got to my feet and went over to the body of Penny Valentine. I had to empty her pockets and remove the ring from her finger; if I didn't Ghorab would, and the less amount of evidence left around the better.

I searched the pockets first and found them empty, then I took hold of the coldly clasped hands stained with dried blood.

The ring was missing.

I called Rafferty over. 'Do you think it was one of the villagers? While we were talking to Ghorab.'

'Possible . . . what about Clay?'

'Doubtful, you moved in pretty quickly after the shot was fired . . . anyway that would have been the last thing on his mind.'

Rafferty shrugged. 'Okay, so we tell Ghorab to search the village.'

'No good,' I said. 'He already knows she was shot. If we start asking questions about diamond rings he might just put two and two together and make five.'

'He might have done that already,' Rafferty replied.

'Damn and bloody blast . . . anyway let's get the body loaded up.'

We called the Arab over and lifted Penny Valentine's body onto the rickety old cart and watched as she was taken away to a pauper's funeral.

'I fear she was a star-crossed lady, Stevie boy. A beautiful star-crossed lady.' Then he slapped me on the back and added lightheartedly, 'Come on, we've got work to do.'

We had spent the remainder of the afternoon removing as much surplus weight as possible from the Commander – passenger seats, carpets and rear ferry tank; finally we defuelled the wing tanks to leave about two hours' endurance. Those two hours would get us across the border into Egypt, to Wadi Halfa at least. Satisfied we had done all we could to lighten the aircraft's take-off weight we dragged the stripped-out equipment to the smouldering wreckage of the Dornier. Then dousing everything in petrol and placing the full fifty-five-gallon ferry tank in the centre we set fire to it and ran.

The explosion was a sound of ripping calico culminating in a dull thunder which echoed dramatically in the confine of palms.

Deep blissful silence followed.

We returned from our cover in the trees to the Commander and I placed the silica gel tube in the bottom of my flight bag. Rafferty dragged our holdalls out of the baggage locker then did a final inspection to make sure all the doors were locked.

'You found the keys then?' I remarked.

'Spares,' he said, 'keep them wired up inside the port wheel-well.'

'Better find the ones that Clay threw away,' I said, dropping my flight bag.

After half an hour we gave up. Either Clay had thrown them further than we imagined or one of the villagers had found them and decided to keep them as a souvenir. We would have to check with Youssef Ghorab on that. Aero Commander's keys in a place an Aero Commander was not supposed to have been was tempting fate. James Valentine and his loose ends. You find enough of them and you end up with a bloody great hangman's knot.

The two-mile walk to the village only seemed that way. In reality it was little more than a mile, but as my left knee had had more exercise in the last day than in the preceding month I had to take things easy. Rafferty found me a stout stick and loaded himself up with the bags.

And that is how we arrived at sunset in the dusty village street.

Youssef Ghorab suddenly materialized from one of the small, squat buildings and hurried towards us.

He salaamed and offered a '*Masail kher.*'

We returned the greeting and followed him into his house. The main room was small, almost square, with thick plastered white walls and a bare stone floor. The furniture was equally spartan, a few chairs with lumpy cushions and a similar number of low circular tables with ornate brass tops. In the corner of the room was an arched doorway with a curtain of multi-coloured beads, through which a mouth-watering aroma of rich spicy food filled the air.

Ghorab waved to the chairs. 'Please, you will sit.'

We sat and he drifted across the room and passed through the coloured beads.

'Cosy little place,' Rafferty observed.

I lit a cigarette and looked up at the window, the only one, as the last of the daylight softened the stark hardness of the room.

'How far do you reckon we'll get tomorrow?'

'How far do you want to go?'

'Well, we could stop off in the Greek Islands after we've refuelled at Wadi Halfa.'

'Have to check the distance on that,' Rafferty replied. 'Haven't got the ferry tank now.'

'Hmm. I'd forgotten about that.'

'Ah well, not to worry, we've got all the time in the world now, and that's a fact.' He settled back comfortably into the chair. 'What would you say to a night out on the town?'

'Good idea. Try me again when we reach civilization.'

Rafferty was laughing as Ghorab returned carrying a pressure lamp which roared softly at the ceiling and spilled a yellow light around the room. He placed it carefully on the nearest table, trimmed the wick, and came to join us.

I said, 'Have you sent someone to guard the aircraft?'

'*Aywa*, I have sent a *walad* . . . a boy.'

Rafferty interrupted. 'One other thing Youssef, we have lost some keys for the aeroplane . . . they were on the ground at the airstrip.'

Ghorab looked puzzled. 'You have searched for them?'

'*Aywa*. Would any of your villagers have picked them up?'

'*Mish mumkin*,' Ghorab said emphatically, 'they are good people. They would not take what did not belong.'

Rafferty gave him a look which said he didn't believe a word of it.

The coffee arrived then, served by Ghorab's rotund and elderly wife. It was Turkish coffee with khardomah seed; thick and strong and green in colour. Rafferty looked in dismay at the miniature cups, then gave an impish smile and produced a bottle of Irish from his overnight bag. Ghorab declined, saying he was a good Muslim. Allah it seemed would permit the odd bit of extortion and thieving; even perhaps a once in a while helping hand to send an unloved one across the eternal river . . . but alcohol! That was something else again. Rafferty and I, however, sipped quietly away as the sunset outside changed to dusk, and dusk to velvet night.

The meal when it came was exceptional. Hommos bithina with unleavened bread to scoop it out of a central dish. This was followed by a mouthwatering local fish which had been baked in charcoal. After that more coffee for Ghorab and more of the Irish for the likes of Rafferty and me.

Ghorab told us about the earlier days in Egypt. About a burial chamber at a place called El Maabda. Apparently an American tourist and a guide had crawled down the hole over sand and slippery black stones until they were standing on a bed of corpses. As much as a thousand years of mummified corpses. It was then that some burning wax fell from the guide's candle . . . or so it was thought. The tourists on the outside of the chamber heard a loud noise, which was followed by black smoke pouring from the opening. The American and the guide were never seen again. The fire lasted for eighteen months before burning itself out.

Rafferty smiled disbelievingly at Ghorab. 'Eighteen months seems a long time,' he said.

'It is true *effendi*, the bodies burn very well. They even used them on the trains many years ago . . . in place of wood.'

Rafferty laughed. Ghorab looked offended. 'I believe you, Youssef,' I said, leaning towards the old Arab. 'So does he . . . just had too much to drink.' I indicated the bottle.

Ghorab smiled thinly, but he didn't speak again, except when he showed us to our room, and only then to express a desire that Allah would bless us both with another sunrise and another day.

I hoped so too as I tucked the silica gel tube under the pillow, pulled the mosquito net back into place, and sank into a deep exhausted sleep.

Chapter Twenty-Two

We went out to the airstrip on the back of Ghorab's cart. It was dawn and the air surprisingly chilly. I was reading up the performance section of the Aero Commander's flight manual as the cart jogged uncomfortably along the deep rutted track. After a few more minutes I snapped the manual closed and handed it back to Rafferty. 'According to that we can't get off and clear a fifty-foot obstacle with the take-off distance available.'

Rafferty looked at me through red-rimmed eyes; the result of too much drink and too little sleep. 'Has anyone ever told you that you take life too seriously? Anyway we have two points in our favour!'

'We do?'

'We do indeed. Firstly the palms at the end of the strip are less than fifty feet now . . . thanks to your man Clay.'

'What's the second?'

The enigmatic smile was back. 'We're both suffering from a terminal illness, Stevie boy, generally referred to as life. Now the medical journals might not agree with my prognosis but they still haven't found a cure for it. And besides you wouldn't want to live forever would you?'

'Not ever, Rafferty, but I was counting on a few more years.'

'Take it as it comes, that's my philosophy. Make your own luck and your own good fortune and blow the bloody lot. Then, when it's gone, and assuming you find yourself still here, you repeat the exercise.'

'You should write a book,' I said. 'Fairy stories; you'd make a fortune.'

Rafferty laughed. 'Perhaps I will,' he said. 'When I'm sitting on my yacht amidst the jewelled splendour of the Cote d'Azur.'

The aircraft was as we had left it, except for the dark-skinned Sudanese boy huddled up to the port main wheel searching for warmth where none existed.

Rafferty turned to Youssef Ghorab and took his hand. 'May Allah give you long life, Youssef.'

Ghorab's watery eyes smiled sadly. 'I have already the long life *effendi . . . maal salama.*'

Rafferty said, '*Maal salama,*' and climbed into the aircraft.

Ghorab turned to me, and held out a frail, bony hand. '*Maal salama,* Youssef.'

'May the road lead to salvation,' he said.

I watched as he and the sleepy-eyed boy led the donkey and cart down the shadowed track; then they reached the bend and were gone. It was almost as if they had never existed. Turning away, my eyes panned down the length of airstrip. Our road. Our salvation. Under the circumstances Youssef's last wish had been a significant one.

Fifteen minutes later, having completed the pre-flight checks, we were lined up at the end of the makeshift runway. Me with my fear; Rafferty standing on the brakes, shoving the throttles inexorably forward. Satisfied with the static power check he nodded at me.

I flicked the intercom switch and raised my voice against the sound of the racing engines. 'You did say we were terminal anyway . . .'

His eyes wrinkled into a smile as he released the brakes. I covered the flap lever with a shaking hand, glad at least that the aircraft vibrated, and therefore portrayed my twitching body as a picture of normality. Slowly, with trance-like quality, we accelerated towards the distant trees and the skeletal remains of the Dornier.

At the halfway point I glanced nervously across at the airspeed indicator – sixty knots! Too slow, we weren't going to make it. Rafferty it seemed thought otherwise, or perhaps he just had implicit belief in what I had told him about the flaps. The story which didn't appear in any book of flying, the one that threw the rule book out of the window, going against all teaching. But it had worked once. Different aircraft maybe, but it had worked. Damn it, I couldn't have dreamt it. Could I?

The crooked, broken palms, which had been there, were now here, as Rafferty pulled the aircraft off the ground. Too bloody slow, insufficient flying speed; the aircraft left the ground then sank back and bounced on one of the main wheels. Then we were flying. I snapped the gear selector to up as we staggered skywards in a semi-stall.

The last time I had been in this position we had crashed and two Filipinos had died. The trees converged rapidly towards the cockpit. We were too late!

'Full flaps!' Rafferty yelled.

I rammed the lever down instantly and we collided with a soft invisible wall, a cushion of air, which pushed us vertically with alarming speed. Now we had another problem, the biggest killer of all. In escaping the trees we had deployed full drag flap, now the airspeed wound rapidly back. Back to the point where we would enter a fully developed stall and fall straight out of the sky.

'Get it down,' I screamed, 'I'm pulling in some of the flap.'

Rafferty lowered the nose and kicked in a touch of left rudder, which sent us skidding down towards the Nile. That was all that was left. Sacrifice height for speed. It didn't matter how little, every few feet is an extra knot.

Down, down, down. Fifty feet, thirty, twenty . . . ten! And that was enough; we had the speed, and the equation of aerodynamics – of thrust and lift overcoming weight and drag – sent the Commander upwards into a long steady climb.

No one spoke for a long time, but there was a smell of fear which took a long time to die. I knew it was fear, a faint breath somewhere between stale body sweat and decomposing human flesh, as individual as people or fingerprints, or even the grave itself.

We levelled off at 11,000 feet and Rafferty throttled the engines back to a low satisfied rumble before leaning the mixtures for maximum endurance.

'It would appear,' he said, passing me a cigarette, 'that we are still breathing the good Lord's air.'

'Nice bit of flying,' I said.

'Thanks to you,' he replied. 'Next time though I'll try those flaps a touch earlier.'

'Next time,' I said, with as much conviction as I could muster, 'next time, my Irish friend, you'll be by yourself. To hell with your take it as it comes philosophy, when my day comes I intend to be a long way away from aeroplanes. They've had half my life and I'm damned if they're going to have the rest.'

He grinned. 'As we're millionaires I reckon you can afford it.'

I exhaled blue smoke at the cabin roof. 'What's the plan? Once we get back to the UK that is.'

'Not the UK for a start. We're going to Eire.'

'Same difference, we still have the customs to worry about.'

Rafferty frowned. 'And that could prove to be one hell of an embarrassment, especially if they decide to rummage the plane.'

'What was your original routing?' I asked.

'Once through Egypt, over to Athens, then Rome, Nice, Dinard and direct to Dublin. Not the most direct but the food's better that way.'

'Okay, we'll stick to that, except your final destination is Shannon.'

Rafferty looked puzzled. 'Why?'

'I'll come to that in a minute, first things first. We can't make Athens direct from Wadi Halfa because we don't have the extra tank any more. Right?'

'Right.'

'So we'll have to stop off again in Cairo; from there we continue as planned, until we arrive in Nice that is. Once in Nice I get off and take a scheduled flight to London and then on to Dublin. Are you with me so far?

'Why the schedule?' Then he laughed, 'It wouldn't be that my flying is that bad . . . would it?'

'I've flown with worse,' I mocked. 'Seriously though, it will look less suspicious if there is only one ferry driver on board, especially as it's a single-crew aircraft. Now we both agree that the customs officers up to Dinard are fairly easy going, in fact the French turn the entire thing into a farce.'

Rafferty smiled. 'Arrive at lunchtime and they're all down the pub, you mean?'

'Exactly. Also as you're just in transit nobody really gives a damn. So going back to the Nice drop-off. We land at about noon during their peak period. You develop engine trouble and stay over for a day giving me a hotel number where I can contact you. I then phone you from Dublin and you depart immediately – having rectified the engine, naturally. The next phase is a touch more difficult. Is the aircraft insured?'

'Yes, I told you back in Nairobi . . . why do you ask?'

'I'm coming to that, you depart Nice early morning, routing Dinard then Shannon. I will have hired a car in Dublin and will be driving along your route, we can check that later on the map. You need to be over land by mid-afternoon, while it's still daylight. That's when your engine trouble returns and you start shouting Mayday.'

Rafferty shifted uncomfortably in his seat.

'It's foolproof,' I said reassuringly. 'You can even mention that you have had problems at Nice and as you will have told the French customs officer all about it, he will verify your story. Now listen carefully. I will have one of those VHF airband receivers in the car with me. We work out the frequencies beforehand and I will monitor your transmissions, right down to the Mayday call and on your position. You then make a precautionary landing in a suitable field, I pick up the diamonds, and you wait for the police to arrive . . . having in the meantime dislodged a magneto wire. I return to a hotel in Dublin, you get the plane fixed and continue on to Shannon. We meet up a few days later. How does it sound?'

'Bloody complicated. Why not just put the diamonds in the fuel tank? I mean what are the odds that the customs will search the aeroplane anyway?'

'And there is your answer,' I said. 'Odds! Because whichever way you look at it there is always the chance, remote even though it might be. And that means gambling with a fortune, and it's the only fortune I've got or am likely to get . . .'

Rafferty mulled the proposition around in his mind. 'You know something, the more you think about it the more plausible it becomes. There is only one part that worries me though, what happens if we miss the rendezvous; either your car breaking down or the weather being clamped?'

'I'll get you a forecast before I phone you in Nice; don't worry about the car, I'll give myself plenty of time.'

'Then there's the question of a suitable field!'

'After what you just did back in Karima I'd say that was the least of your problems. I take it you're familiar with the terrain up to Shannon?'

'Reasonably so,' he said.

'Christ I'm an idiot! Slight amendment to operation. You hang fire in Nice for an extra day while I drive down the route. I'll find the field for you, then all I have to do is work out the lat. and long. and pass it over the phone with the weather report.'

Rafferty reached down and took a half empty bottle of whiskey from his flight bag.

'And I thought it was just me with the devious mind.'

'Not devious,' I said. 'Trained. A part of the way to becoming an officer in the Royal Air Force . . . they call it initiative.'

'Drink?'

'That wasn't part of the doctrine according to Lord Trenchard, but thanks.'

Rafferty said, 'So that's it?'

'More or less, there are sure to be one or two refinements I can think of before we put it into operation, but in essence that's it.'

Rafferty looked at his watch. 'Better give Wadi Halfa a call . . . fifteen minutes to run.'

The Arab's voice was annoyed at first. Annoyed that he had not received a flight plan on our movement. Rafferty assured him, with the air of a well-rehearsed liar, that we had left Khartoum that morning and had naturally filed a plan. He even went as far as suggesting he contact Khartoum to verify the story. The Arab gave a grunt and said it was not possible as the HF link was not working. Rafferty gave a bemused smile and waited. Then the Arab asked the purpose of our flight.

Rafferty said, 'Ferry flight, we are just stopping for fuel.'

'What sort of fuel?'

'Avgas.'

'We have no avgas,' the Arab replied with satisfaction. 'You try El Qasr . . . they have fuel.'

'Roger, we are diverting to El Qasr. Maintaining flight level one one zero.'

'Copied Mike Mike Romeo, you will advise me before leaving this frequency.' It was more of an order than a request.

'Yes sir,' Rafferty said with ingratiating humility. 'We will advise.'

'The best-laid plans of mice and men,' I started. 'Where the hell's Al Kasar?'

'El Qasr,' Rafferty said correctively. 'Arab name for Luxor. I think it means castle or military camp. Probably from the time of the Romans.'

'How far?'

He consulted the airways chart. 'About two hundred and twenty.'

I looked at my watch and the airspeed indicator. 'And we've been airborne for fifty-five minutes to date . . . let me have your computer.'

He passed me the circular slide rule, the one which every pilot must learn to master, and I lined up the information. Outside air temperature plus fifteen against pressure altitude of 11,000 feet, then indicated airspeed on the inner scale of 145 knots showing a true airspeed of 178. Say 180! Three miles a minute, with 220 to go.

'Seventy-three minutes to Luxor,' I said. 'What do you reckon on the fuel?'

'I'd say with a few "Hail Marys" and the odd "Our Father" we might make it. We are in the right corner of the world for miracles after all.'

I didn't answer but just sat uncomfortably on the edge of my seat. Below, the white rocky desert; above, sunlit silence. The green fields of England were still a long way away; as much as a lifetime. And in the end it was for the most basic of errors, running out of fuel – just about the worst sin in the book. The accident report would be scathing in its findings and the conclusion of pilot error would for once be justified.

Eleven thousand feet away and unnoticed we crossed the border between northern Sudan and Egypt.

Chapter Twenty-Three

Sixty minutes later we were still there, praying for tailwinds; listening to engines and the constant hiss of airflow. Watching a fuel-gauge needle which had long since pointed at empty.

'I make it about twenty miles,' Rafferty said.

I didn't speak, preferring instead the companionable rumble of the engines. As long as we had that we were winning. I think Rafferty must have sensed my feelings and got on with tuning in the Luxor radio beacon and calling up the tower on 118.1. Through my headset came another voice of another controller running through the litany of circuit-joining procedure.

'Cleared direct to finals double Mike Romeo . . . runway in use zero two . . . surface wind three fife zero at one zero . . . QNH one zero one fife or two niner point niner seven inches . . . outside air indicating plus two six . . . advise beacon inbound or runway in sight, over.'

Rafferty flicked his transmit switch: 'Roger cleared finals zero two, one zero one fife and call the runway . . . *shukran*.'

'*Afwan sadeek*.'

Rafferty said to me, 'Good controller!'

I nodded.

'I'll leave the descent for a while . . . might need the extra height.'

Fate had been tempted and the port engine missed a beat. Distinctive, unmistakable! Rafferty checked the sudden slight yaw and eased the mixture levers gently forward.

'Come on, old girl, you can make it . . . you wouldn't want to end your days in such a godforsaken hole as this now, would you?' The Irishman spoke to the aeroplane and patted the instrument panel with great tenderness, as

224

if trying to reassure her that she was the most beautiful lady in the world.

I ceased to exist as of that moment. Now it was just the pilot and plane. And in any plane the pilot's life comes first.

We were less than five miles out when the port engine started playing up again, only this time it jumped and backfired. The corresponding engine gauges fluctuated wildly. Rafferty pushed the mixtures to full rich and lowered the nose. We were into the descent as the engine caught.

Three miles out.

The usual expression on Rafferty's face, depicting carefree nonchalance, had changed to one of survival as he pressed the transmit switch and gave the finals call. I felt the gritty sweat on my face and neck as I stared at the ground below. It was too far to fall. I screwed myself into my seat and clenched my hands until they hurt. This had to be it! It had to be!

Two miles out.

They both went at the same time – dramatically. Belching and spitting and backfiring. The aircraft's nose swung violently in yaw and pitch, defying all attempts to be controlled. The spasms of a dying man, or woman . . . or aeroplane.

One mile out.

In my mind I told Rafferty to keep going, as the gauge needles jumped and stuttered and died. Told him that he could have my share of the diamonds if he got me out of this. But he wasn't listening, he was still talking sweetly to his aeroplane, lost in his own little world of Irish magic.

Four hundred yards out.

Air lock? I reached for the mixture levers and pulled them both back.

Rafferty grabbed my hand. There was frenzy in his voice when he said, 'What the hell are you doing?'

'Shut up . . . get the nose up . . . now!'

He pulled the control column back and I slammed the mixtures to full rich. There was a moment's hesitation, as the last dregs of fuel swilled towards the back of the tanks, and down into the engines. Then they caught, loud and clean and healthy.

'Keep it fairly flat,' I yelled. 'I'm giving you the gear now.' Three green lights flickered on. One . . . two . . . three. Like fairy lights on a Christmas tree. I looked up as the tyres screamed onto the runway. We were down.

I flopped back in my seat, feeling for all the world like a sweat-stained, worn-out rag doll.

'Thanks,' Rafferty said.

'Don't mention it . . . nearly cost me a lot of money . . .'

'I don't understand . . .' he started.

'Forget it, let's get to the terminal before they pack up for good.'

The airport was a vast, sprawling emptiness, as big as Gatwick or Manchester, except there were no aeroplanes. Just our Aero Commander. The terminal building was impressively large. A sand-coloured feat of beautiful architecture. The control tower on the north end pointed skyward like a misplaced minaret. The entire place looked deserted.

Rafferty taxied to a stop, applied the park brake and cut the engines. The propellers shuddered to a stop, leaving us with needles drifting down dials and the familiar tinkling running-down noises of aeroplane cockpits. That and the post-flight sound of engines inside your head. The one that took longer to die.

I took out my cigarettes and passed one to Rafferty. He accepted it without a word.

'It's becoming a habit,' I said.

'What's that?'

'Well, that's nearly two in one day . . . most pilots last a lifetime without even coming near to an accident.'

'And most pilots,' Rafferty said simply, 'don't ferry aeroplanes for a living.'

'Any whisky left?'

'About three fingers, not much to celebrate on . . . but enough.' He rummaged in his flight bag. 'After you,' he said, handing me the bottle.

We were still sitting when a blue-suited little Arab and a soldier appeared from the terminal about fifty yards away.

'Reception committee,' I said.

'Looks that way. I'll do the tower duties, landing fee and flight plan, it would be a mighty climb for that bad leg of yours.'

'Thanks.'

'I'll meet you in the baggage hall afterwards.'

'Where's that?'

'I'll show you on the way in, it's the place you go for immigration and passport control. You'd better take my passport as well.' He reached back into his flight bag. 'And you'll need this.' He handed me two Egyptian ten-pound notes. I tucked the pink-tinged paper money in my shirt pocket and his passport in my flight bag.

'Reference our visit to Ireland,' I said, climbing out of my seat. 'It might be better if I take a British Airways flight direct from Cairo to London. That way I'll make up a day while you're in transit to Nice.'

'Sounds good to me, we'd better run through it again on the way up to Cairo. You'll want a contact number for me in Nice.'

'Damn . . . the hotel you mean?'

'Not too important, there's a handling agent I sometimes use . . . I'll check my address book later for the phone number. If the worst comes to the worst I know one or two hotels in Dublin where you could stay. Then I could phone you once I've arrived in Nice.'

'Might be the best way.'

'Of course you're being very trusting,' he said, following me back to the passenger door.

'I am?'

'You are! I could always slip away to South America!'

I stepped down onto the bleached white concrete. 'But being such a good Catholic,' I said, 'you wouldn't dream of it, would you?'

He laughed, 'You're not wrong, Stevie boy . . . we may be a lot of things, but we do keep our word.'

227

The little Arab greeted Rafferty like a long-lost brother, then posted the soldier to stand guard over the Commander. That non-essential act would require at least a couple of packets of cigarettes before we parted.

We were led across to the terminal where the shifty-eyed little Arab said he would go and arrange the fuel. Rafferty waited until he was out of earshot before saying, 'A sly one and make no mistake. Now down to business, you go through that doorway, the offices are on the left. I'll see you there in about ten minutes.'

Rafferty's footsteps were echoing down the stone stairs as I pushed open the tall grey doors which led to the baggage hall. Baggage hall? It was more like a vast empty cathedral with tall stone columns reaching majestically upwards to a high roof; the darkness and silence borrowed from the tombs of ancient Egypt. To my left, and the left of the colonnade, a low baggage ramp stretched away into the shadows.

As I rounded the first pillar I saw the shaft of daylight beaming vertically downwards from the high roof window, capturing millions of dust particles which glittered with the magnificence of miniature jewels. The grey-suited rotund figure was standing quite still, the light reflecting from his shiny bald head like a halo.

I walked slowly towards him.

'*Sabahil kher*,' he said. His voice was almost a whisper.

'*Kayfa halik.*'

'*Bikher . . . wa inta?*'

'*Kwayyisa.*'

Near enough. We had asked how each other was. It seemed we were both fine; except I had just about run out of Arabic.

He must have guessed as much when he said in English, 'You are the pilot?'

'One of the pilots, there are two.'

'*Itnen* pilot?'

'*Aywa . . .* two.'

He moved his left hip away from the baggage ramp.

'We go to my office.' He waved expansively towards a

white-painted door which was covered in Semitic squiggles.

The room was small, square, and furnished to a bare minimum. I sat on one side of the desk, he on the other, copying details from my passport into a giant ledger. When we had finished I passed him Rafferty's and watched him go through the same procedure. He wrote with a slow, careful hand.

'I think that is all,' he said, handing back the passports, 'except you will now go to the next office.'

'*Shukran*,' I said, getting to my feet. He didn't answer. Then I noticed the ledger was still open before him. His eyes were expressionless and unblinking. I reached into my shirt pocket, took out one of the notes and placed it neatly between the pages.

He closed the book with careful precision.

'*Afwan*,' he whispered.

He followed me out of the office, switching the light off as he left. Then he went past the end column and out of the main door. His footsteps were as soft as his voice.

The next office was a carbon copy of the first, except there were two Arabs and they were both dressed in clean white *galobeas*. A similar procedure was followed with the vaccination certificates. Satisfied all was well, the Arab who had been doing the writing edged his book towards me. I slipped the note between the pages.

'May Allah go with you,' the scribe said.

'And with you my friend.'

'*Shukran*.'

'*Afwan*,' I replied.

They both smiled with the innocence of choir boys and followed me out into the baggage hall, closing their office door behind them. They left hand in hand, giggling and talking in low effeminate tones. I sat on the baggage ramp and lit a cigarette. It might cost a few Egyptian pounds but at least it was friendly and totally painless. Smuggle what you like, and as long as you pay your way your passage will be swift and unhindered.

I put the cigarette packet back into my shirt pocket and felt a small crumpled sheet of paper. The list! I

229

straightened it out and moved into the shaft of daylight. The pain started again. The pain of lost love; the sort of pain I thought only affected the young. The only difference now was that she would be in my mind forever . . . home for good.

Now I had to sort out a flight from Cairo to London, and from London on to Dublin. By Christmas I could be searching for a country cottage in the depths of Cornwall, or Devon, or Dorset; and a dark blue Aston Martin.

The dream shattered suddenly, like expensive lead crystal. One minute it was whole and totally believable – the next, a million fragments scattered on a dusty airport floor in Egypt.

'Mr Stephen Ritchie?' The voice had asked a question. Coldly. And the question was still echoing between the tall pillars. But it wasn't the question that made my heart stop, it was the voice. English with the faintest trace of American. The voice on the telephone. The voice from Paris. Max Goldstein.

I sat there frozen in fear. How the hell did he know it was me? How did he know I would be here today? Then I remembered the line from his letter of instruction, something about 'there is a possibility that I will meet you along the way to accompany you to the final destination'.

'Max Goldstein,' I said hesitantly. 'Is that you?'

'Full marks, Mr Ritchie, full marks. Now perhaps you could explain exactly what is going on?'

'The Dornier you mean?'

'Amongst other things, yes,' he said matter of factly.

'As you seem to be aware of my movements,' I said, trying to put a little composure back into my voice, 'I would have thought you would have known it was stolen in Nairobi.'

'Possibly.'

'So I coopted a ferry pal of mine to try to get it back. It's as simple as that.'

'Perhaps, but why didn't you contact me from Nairobi?'

'I didn't have time. I was at the airport when the Dornier was stolen. Rafferty – he's the ferry pilot I mentioned – and I saw it turn into the Rift Valley after takeoff, so we picked up our things and tried to head him off at Khartoum.'

'Him, Mr Ritchie, how do you know it was a man?'

'Okay her, him, it, say what you like . . . I don't know. Just a figure of speech.'

'So you went to Khartoum?'

'Almost had him as well,' I said. 'We saw the plane overflying at about ten thousand feet, but by the time we got airborne we didn't stand a chance of finding him. We headed this way on the off chance, that's all.'

There was silence, then Goldstein said, 'Why did you think he was coming this way?'

'The clearances. The clearance telexes were inside the aircraft, so whoever stole the plane would obviously stick to that route, or so I thought.'

More silence.

'And you have no idea why anyone would steal the Dornier?' he said.

'Why does anybody steal anything . . . ? Personal gain, I imagine.'

'Why didn't you telex me from Khartoum?'

'Time, we didn't have the time. We'd just refuelled and contacted the tower to try to find out if they had anything on the Dornier, when it overflew on a northerly heading. Anyway, as you're here it wouldn't have been much good to contact your Paris office would it?'

'But you didn't know that, did you, Mr Ritchie?'

'No, but I was going to get in touch with you as soon as possible,' I lied. 'Anyway, why all the melodrama?'

'Melodrama?'

'Yes, why don't you come out of the shadows, this bloody place is eerie enough without me talking to a voice in the darkness.'

'In good time, Mr Ritchie, in good time.'

'Look,' I said 'it's about time I went and found Rafferty. He's just gone to check with air traffic, they might have something on the Dornier.'

'Don't worry about your friend Mr Rafferty, someone

is asking him a few questions at the moment. He will join us shortly.'

I should have known. Max Goldstein, heavily into diamond smuggling and God knows what else, would at least have a helper. And Rafferty and I were unprepared. We hadn't even planned for this contingency. How the hell could I have forgotten about Goldstein? Perhaps I hadn't, perhaps subconsciously I felt he wouldn't be waiting. And even if he had he would be looking for the Dornier. And as he had never set eyes on me before . . .

'How did you know it was me?' I asked.

'I have my ways,' Goldstein replied. 'The passport officer is a personal friend of mine.'

I finished my cigarette and dropped it onto the floor.

'How long will your . . .' I'd just started the question when the tall entrance doors banged open.

'Wait there Mr Ritchie, I won't be a moment.'

I heard Goldstein's footsteps moving towards the doors. In a pig's eye I'd wait here. Rafferty's story would have been different for sure. There was no way we could have said exactly the same thing, which meant Goldstein would smell a rat straight away. I picked up my flight bag and eased myself off the baggage ramp and moved into the darkness. There had to be another way out. But where?

I was still moving towards the opposite end of the hall when the lights suddenly went on. Bright white lights reaching down from every corner.

'That's far enough, Mr Ritchie,' Goldstein shouted. 'I suggest you start walking this way . . . immediately.'

'What the hell are you talking about?' I shouted.

'I think you know,' he said angrily. 'Karima? You forgot to mention Karima.'

I dodged behind a column, still looking for a door to the outside world.

'Karima?' I called out. 'We did drop in as a matter of fact, just tying up loose ends . . . I mean it was possible that the Dornier could have stopped off there.'

'And crashed, Mr Ritchie?'

232

'What the hell are you talking about now?' I shouted back.

A distant muttering of voices.

'You have ten seconds, Mr Ritchie. In ten seconds your friend Mr Rafferty will be killed.'

'Okay, I'm coming out.' I moved back to the aisle between the offices and the baggage ramp and started walking. The only sound was my footsteps echoing between the columns. I was little more than halfway when I heard a slight scuffling sound behind me. The sound of a shoe or sandal being scraped lightly over sanded concrete.

I spun round and caught the impression of sudden movement as something crashed into my skull. There was no pain, just a flurry of stars giving way to unconsciousness.

Chapter Twenty-Four

My return to consciousness found me propped up against a rough cement wall, the heat of midday and the dry dusty desert chafing gently against my face. I struggled to open my eyes, blinking back double vision and the dull throbbing ache inside my head.

'What the hell's going on?' I said, turning to the figure sitting beside me.

Rafferty managed a laconic smile before replying. 'Same question I asked when I was dragged out of the tower twenty minutes ago!'

The pieces came together then. Slowly and painfully unshrouding the shadow of memory. 'Where's Goldstein?' I said.

Rafferty lifted his head. 'Over there . . . at the plane.'

My eyes focused across the glare of concrete apron, to the Aero Commander and the refuelling truck. A white-suited figure was watching an Arab pump fuel into the wings. The heat haze gave it that unreal quality of a mirage shimmering up out of a silver sea.

'What's he doing, why's he refuelling?'

'Would you believe we're going to Cyprus?'

'Cyprus?'

'That's what the man said. Larnaca to be exact; apparently he's got a boat to catch.'

I looked beyond Rafferty, catching the movement in the shadows at the corner of the building. 'Who's that?'

'The guy who banged you on the head,' Rafferty replied without turning around. 'And if you've got a notion to even up old scores I'd forget it . . . he's got a Browning nine millimetre, and I get the distinct impression he knows how to use it.'

I slumped back against the wall. 'Got a cigarette?'

Rafferty dug around in his pockets and threw me the pack.

He said, 'What puzzles me is how this guy just happens to be here . . . if I remember correctly wasn't he the one who set up this ferry trip of yours in the first place?'

'Yeah . . . he's based in Paris.'

'That's what I thought you said. So what's he doing here?'

'Something I forgot to mention, in fact something I'd forgotten myself. In his original letter of instruction he said there was a strong possibility he might meet me en route and accompany me to the final destination . . . Tel Aviv!'

'Sweet Jesus . . .' Rafferty said dejectedly.

I ground out the cigarette. 'Don't remind me,' I replied bitterly. 'I'd just got it into my mind that Goldstein was nothing more than a middle man in an aircraft sales deal. Then after what happened in Zomba . . . and Karima, it went clean out of my mind.'

Rafferty studied his long slim fingers for a moment, then ran them back through his hair. 'So you figure your man here is the key figure in this diamond operation?'

'One of them at least . . . has to be.'

'What the hell, no use crying over spilt milk now, is there!'

'Perhaps not . . . what happened to the luck of the Irish by the way?'

Rafferty pulled his facial muscles into the remnants of a smile. 'Only so much in a day Stevie boy; precious stuff you see.' The smile vanished at the thought, being replaced by a concentrated frown. 'Now there's irony for you,' he added.

'What's that?'

'The Serena bar in Nairobi. Do you recall asking me what *mazel und broche* meant and I said luck and blessing.'

'So?'

'So! So now it all comes flooding back. The expression is used by *diamantaires*, they seal every business transaction with a handshake and the words *mazel und broche*.'

Rafferty laughed quietly to himself. 'Now if you'd said at the time it was to do with diamond smuggling, or better still if only I'd remembered when you did . . . ah well, there you go. All part of the tapestry Stevie boy, deception in every weave.'

'I've a feeling it's going to be more than that . . . what's going to happen when we get to Cyprus?'

'Your man Goldstein didn't say.'

'As far as I'm concerned he doesn't have to . . . I already know. What's the distance to Cyprus?'

Rafferty mulled the question over in his mind for a few moments. 'About six hundred nauticals give or take a bit. Have to go north initially to clear Egyptian airspace.'

I said, 'And if I remember the Commander's range figures she'll go over eight hundred miles to dry tanks.'

'At sixty-five per cent power . . . yes.'

'What speed will that give us?'

'Hundred and eighty knots.'

'So our time en route will be over three hours.'

Rafferty looked at me. 'That sounds right . . . so what are you getting at?'

'The way out,' I said quietly.

Max Goldstein joined us fifteen minutes later. The bowser, having completed the refuelling operation, chug-chugged noisily away in a cloud of dirty black smoke.

'Mr Ritchie,' he said, stopping a safe distance away from Rafferty and myself, 'I'm pleased to see you have recovered from your unfortunate little accident.'

I levelled my eyes at his. 'Forget the niceties Goldstein, they don't suit you. Now perhaps you will tell me what exactly is going on?'

He considered the question; the depressions in the corners of his mouth giving him a slightly cynical expression. Then he said, 'For a man of your obvious investigative zeal, Mr Ritchie, I would have thought the answer was self-explanatory.'

'Meaning?'

'Meaning,' he said coldly, 'we are going to kill you.' His

236

dark eyes twitched towards Rafferty. 'And your Irish friend, of course.'

I stared at the dark brooding face; the too-big Roman nose which curved round like a giant beak. Between his eyes, which looked almost black in colour, a strongly etched vertical line marked him out as a man of perseverance. The hair was oily black, combed straight back, giving the ugly features that final raw and brutal severity.

'You've obviously found the diamonds!' I said at length.

The start of a smile moved across the thin lips, exposing badly decaying teeth. 'In the flight bag, yes. Not a very ingenious place Mr Ritchie . . . I was somehow expecting more from you.'

'But you forget,' I said, 'I wasn't expecting anything from you. In fact I was under the impression it was Valentine all along.'

Goldstein flicked away a persistent fly. 'Valentine! Ah yes . . . a pawn with dreams of grandeur; a pawn who had promoted himself to a knight or even a bishop.'

'And you! What's your position on the board . . . king?'

'More important than that; in fact you could say the power behind the throne.'

I said, 'The queen!'

'Indeed, Mr Ritchie, indeed. The controller of the game. I like to think life is very much a chess game on a grand scale. Opening gambit; middle game; and end game. The middle game of course is where you win . . . if you're going to win at all, that is.'

'From that I take it you're calling check.'

Goldstein laughed; an evil piratical laugh. The non-musical echo of a cracked bell. 'Check! Check! Surely checkmate.'

'If the game was over . . . maybe!'

The laughter was still there when he said, 'Over, Mr Ritchie, over. It was over a long time ago. In fact it was over before it even started . . . you see I own all the pieces.'

'And you make up the rules as you go along, I suppose?'

'Perceptive as well, I see.'

'So when do we leave?'

'Right now,' Goldstein replied. 'The sooner the better.'

Rafferty stirred. 'Would it be possible to get a bite to eat before we leave? It's been a long day and looks to be getting longer by the minute.'

Goldstein turned impatiently to the Irishman. 'We haven't the time,' he said sharply. 'Besides there are no catering facilities at the airport.'

Rafferty persisted. 'How about the town?'

'Too far.'

'Then pal, I'd say you've got a problem, because until me and the Captain have eaten we're not moving an inch.'

Goldstein clenched and unclenched his fists with the menacing air of high explosive on a fast fuse. 'You've got exactly one minute,' he hissed. 'Sixty seconds!'

'Then what?' I said, climbing slowly to my feet. 'Then you'll shoot us, I suppose. Kind of defeats the object, wouldn't you say . . . after all you're the one who has to get to Cyprus.'

Goldstein gave a twisted little laugh. 'Don't concern yourself with my travel problems, Mr Ritchie . . . they can be overcome.'

'Hire another pilot, you mean?'

'Why not?'

I laughed. 'Because,' I said. 'Because this is bloody Egypt, not downtown Miami on a sunny afternoon. And when it comes to East-of-Suez Arabs flying aeroplanes you've got problems.'

'You overestimate your worth, Mr Ritchie . . . people like you are ten a penny . . . and even then I consider the price too high.'

I shrugged. 'Bullshit, Goldstein, and you know it. These clowns don't even have the coordination to use the rhythm method, never mind fly the white man's big metal birds . . . I therefore suggest if you want to get to Cyprus you do as we ask.'

Goldstein took a black cheroot from a leather case, lit it, and then paced slowly back and forth. After a while he stopped. 'As you wish,' he said quietly. 'I will send Mustafa into Luxor . . .'

I turned to the shadows. 'He's an Arab then?'

Goldstein grinned. 'He is many things to many people. By profession however he is simply a killer . . . a thief who steals life. And if you have any ideas that this concession of a few more hours is going to help you with your obvious escape plans, I'd forget it.' He inhaled deeply on the cheroot before adding, 'No one gets away from Mustafa!'

We were still sitting nearly an hour later. Goldstein had allowed us the luxury of moving into the shadow of the building; away from the fierce heat of early afternoon. My mouth and throat were cracked and dry, even the bodily function of making saliva seemed to have given up the ghost. My eyes moved across to Goldstein, sitting against the wall next to the main terminal entrance door. The Browning hi-power rested gently on his knee. 'You find it hard to believe!' Goldstein said tonelessly.

'Once I might have,' I said. 'Not any more. One thing you didn't tell me, though; what about Valentine? This was the last shipment after all.'

'He would have been eliminated as it happens, but as we have been saved that minor task . . .'

'And you masterminded the entire operation?'

'In a manner of speaking, yes . . . the ultimate insurance swindle, wouldn't you say?'

I played along, preening his ego, letting him talk himself into a corner. My corner! 'Indeed. First you con the world by manipulating its emotions, and then when the illusion begins to falter . . . this!'

Goldstein smiled openly. 'As you so rightly put it, Mr Ritchie, conning the world. And that was the only reason it worked . . . because of people's gullibility.'

'There is a question to which I don't seem to have an answer,' I said. 'Why Tel Aviv with the final shipment?

239

The diamonds are cut and polished, after all.'

'Who said anything about Tel Aviv,' Goldstein replied. 'We are going to Cyprus.'

'And the Dornier deal with the Israelis?'

Goldstein shrugged. 'An idea for counter insurgency measures that went wrong. Now they will probably buy up a bunch of equally old Skyraiders from the Americans.'

'With the insurance money from the crashed Dorniers you mean?'

Goldstein laughed. 'The way of the world, Mr Ritchie . . . the way of the world.'

The rain started north of Baltim; a light fine drizzle which hissed persistently against the windscreen. By then it was night. Black, endless, lonely. A place I should never have been. A place which made my skin crawl with fear. A fear which stops hearts; a cringing, sweating, whining fear which reduces men to gibbering imbeciles. A skytrap. A rotting, stinking death hole, full of pilots who had once been afraid of the sky. Now their spectral images had sent out the angels of death to lead me inexorably towards the final landing place.

The Commander shuddered as it hit a patch of light turbulence. I felt my bladder weaken and nearly give way; felt the uncontrollable shakes start up in my legs; felt my mouth go dry; felt the sweat run cold on my body. Throughout it all the tiny voices inside my head were screaming at me to go back . . . pleading . . . begging . . . crying! But now the inner torment was acting as a spur, driving me on; forcing my hands to keep a steel-like grip on the control yoke. There could be no going back . . . not any more.

From somewhere in the dull red glow of the instrument panel I thought I saw Sally's face smiling back at me. Then there were other faces; faces from the past sliding slowly by like an endless family of mourners. The faces ended at Luxor and the unforeseen meeting with Goldstein. From there it became the reason. The reason for it all. How a large South African diamond cartel had created a worldwide belief that diamonds were scarce and therefore precious. Then linking the rarity value with romance and legitimacy and investment potential, had conned the world for years. Their problems began when massive deposits were discovered in Australia. That and a journalistic scoop by some nosey reporter who had confirmed that the rumour about Israeli dealers was true. The rumour that by careful stockpiling they had undercut De Beers' control of the market. The final collapse of world diamond prices was suddenly only a matter of time away.

Goldstein however, being one and a half steps ahead of the rest of that world, had foreseen it all years ago. It was when diamond prices were at their peak that he decided to take out his insurance for old age. In more ways than one! It had started when Felix Schmocker had applied for the post of chief security officer at the Williams Diamond Corporation; the company of which Goldstein had controlling shares. On checking Schmocker's record he accidentally uncovered one or two bent deals with minor gangsters. Schmocker's qualifications were therefore impeccable. Once in, he was easily bought off by Goldstein. They then planned the robbery, which being an inside job was not an altogether impossible task.

Following the robbery Schmocker had been arrested. Everything was running to plan. Naturally the evidence was sufficiently threadbare and, with Goldstein vouching for his employee, he was subsequently found not guilty. For Felix Schmocker, it was all working out perfectly; right down to his premature retirement on a substantial pension. What he didn't know, however, was that his days had been carefully numbered. What he also didn't know was that the police tail, which Goldstein had fobbed off as short term, had in fact been instigated by Goldstein. What better way to prove the integrity of his company? Help the police and the insurance agents to lay a false trail and then catch the thief red-handed with the ten-million-dollar diamond shipment.

Goldstein being Goldstein, however, then engineered a

241

perfectly normal car smash in the middle of Johannesburg – before the very eyes of the local police. The only victim of that smash, the victim who was incinerated at the wheel of his car, was none other than Felix Schmocker. The diamonds it appeared were lost forever. Following that, the insurance company paid up and Goldstein went away a happy man. Happy, because in the interim period he had stashed the diamonds away in southern Zimbabwe; he had also found the vehicle to transport them to Tel Aviv. That vehicle had been uncovered accidentally in a conversation he had had with Felix Schmocker; a conversation which had concerned James Valentine. A conversation which had given Goldstein the ultimate weapon – blackmail! James Valentine had had little choice. Either do as he was told, or risk public scandal and disgrace which would wipe out a lifetime of work. Valentine had succumbed. Homosexual relationships, no matter how far away in the recesses of a distant, cobwebby past, were still damning enough to end careers . . . and lives.

I looked down into the black night and felt a wave of dizziness sweep over me. Why the hell had I insisted on doing the flying! Rafferty could have managed just as well. A distant lightning flash ahead of the nose lit up a long seething corridor of cumulonimbus. The skytrap was closing in.

Rafferty said, 'Looks pretty bad!'

'Take over a minute.'

He took control, while I slipped my headset down around my neck and turned back to Goldstein and his henchman. They were both sitting on a number of squares of foam packing we had scrounged from the freight sheds at Luxor. As the passenger seats had been burned at Karima, it was all we could find. Now with the unheralded bad weather my plan might stand a better chance of working. Neither of them had seat harnesses.

I said to Goldstein, 'Might be a few bumps ahead . . . shouldn't be too bad though.'

He leaned forward until the ugly features of his face were caught in the soft red glow of the instrument panel. 'For your sake,' he said meaningfully, 'it had better not be.'

I looked across at Mustafa, the silent Arab with the gun. He betrayed no emotion, his saturnine face set with the permanence of granite. The true professional in every sense of the word. A cold, calculating assassin.

I turned back to Goldstein. 'Nothing I can do about the weather . . . you'll just have to hang on.'

His eyes narrowed. 'How long before we reach Larnaca?'

'About forty-five minutes at a guess.' And as much as a lifetime, I almost added. He shrank back into the shadows.

'I've got it,' I said to Rafferty, and took over control.

'Do you want me to try Larnaca approach?'

I turned the instrument panel lights down to their minimum intensity and peered ahead into the night. The lightning flashes were getting near. 'Five minutes!' I said. 'Give it another five minutes.'

Rafferty nodded. He understood.

That five minutes was the longest I had ever known. Three hundred seconds taking an eternity to sweep around the clock face. Three hundred soundless ticks to what seemed certain death. I moved my right hand to cover the two throttles. I was as ready as I would ever be. I ran over the sequence again in my mind. Something an Air Force instructor had taught me over twenty years ago. The loop is one of the four basic manoeuvres which make up all aerobatics. On the face of it it appears to be an easy enough exercise . . . on the face of it! To do it well; to describe 360 degrees in the vertical plane and hit your own slipstream at the bottom requires many hours of patient practice. Not that I intended to complete a loop, I doubted the Commander would get round; especially as I hadn't done aerobatics for what could have been a thousand years. What I was banking on was the sudden effect of positive g on the two passengers. Normally an average pilot will black out at between 3 to 5

243

g, although he may momentarily withstand an acceleration of 8 g. Passengers however, not being able to anticipate the imminent g loading, will always go before the pilot. As Rafferty was aware of the five-minute signal, he would follow me through mentally and hopefully stay conscious to carry out the final part of the operation.

At four minutes and thirty seconds on the stopwatch I eased the nose gently down and watched the airspeed gradually increase. The altimeter slipped silently out of 10,000 feet; 155 knots indicated gave us a true airspeed, when rectified for temperature and altitude, of 195 . . . I tried to keep it steady at that . . . sweat running down my face. The aircraft jostled violently as we hurtled into an embedded cumulonimbus; the rain turned to hail and suddenly the instruments were alive, shaking, dancing, totally unreadable. Ten seconds to go. Christ, I couldn't go through with it. I couldn't! I saw Rafferty's hands in my peripheral vision; sliding down beneath his seat . . . unclipping the fire extinguisher. Five seconds . . . four . . . three . . . two . . . one . . . GO! I bit my lip savagely, feeling the salty blood run into my mouth as I heaved the control column back in a vicious whiplash movement. The effect was devastating . . . I'd overdone it. I felt my body slam down into the seat; felt my eyes pushing down my cheeks; felt my mouth forced open, pulling my bottom lip beyond my chin. As the Commander hit the vertical I stabbed the controls forward and almost floated out of the seat. Now it was negative g. Rafferty had spun round as the g eased up and fired the bottle. The bottle which contained CO_2 powder. And I had forgotten! Forgotten the effect . . . the anomaly. Not to be used in a confined space; and what was a cockpit? Now it was too late, the white powder swirled around me like a fog. An irritant which burned into the eyes . . . I was blind! The plan had backfired. I couldn't see a damn thing. I heard an earpiercing scream. It sounded like Goldstein. What about Mustafa . . . get the bastard . . . perhaps he's still blacked out. Jesus . . . what was happening? I tried to rub the stinging pain out of my eyes, but it became worse.

Through a watery red haze the instrument panel wavered gently. The dust cloud was beginning to settle. That was when I saw the airspeed! Or what little was left of it. I kicked in full left rudder . . . what the bloody hell was happening? We were inverted. The thunderstorm . . . the turbulence! Altimeter . . . altimeter: 8,000 feet. Going down fast . . . which bloody way? Which way? Airspeed . . . watch the bloody airspeed . . . caution range . . . watch the red line!

The explosion was like a bomb going off inside an empty room. The sudden white-lit blast shattering eardrums; drowning out the screaming engines; the thunderous hiss of airflow. The Browning hi-power! I turned from the controls and grabbed Rafferty by the shoulder. He slumped forward into the seat, falling hard against the controls, pushing the plane into a near vertical dive.

Chapter Twenty-Five

Rafferty couldn't have weighed more than 150 pounds; but 150 pounds of dead weight can be ten times that much. Or so it seemed. 'Come on, Rafferty . . . for Christ's sake . . .' I took hold of him with both hands and hauled him back into his seat. He was half against me as I grabbed for the controls. Altimeter 3,500 . . . 3,000 . . . 2,500. Airspeed . . . through the red line . . . Jesus Christ we had exceeded VNE; the manufacturers' 'never-exceed' speed. Bloody, bloody throttles, you stupid bastard . . . I slammed them closed. The engines crackled and backfired viciously. Level the wings . . . level the bloody wings . . . now back on the column . . . come on pull . . . pull. Easy! Easy! We still need to keep it in one bloody piece! The altimeter rocketed through 2,000. Jesus God, we weren't going to make it . . . we weren't going to make it!

Wheels! . . . get the wheels down . . . extra drag . . . probably lose the bloody lot in the slipstream . . . Sod that, just move. I rammed the gear selector down and heard the terrifying scream of the aircraft coming apart.

Except it wasn't the aircraft – not yet at least. It was the undercarriage doors being ripped away. I saw the sea as the frightening image of further structural break-up flashed through my mind. There was nothing left; nothing until my hand reached unconsciously for the flap lever and pushed it all the way down. The thought that one flap might be ripped off and the other remain never entered into it. The thought that when that happened we would commence a final series of rolls to instant death. It was all that was left; the only way of slowing down the uncontrollable dive.

They went, both at the same time; but not before they had ballooned us back towards the sky. Then they ripped away, hitting the tailplane as they went. Now the bloody elevator was playing up. 'Rafferty!' I screamed, and shook him violently. He fell sideways towards his side of the cockpit. Behind me all was silent. We were down to about one hundred feet. It was still raining or perhaps it was sea spray. And the aircraft wanted to climb! I wound on full nose-down trim . . . nothing . . . nothing . . . nothing! It was still going up. Now it was taking all of my physical strength to stay straight and level. Which way was Cyprus . . . and how far? I looked up at the standby compass, bathed in its own little pool of red light. It read 045 degrees. I laughed like a maniac; a great wild, convulsive fit of laughter. We were still on bloody course! After all that . . . we were still on course!

Rafferty began to make low moaning noises about two minutes later. I went to shake his left shoulder, taking my right hand away from the control column. The Commander reared up like a frightened stallion. Forget Rafferty . . . just keep pushing . . . pushing . . . pushing. There was a sharp stabbing pain in my chest now; that and the muscular ache in my arms as the exertion slowly began to tell. The sweat still continued to run into my eyes, adding to the pain from the extinguisher's carbon dioxide; the agony of a thousand tiny abrasions giving everything a blurred watery image. I started praying at that moment; my own version of the standard pilot's prayer. Dear God, get me out of this . . . anything but drowning . . . and burning . . . crashing in aeroplanes . . . any bloody thing. I mean what good is a crippled angel who's afraid of flying for Christ's sake . . . just get me down and you can name the deal . . . I'll even go to church on Sundays . . .

He didn't answer, he never did. But then I knew he was there; knew he was watching . . . thinking . . . making the final decision.

My arms were slowly giving out when Rafferty rolled his head towards me. I saw his eyes flicker, then blink, then again, and again. There was a mask of dried

247

congealed blood around his nose and mouth. 'What . . .' he started.

'Controls,' I screamed. 'Push the bloody control column.'

He dragged himself up into a sitting position and pushed. The relief swept through me with an almost sexual intensity.

'What happened?' he shouted. I reached over, found his headset, and slipped it on his head.

'Lost the undercarriage, or some of it at least. Then the flaps ripped off. Must have damaged the elevators . . . can't stop it from climbing.'

'Have you called Larnaca?'

'No . . . too busy praying. Hang on to the controls and I'll try them.'

I dialled up Larnaca approach on 119.4 mhz and started transmitting. 'Mayday. Mayday. Mayday. This is Five Hotel Mike Mike Romeo, we have serious flying control difficulties; position approximately thirty . . . three zero miles southwest of Nicosia; level one thousand feet . . . heading zero four five . . . possibility of ditching imminent . . .'

I waited for almost a minute but there was no reply. Only the crackling static in the headset. I thumbed the transmit button again: 'Larnaca approach, Mayday, Mike Romeo changing to one two one point five, out.'

I clicked the dials round and started again. This time on the international distress frequency.

Rafferty looked uncomfortable. 'Any joy?'

I said. 'Nothing . . . still could have picked us up, though.' I took some of the control load.

'I think it's getting worse.'

'Fuel burn-off!' I reached forward and reduced power.

'Something like "coffin-corner" on the jets,' Rafferty remarked.

'Yeah . . . I think we'd better start going down before it turns into a complete can of bloody worms.'

We both pushed, and the Commander sank down towards the raging sea. Each of us with his own private thoughts. Pilot's thoughts; thoughts of: as the fuel burned off so did the weight. And as that simple equation – of thrust and lift equalling weight and drag – had to be maintained to stay level, we were on a hiding to nothing. Because as the weight reduced so we had to reduce the power. The same power that was giving us extra speed with weight reduction; and that extra speed added up to extra lift. With the damaged elevators we didn't have sufficient control movement to compensate for that. Which left us reducing power. And if you keep on reducing power, you keep on reducing speed. And if you keep on reducing speed you finally stop flying. You stall! The airflow breaks up over the wings and you fall out of the sky.

It was now a matter of reaching Cyprus while we still had some control over the plane . . . either that or realizing we weren't going to make it, and coming to terms with an eleventh-hour ditching. With a heavy sea running on a dark wintry night, ditching was another way of saying dying.

We were at 500 feet when I realized the eleventh hour had come. The speed was back to eighty-five knots. 'Life-jackets!' I yelled. 'Get yours on . . . I'll hold it.' Rafferty moved quickly, then took over while I pulled my bright yellow life vest over my head and tied it securely around my waist.

'What about Goldstein?' Rafferty said.

'Is he still alive?'

'Think so . . . I slugged him about the same time he slugged me.'

'And the Arab?'

'Got in the way of his own Browning.'

I lifted my right knee and pressed it tight against the centre of the control column. 'Okay . . . check on Goldstein, but before you do that find that bloody gun, I'm not having that silly bastard shooting me at this stage of the game.' He began to move back. 'Only thirty seconds,' I added. 'Doubt I can hold it for much longer.'

Thirty seconds later he was back, dropping the heavy Browning automatic into my lap. 'Still out cold, but I've tied a lifejacket to him,' Rafferty said, straining on the controls.

I slid the gun into the map pocket by my left leg and passed a final mayday. No reply. 'Harness tight,' I said.

Rafferty gave a final tug. 'I'm okay . . . what about the wind?'

'I'm turning now . . . from the drift we were getting earlier I reckon it's westerly . . . have you ever ditched before?'

Rafferty gave me a wintry little smile. 'Not this week, Stevie boy.'

I snapped on the landing light. 'Right, slide your seat back a couple of notches for a start; be easier to get out that way. Next, just before touchdown I'm going to feather the engines and crack the door open. Normally two impacts . . . the second will be the big one. When that happens the windscreen will probably split . . . water pressure. Once we've stopped, release your harness and follow me out of the door. Don't inflate your jacket until you're on the surface. Got that?'

'What about your man in the back?'

'Sod him,' I snapped. 'If we float for long enough I'll try to pull him out . . . How are the arms?'

'Can't feel a bloody thing.'

The landing light picked out the angry black sea seconds later. And suddenly I wasn't afraid. Not any more. It was as though I had faced the worst that life had to offer and come out in front. Now at the end of it all, it was between me, an aeroplane and the sea. All that was needed was one successful ditching.

I said, 'Ease up now.'

Rafferty released pressure and the nose rotated gently into the flare. 'Okay . . . I'm feathering . . . Now!' I reached out and pulled the two blue-topped propeller levers back through the gate. Then quickly snapped the mixture levers to idle cut off. There wasn't time for anything else . . . except the door. I released the catch and felt the sudden rush of slipstream.

'I've got it now . . . brace yourself!' I held the Commander just above the breaking waves, letting the speed decay. The wheels or what was left of them touched a wave top . . . I felt the momentary jerk. Come on you bastard, get down. I jerked the stick forward and back.

The next moment we hit. The metallic bang was reminiscent of a power boat slamming down into the water, or the empty echo of a metal drum. Then the nose dug in and the aircraft pitched down. The windscreen shattered in that instant; black foaming water rushing into the cabin.

Seat harness . . . seat harness . . . where's the bloody clip? I fumbled for long seconds before successfully releasing it. By then the cabin was totally submerged in cold swirling water. I pushed the door open and swam out; my hands making contact with the bent propeller. I pulled myself up and inflated my jacket. Rafferty bobbed to the surface two seconds later. 'Here!' I screamed. I reached out and caught his arm.

'Still . . . still floating,' he cried. 'Can we get Goldstein?' I looked back at the breaking waves crashing against the high fin. The rotating beacon was still working. The red light sweeping in lazy circles.

'You try to get him to the pilot's door . . . I'll reach down and pull . . . you push . . . not much time.'

Rafferty moved back inboard of the propeller and submerged. I followed, clinging to the prop until the last second . . . then reaching for the top of the open door. The hands began pulling at my feet long agonizing seconds later. I felt for them in the cold water and pulled. Rafferty's face bobbed up in front of me.

'Where is he?' I spluttered, swallowing a mouthful of sea water.

'Can't move . . . stuck . . . think he's dead anyway.' The Commander lurched sickeningly in the violent seas.

'Let's get away . . . going down . . . inflate your bloody jacket.'

Rafferty pulled the toggle, the jacket lifted him higher in the water. I shouted: 'Hang on to me . . . let's go.'

We eased slowly away as the aircraft burbled slowly downwards to a watery grave. The last thing I saw was the white beam of the landing light fading in the greeny blackness.

Suddenly, quite, quite suddenly it was all over. The plane had gone and we were totally alone. Alone in a cold and stormy sea. And nobody had seen us go in. Rafferty tugged my arm. 'Got two of these . . . glove compartment.'

I reached for his hand and felt the small cylindrical tube. 'What is it?'

'Flare . . . know how to use them?'

Still clinging to Rafferty with one hand I rubbed the flare against my cheek. 'Knurled end . . . Night.' I laughed, the Air Force might have been a long time gone, but the teachings remained. The laughter stopped as the sea rushed into my mouth.

'What?'

'Knurled end . . . if . . . see a ship twist off knurled end and hold it out away from your face.'

'What are the chances?'

'Not good . . . best to stay still so that your body warms water around you.'

Rafferty looked at me, his face caught in the glow of the tiny white light of his lifejacket. The light activated by contact with the water. 'How long?'

'Hour . . . two.'

He smiled sadly. 'Yeah . . . figured about that.'

I could feel my hands and legs getting colder; numbness would be next; then nothing. Nothing but a pleasant warm sensation . . . tiredness . . . closing eyes . . . I reached down and pushed the flare tightly into my belt, then felt for my shirt pocket. It was still there. Goldstein hadn't even bothered to search me. I took the diamond out carefully, gripping it with all my strength.

'Rafferty!'

His face turned towards me. Cold and haunted.

I held out my free hand. 'Not much good . . . now. But thanks for everything.'

He took it from me and held it in the glow of his mae-west light. 'I'll say one thing, Stevie boy . . . you're a gentleman.' Even as the words left his lips, a wave crashed over our heads. We clung to each other two-handedly . . . neither wishing to die alone. When we bobbed back to the surface the diamond had gone.

Rafferty smiled, then started laughing. Swallowing salt water and choking at the same time. 'What the hell . . . plenty more where that came from.' He pulled my hand down beneath the water to his waist; that was when I felt the familiar shape of the silica gel tube. 'No point leaving them, now was there?'

My teeth had started to chatter when I said: 'What . . . what you going to do . . . with your half?'

'Start a little airline . . . based in Dublin . . . and then I'll ask Annie girl to marry me . . .' In the ghostly white glow his eyes seemed to be full of tears. After a while he said, 'You . . . what about you?'

'Fishing boat . . . in Penzance . . .'

'Didn't know . . . you liked fishing.'

I gave a tired laugh. 'Neither did I.'

We stopped talking then. The effort had been too much. Cold and fatigue had taken over; sapping our strength . . . as it would eventually our will to live. And then above the wind and the sea, a regular heartbeat. The steady wap-wap-wap of rotor blades. I strained to listen as the sound grew steadily louder. Then I jerked Rafferty around. 'Hear that . . . do you hear that . . . ? Chopper . . . search and rescue guys.'

We both looked towards the sky and saw the brilliant white searchlight beaming down through the grey slanting rain. I pulled the flare from my belt, released the end and held it out.

The blinding orange light reached out across the night . . . forging the final link.

THE END

ALFRED COPPEL

THE APOCALYPSE BRIGADE

A world on the brink of disaster . . .
A private army willing to fight to the death . . .

The Apocalypse Brigade describes the world as it may be
a decade from now, where superpowers are held in thrall
by both terrorists and OPEC. It is a world on the edge of
apocalypse, where private citizens are prepared to act
when their weakened governments are not . . .

"Mr Coppel is a wily writer. He knows how to keep things
churning . . . and he knows when and how to spill a little
blood and when and how to turn back the bedclothes . . .
That he has a certain and unswerving understanding of
the true nature of the world today is clear almost from the
very first page"

The New Yorker

0 552 12079 0   £1.95

CORGI BOOKS

GiRi

義理

MARC OLDEN

"Ludlum, look out, Marc Olden is here"
Walter Wager, author of *Telefon*

GIRI
to the Japanese, a term meaning duty or loyalty, the most binding obligation of the samurai warriors. But to an American, it means something else – revenge!

Combining international intrigue, Oriental philosophy, deadly violence and burning passion, *Giri* is a gripping, fast-paced thriller in which East clashes with West, and the ageless code of the hunter versus the hunted is put to the ultimate test.

"Anybody who loved *Shibumi* and *The Ninja* shouldn't miss it"
James Patterson

0 552 12357 9 £1.95

CORGI BOOKS

A SELECTED LIST OF FICTION AVAILABLE
FROM CORGI BOOKS

□	12187 8	Nightworld	**Robert Charles**	£2.50
□	12394 3	34 East	**Alfred Coppel**	£1.95
□	11982 2	The Hastings Conspiracy	**Alfred Coppel**	£1.75
□	12079 0	The Apocalypse Brigade	**Alfred Coppel**	£1.95
□	12478 8	The Dragon	**Alfred Coppel**	£2.50
□	11661 0	Control Tower	**Robert P. Davis**	£1.25
□	10683 6	The Pilot	**Robert P. Davis**	£1.75
□	12180 0	The Man from St. Petersburg	**Ken Follett**	£1.95
□	11810 9	The Key to Rebecca	**Ken Follett**	£1.95
□	12393 5	Balefire	**Kenneth Goddard**	£1.95
□	12160 6	Red Dragon	**Thomas Harris**	£1.95
□	12255 6	Worldly Goods	**Michael Korda**	£1.95
□	10174 5	The Attorney	**Harold Q. Masur**	£1.75
□	10595 3	Dubai	**Robin Moore**	£2.50
□	12357 9	Giri	**Marc Olden**	£1.95
□	12574 1	The Price	**Peter Ransley**	£1.95
□	12583 0	Submarine U-137	**Edward Topol**	£2.50
□	12307 2	Red Square	**Edward Topol & Fridrikh Neznansky**	£2.50
□	12271 8	The Assassin	**David Wiltse**	£1.95

ORDER FORM